Praise for Nell: Marshal of Bodie

"John Mullen has a Western-mystery winner in *Nell: Marshal of Bodie*. Nell is an intrepid, determined protagonist who allows nothing to stand in the way of her dream to become a Pinkerton agent—not murder, mayhem, or missing gold. Mullen portrays the late 19th-century gold-rush town of Bodie, California, with a nuanced and enthusiastic eye, while weaving a twisty mystery replete with suspects and red herrings. Readers who love mysteries featuring strong female characters set in the iconic West will find much to enjoy in *Nell: Marshal of Bodie*."

—Ann Parker, author of the
award-winning Silver Rush mystery series

"I loved this book. A real gem. Wonderful voice, wonderful prose. A strong female protagonist who easily carries the story. The three-dimensional characters so well drawn they could walk off the page and have a cup of coffee with you."

—David Putnam bestselling author of the
Bruno Johnson series

"*Nell: Marshal of Bodie* is an engaging and rollicking tale with a plucky heroine."

—Anne Louise Bannon, author of the
Old Los Angeles mysteries

Nell: Marshal of Bodie

ALSO BY JOHN EDWARD MULLEN

DIGITAL DICK

"In *Digital Dick*, John Mullen has created one of the most unique sleuths in the mystery world. Suspenseful, funny, and heartwarming. Digital Dick is a winner!" — Matt Coyle, author of the Anthony Award winning Rick Cahill crime novels

"Digital Dick is a terrifically funny take on how a computer might view our world. With precise analysis and observation, the ability to compute probabilities and scenarios in nanoseconds, and a Satisfaction Index that gets knocked around faster than a ping pong ball, Dick solves crimes with blazing speed — but also learns that even a computer can have a heart." — Terry Ambrose, author of the McKenna Mysteries and the License to Lie thriller series

"... an exciting murder mystery .... In addition to taking the prize for originality, this book is a great piece of story-telling and a good read. I highly recommend it." — Lois Wells Santalo, Midwest Book Review

Nell: Marshal of Bodie

A Nell Doherty Mystery

John Edward Mullen

MURDERS IN TIME
1895

Published by Murders in Time Press
www.murdersintime.com

Library of Congress Control Number: 2022911658

Names: Mullen, John Edward, 1949- author.
Title: Nell: Marshal of Bodie / John Edward Mullen
Description: San Diego, California: Murders in Time Press, 2022.
Identifiers: ISBN 9780996290722 (paperback) | 9780996290739 (ebook)
Subjects: Women detectives—Fiction. | Murder—Investigation—Fiction. | BISAC: FICTION / Mystery & Detective / Historical. | FICTION / Mystery & Detective / Women Sleuths. | FICTION / Westerns | GSAFD: Mystery Fiction.

Cover Design: Hannah Linder
Interior Design: Catherine Posey

.

Chapter One

January 30, 1892

Mama didn't look me in the eye, only stared at her lye-reddened hands resting in her lap.

We sat side by side on the upholstered couch in the room that served as our parlor, dining room, and kitchen. Outside the window, icicles melted along the eaves, spattering the wet snow on the ground. On the hill above town, the harsh bray of the Standard Mill's whistle announced the noon meal.

"I don't mean to be cruel, Nell." Mama's gaze finally met mine. "But you'll most likely have to support yourself. A school teacher is a respectable position for an unmarried woman in your situation."

My situation. Mama's most irritating, most oft-spoken phrase. "Do you really think me so unattractive no man will have me?" *Rags would have me.*

"That's not what I meant, dear. You're a very pretty girl. But now that you're eighteen, you need to think of your future."

Mama's hand hovered over my leg before she patted me high up on the thigh. I had reached the couch first and sat in her place out of obstinacy. When we had our mother-to-daughter talks, she always wanted to sit on my left, so my wooden leg was as far away from her as possible.

"Don't be so stubborn. You can live with your aunt Agnes while you earn your teaching diploma in San Jose."

I took a deep breath and counted to ten. "I don't want to be a teacher. I want to be a Pinkerton detective."

"Nell, be serious. Your leg ..."

I gritted my teeth. "My leg doesn't keep me from doing chores or riding a horse. It won't keep me from being a detective." I hoped.

Boots scraped on the warped wooden boards of the front porch. Papa opened the door, stepped inside, and quickly closed the door behind him. He flashed his gap-toothed smile, the one Mama said won her heart. "How are my beautiful angels?"

Mama glared at me. "Your daughter is talking her same old nonsense. She still thinks she can be a detective."

"Papa," I said, happy to change the subject, "have you learned anything new about the gold robberies?"

He removed the curved pipe from his mouth. "I sent Vern to check on something." He pulled once on his pipe and exhaled the cherry-scented smoke. "Should know in a day or two if it'll pan out, but that's all I'm willing to say."

"Not even the veriest little hint?"

"No, darlin'." He hung his derby, coat, and gun belt on the rack. "Something smells good." He strode to the couch and leaned down.

Mama tensed as he kissed her cheek. They must have been having their "troubles" again.

"I like how you've fixed your hair, Mother. Bangs look good on you."

Mama's gaze remained cool and sober, like she looked in photographs. "Talk to her, Sam. Tell her she can't be a detective. I'll serve up your dinner."

2

Mama went to the kitchen area at the back of the room. She ladled lamb stew onto a plate from the pot on the cook stove and sliced bread at the counter.

Papa sat next to me on the couch. "Are you sure that's what you want, Nell? Do you remember what I've told you, that real detectives' lives aren't as exciting as they appear in the stories of Sherlock Holmes and Nick Carter?"

"It's my heart's desire. How could I not wish to put on a disguise and worm my way into a criminal's confidence? How could I not want to put outlaws behind bars, like you do as Bodie's marshal?"

He puffed his pipe for a long minute. He patted my wooden leg. "Mother, I had a thought."

"The answer's no," she said.

"Hold on, now. Don't you think our special girl deserves a chance at her dreams?"

Mama banged the knife handle on the counter. The bread plate rattled.

"Being a detective is unladylike." She turned a red face toward us. "And we shouldn't give her false hopes. Her best chance, practically her only chance at making a respectable living, is to become a teacher. She has a natural bent for it. She's done wonders with those ... those Chinese."

I squeezed my eyes together to block Mama from my sight. Always "those" Chinese, as if they were different from us.

Papa went to the wood stove next to the kitchen counter, opened the grate, and emptied the ash from his pipe. "Suppose we give Nell a year to make good as a detective. If it doesn't work out then she agrees to become a teacher."

I crossed my fingers, hoping Mama would agree with Papa. To no avail.

She stormed past Papa into their bedroom.

I flinched when she slammed the door. "I'm sorry. I didn't mean to cause a fight."

"It'll be okay." Papa tapped on the door to their bedroom. "Mother." He went in and shut the door.

I didn't understand much of what they said, but a few times Mama's voice rose. I caught an angry 'detective,' and the word 'harlot.' I assumed she was saying I would fall into sin if I became a Pinkerton. That wasn't fair. Mama had no cause to call a female detective a harlot. I leaned forward. Papa spoke too softly. Did I dare to sneak up to the door?

Mama sobbed. She never cried. Could she really be upset about me becoming a detective? Could Mama be right? No. I didn't have a choice. If I became a teacher, I would wind up old and alone, a spinster, proper but sad. I wanted a bigger life than I could have in Bodie. I would get it with or without her help.

After ten minutes, their conversation ceased. Papa came out alone. I held my breath.

"You have a year."

"Oh, thank you. Thank you."

It's going to happen. I get a chance to be a Pinkerton. I wanted that more than anything, more even than getting my leg back.

I grabbed the arm of the couch and pulled myself onto my feet to give Papa a hug. He took a swing at me, a slow swing. I ducked under it and jabbed him in the stomach with my right and then my left fist. He pulled me into a hug.

"You'll need to be tough out there on your own."

"I can take care of myself."

"Your mother and I know you can handle rough, crude men. You've met plenty of that sort here in Bodie. Your mother worries most about you meeting a sweet-talkin' man."

"A sweet-talking man would take one look at my leg and disappear."

"Maybe, maybe not. You mind your mother's worries, you hear?"

4

"Okay." Speaking of worries, a serious one came to mind. "Papa, is it true Erastus Kohl is back in town?"

"Yup. Saw his pale, pinched face on Main Street yesterday."

"Are you afraid?" I was. Kohl had threatened to get even with Papa for sending him to prison.

Papa squeezed me tighter for a second. "Darlin', Kohl's had two years in prison to think about what a folly it is to break the law. I expect he'll behave himself, except maybe cheating a little when he weighs out a cut of beef."

"You sure?"

"I'm sure. Now, I've got to eat and get back to work."

I hoped he was right not to fear Kohl. I poured coffee into Papa's favorite cup. It was cheap and made of tin, but it was special because I'd given it to him for his birthday with the dime I'd won in a spelling bee when I was ten. He liked it best because it held twice as much coffee as Mama's China cups.

Papa took a sip of his coffee. "I know you're excited by the prospect of becoming a detective, but Pinkertons don't spend every minute slapping handcuffs on desperados. Pinkertons I've worked with spend a lot of time watching and listening. For hours and hours, sometimes for weeks on end. And they write reports, lots of reports. Every day, in great detail. There's a lot of humdrum to detective work."

"I won't mind." Unless it was always boring. But that couldn't be. In Mr. Pinkerton's books, detectives chased thieves, blackmailers, and murderers.

Papa blew on a spoonful of stew to cool it. After swallowing, he asked, "How do you intend to get hired by Pinkerton's?"

"I'll go to their office in Chicago and apply for a job, just like Kate Warne did."

"And your leg?"

I sat up straighter in my chair. "In one of Allan Pinkerton's books, he says women operatives mostly work at gaining the confidence of others. So, what I plan to tell them is my wooden leg will make that easier because people will have sympathy for me. Plus, my leg will make me less suspicious. No one would think a detective agency would hire an operative with a wooden leg."

Papa grinned. "I'm happy to see you've given this some thought. I hope your dream comes true, but I will miss you."

"I wish Mama felt the way you do about me becoming a detective."

"Darlin', you're her baby. She wants to protect you. She can't do that if you leave us."

"I'm not a baby."

"You'll always be your mother's baby."

After a few minutes, he finished his stew and left. Mama came out of their bedroom, her cheeks tear-stained. She joined me at the sink where I was doing up Papa's dishes.

"I'm sorry I upset you, Mama. I may not be successful as a detective, but I have to try."

"You think chasing outlaws sounds adventurous. It could get you killed. Besides, only disgraced women become detectives."

I huffed. Mama was so old-fangled. "Mr. Pinkerton said being a detective is an honorable profession for a woman. Kate Warne helped protect President Lincoln on his inaugural trip to Washington."

"Your father should never have given you those detective stories. Ungodly foolishness, putting such fancies in a young girl's head." Mama grabbed my shoulders. The intensity of her stare shocked me. "Your father thinks that because he can get away with doing what he pleases, you can, too. He's wrong. He forgets you're not a man."

Chapter Two

I stood over the ironing board until two o'clock, smoothing away creases in shirts and shirtwaists. I then took both flat irons off the stove and set them on their stands on the kitchen counter to cool. In the bedroom I shared with my brother Patrick, I laid red paper from Yong Liao's Mercantile on my narrow bed and wrapped the Chinese New Year's gifts I had purchased for Rags and his brothers. I looked forward to the parade and fireworks. I couldn't wait to tell Rags that Papa had approved my becoming a detective. Would he be sad?

I slipped out of my faded house dress and into my newer blue Sunday dress. I did not own a Chinese dress appropriate for the festival. The owner of the Chinese mercantile had tempted me last week with a red silk dress, offering to sell it to me at the 'Chinese' price. Even that was too expensive. I brushed my hair for the obligatory hundred strokes, kissed Mama goodbye, and left the house.

On each step down Park Street, I waited a fraction of a second after planting one boot in the mushy snow before raising the other. Plant left. Swing right hip. Plant right. Plant, swing, plant. I mustn't fall. I carried not only my Chinese New Year's presents, but, also wrapped in brown paper, a shirtwaist Mama had sewn for Mrs. Taylor.

I turned east onto Green Street and hitched past the high-walled corral full of stacked firewood.

I stopped in front of what was left of Lucy Barnes's house. So many homes like hers had been abandoned years ago when most of the mines closed. The house where we played, now a ruin, the wooden sides weathered gray and leaning like that tower in Italy. The roof stove-in by last winter's snows. Lucy had been my best friend and my only confidant. Ever since she left town in '87, I had missed her mightily. *I'd give anything to have another girl-friend to talk to. Thank God I have Rags.* I trudged on, the slush beginning to crust up under my boots.

I approached the boardwalk in front of the Bull's Head Market. Mrs. Taylor stood inside, feather-dusting a porcelain tea set displayed in the front window. The shop was empty of customers. I tapped on the window and she opened the door.

"Hello, Mrs. Taylor."

"Afternoon, Nell."

"Here's the shirtwaist Mama sewed for you."

She unwrapped the brown paper and held the shirtwaist of spotted blue cambric at arm's length. "'Tis lovely. Thank your Mama for me. Have you heard the news about the Second Chance Mine?"

"No. What happened?"

"They've hit pay dirt! The Dear knows it's just what Bodie needs."

"That's fabulous." More gold meant more people would come to Bodie, more customers for Mrs. Taylor, and maybe a new girlfriend for me.

"Tell your Mama to buy Second Chance stock before the news gets around."

"I'll be sure to let Mama know. Thank you." Though we didn't have any money to spare.

8

I waited until Mrs. Taylor pulled her accounts book from underneath the counter and deducted $1.75 from what we owed her. I clasped the remaining packages under my left arm and tramped on toward Main Street.

On the snow-covered hill east of town, the stamp mills of the Standard and Bodie mining companies thundered. Their thousand-pound stamps pulverized melon-sized rocks into a fine powder. The din could be heard miles away. Mill workers suffered terrible hearing loss. It saddened me to hear young men shout greetings to each other when they met on Main Street.

The stagecoach from Hawthorne pulled up in front of the City Livery Stables. Small wisps of steam rose from the bodies of the horses. After setting the brake, the driver spat tobacco into the brown mush of the street and climbed down from his box. He pulled two battered leather suitcases from the rear boot and set them on the boardwalk. Then he helped a pretty young woman out of the coach.

"Here ya go, miss. This is Bodie."

A curl of blonde hair had escaped from under the woman's bonnet. Her coat, trimmed with fur at the collar and wrists, was frayed where it brushed her button boots. She looked to be older than me—in her mid-twenties.

"Excuse me," she said. "Can you tell me where Smith's Dance Hall is?"

The dance hall? She would be popular with the men there, but Mama and her friends would consider her unladylike, at best.

One of three drunks that had stumbled out of the Champion Saloon next door doffed his plaid cloth cap and bowed at the waist. "Let me assist you, my beauty." He lost his balance and fell off the boardwalk into the muddy slush.

The stage driver and the drunk's two companions pointed, slapped their knees, and guffawed. The young woman covered her mouth with her gloved hand. I stood next to her shaking my head. Just yesterday, Papa had released these three drunks from jail.

"Smith's Dance Hall is down Main Street," I said, "past the bend in the road. I'm headed that way. I can show you."

The woman turned to pick up her suitcases, but Micah Pettibone, the oldest of the drunks, gray-bearded and wearing an ancient Union Army cap, had already grabbed them. "At yer service, miss."

The third drunk, pudgy, red-nosed Bill Hoffman, tried to take one of the bags from his friend, but the elder man held tight. "I got 'em."

Bill smirked. "Well, then, I'll just bring up the rear." He grabbed the young woman's bottom.

She spun around with her hand raised to slap Bill.

He threw up his arms and cringed. He had always been a coward.

I curled my right hand into a fist and waved it in front of him. "You behave yourself, or I'll break your nose again."

"You would, wouldn't ya, Pencil-Leg?" He stepped away from me and saluted my right leg. "Hello, ol' Tom."

My face burned. "Ol' Tom" was Bill's nickname for my newest wooden leg. No mere stump—it had both an articulated knee and ankle. I had received it as a hand-me-down, a gift from Doc Boyle who had removed it from the body of Tom Small, a dead miner. I was grateful for the leg because it allowed me to get around without crutches. Wearing a dead man's wooden leg embarrassed me at times, and, as at that moment, the leg was sometimes a cause for others to torment me.

I'd taken all of that I would take.

One quick step brought me face to face with Bill Hoffman. Papa had told me never to start a fight when my anger was hot. Always count to ten, he had told me. I counted under my breath: two, four, six, eight, ten. Bill must have seen the remaining fury in my eyes. He covered his nose with his hand and turned to help his friend who'd fallen in the slush.

The stage driver told Pettibone to put the suitcases down.

"I could've gotten a tip," Pettibone said. "Worth a beer, mebbe." He shuffled off after his friends.

"Thank you," the young woman said to the driver. To me, she said, "I'm Mrs. Irene Lockhart."

"Nice to meet you. I'm Nell Doherty. I should warn you, some of the customers at Smith's Dance Hall are brutes like Bill Hoffman."

"I've been told I might find work at Smith's," Mrs. Lockhart said. "And you needn't worry about me. I've dealt with men worse than Bill Hoffman. A lot worse."

Chapter Three

Mrs. Lockhart and I proceeded side by side down Main Street's boardwalk. Sunlight glinted off untrammeled patches of snow on the edges of the street. Many of the buildings we passed stood empty. Inside an abandoned saloon, a thick layer of dust covered the bar, the upright piano, and a pair of roulette wheels. I stole a glance at my companion.

What would Mama say if she knew I had strolled down Main with a dance-hall girl? She'd probably think Mrs. Lockhart a harlot. And perhaps she was, though she didn't swing her hips when she walked like other fancy ladies I'd seen. *It might be fun to know a harlot, unless she led me astray.*

A sleigh bringing mail from Bridgeport slid past, pulled by two horses wearing square, wooden snow shoes. The mailman sat hunched over the seat. A blanket covered his legs. He slowed the sleigh and leered at Mrs. Lockhart and me as he passed.

"Such a bore." Mrs. Lockhart groaned. "Much like that other bore, Bill Hoffman. I've been thinking about what you did a minute ago. Confronting an ill-mannered drunk like Bill Hoffman took courage. You're very brave."

Brave. I liked that. Mama would have called me bullheaded

and unrefined. Being brave was something that could win me a job with the Pinkertons.

The wind picked up and I leaned into it. Mrs. Lockhart shivered. "Is it always this cold?"

"This is mild for a Bodie winter."

"I'll need warmer clothes."

We trod through moist snow as we crossed a gap in the boardwalk and passed a deserted barber shop. Mrs. Lockhart asked. "Did you really break Bill Hoffman's nose?"

"In school, not long after my accident. Bill wanted me to show him my wooden leg. He teased me again and again, but I ignored him. Until, one day, he pointed at my leg and said: 'You may not wind up an old maid on account o' yer wooden peg. All you have to do to catch a husband ... is bash 'im over the head with it.' That lit my fuse."

Mrs. Lockhart shook her head. "What did you do?"

"I hitched myself over to where he stood surrounded by his friends, laughing at his joke. One of his cronies made room for me in the circle of school boys. Bill turned his head and my fist met his nose. Everyone on the schoolyard heard it crack."

"I imagine," Mrs. Lockhart said, her green eyes sparkling, "breaking his nose was deliciously pleasing."

I bowed my head. "It was."

We were neither of us school girls, but we both giggled. I didn't care if Irene was a harlot, I liked her.

"I take it you lost your leg in an accident."

I swallowed hard. "I was twelve. A wagon I was riding in turned over. My leg got crushed ..." I stood still. For some reason, telling the story out loud scared me. My body trembled.

Mrs. Lockhart put down her bags and gave me a hug. "I'm sorry. I didn't mean to cause you any pain." She handed me her handkerchief and I wiped the tears from my face.

"I'm okay."

Mrs. Lockhart picked up her bags and we continued down the boardwalk. "You're an unusual young woman."

"Because I'm a cripple?"

"You're not a cripple where it counts—in your mind. I sense a fierce independence in you, uncommon for a woman."

"Well, if I don't stick up for myself, I won't be able to do what I want to do."

"Which is?"

I chewed my lip. Will she laugh like most everyone else? "I want to be a detective."

"Really?" Mrs. Lockhart's eyes widened. "That exactly proves my point; you are unusual."

She hadn't scoffed or laughed at my dream. I breathed a bit easier.

We passed the billiard parlor. The Justice of the Peace, Odysseus Superbus Snethens, stood inside, cue in one hand and whiskey glass in the other. He lifted his glass in salute and I waved back.

"Mrs. Lockhart," I said, "As a dance hall girl, you lead an unusual life, too."

"I had no choice. After being widowed, I had to find work."

"I'm so sorry."

Two young boys bolted out of a lodging house ahead of us and ran past us on the boardwalk. The one in the rear yelled, "Gimme my marbles!" The boy in front took off across rutted Main Street, dodging between a buggy and a freight wagon loaded with iron pipe.

Mrs. Lockhart and I passed the Parole Saloon and Chop Stand. The smell of charred pork filled the air. Mrs. Lockhart stopped to inhale. She licked her slightly blue lips.

Like me, Mrs. Lockhart had known tragedy. She was living an unconventional life. *Might she know what my future life will be like?*

"Do you want to know a secret?" I asked.

"I adore secrets."

"A lot of people, including Mama, wouldn't understand, but losing my leg was a gift in disguise. Because I'm different physically, I've been allowed to be different in other respects. Being considered unmarriageable has meant I have a chance to follow another path, one I choose."

"Life isn't easy for a woman following her own path. Independence comes with a price. We've no husband to rely on, to help support us, no one to share life with."

Loneliness was something I knew and could abide. I looked at Mrs. Lockhart's worn coat. I wasn't sure I wanted to hear the answer, but I had to ask. "But you're able to manage?"

"Yes, I get by all right."

"I'm so glad you said so." *I may have just met my new best friend.*

A minute later, we stood before the frosted glass doors of Smith's Dance Hall.

"If anyone gives you any trouble," I said, "tell them you're a friend of Marshal Doherty."

"Thank you, I will." She smiled as if amused.

Odd. Maybe, if she is a harlot, she wouldn't seek help from a policeman.

I hitched back down Main until I reached King Street, the narrow lane where most of Bodie's Chinese residents lived. New red paper lanterns hung in front of Yong Liao's Mercantile and several of the two-story, wood-framed boarding houses across the street. Red scrolls bearing Chinese characters in gold adorned many windows. From the boarding house across the street, the wind carried the overly sweet, flowery scent of opium.

I climbed the stairs at the back of Yong Liao's Mercantile. Every other step, I gripped the banister and hauled myself upward. When I reached the landing, I entered the second-floor hallway. I knocked on the door to the three-room apartment Rags shared with his family. His fourteen-year-old brother, Wu Bo, also called Bobby, opened the door and we bowed to each other.

"Nay hoh, Bobby. Happy New Year."

"Sure'n it's a grand day," he replied, in his mother's brogue. "Oh, come in, come in. You're lookin' lovely, and it's no mistake." He stared at the red packages I had brought. "Would you care for some tay?"

"Please."

Bobby stood three inches taller than I, almost as tall as his oldest brother, Rags. Unlike Rags, Bobby took after his mother. His eyes were a mischievous blue-gray. And while Rags had black hair, Bobby's was brown. Unlike most of the Chinese who lived in Bodie, Rags and his bothers did not wear the traditional long plaited queue.

While Bobby fetched China cups and poured tea, I set my gifts on the dining table and removed my coat. In front of the shrine to the family's ancestors on a table against the wall, a pair of joss sticks set in a sand-filled vase sent tendrils of sandalwood-scented smoke to the ceiling. Bowls of fresh oranges and nuts sat in front of a pair of small stone tablets inscribed with the names of Mr. Wu and his forebears. A photograph of Mr. Wu stood between the stone tablets. A crucifix and a bright green Fenian flag bearing a gold harp had been newly tacked to the wall above the shrine, the latter to honor Mrs. Wu's rebellious Irish ancestors.

Using both hands, Bobby offered me a cup of tea. I inhaled the vapor and took a sip. "Wonderful, Bobby. Thank you." He got himself a cup and we sat side-by-side at the dining table.

"'Tis a pleasure spending time with my favorite teacher."

"I'm your only teacher."

Bobby blushed. "Oh, if'n I had a hundred teachers, you'd still be my favorite. You're the best that could be."

"Thank you."

Bobby leaned toward me. "I know Rags's secret," he whispered. "But I'm not supposed to tell anyone." He sipped his tea, peering at me over the rim of the cup. He loved to tease.

I raised my cup and feigned disinterest. I turned toward the window. King Street was empty save for a pair of Chinese in blue coats carrying a drum and a flute. Virgin Alley, which dead-ended at King Street, was quiet too. It was much too early for the alley's customers to be prowling.

"Nell?" Bobby said, irritated that I hadn't taken the bait.

"Hmm?"

"You would want to know the secret, if I could tell you."

"I imagine if it was something of interest, Rags would tell me himself."

"He's too embarrassed."

"Too embarrassed to tell his oldest friend?"

Bobby pressed his lips together, straining his jaw muscles. He held his breath for twenty seconds before blurting, "Oh, I haveta tell ya. He's in love."

Heat spread across my cheeks.

"I can't tell you who," Bobby said. "Sure'n he'd skin me alive if I told."

I tried to cover my excitement by making a show of drinking from my cup. Could it be Rags felt as I do? He had given no hint of great affection toward me. Well, there had been the one kiss. But that was but a lark, the result of a dare, and three years ago when we were fifteen.

"Bobby, while we wait for your brothers and your mother, let's continue your lessons."

"Oh, if'n I must."

"You must, or I won't have earned the quarter your mother will give me on Friday. Open your book and read the next selection."

"'Tis a laborious legal speech. I'd read better a pirate tale." He looked at the red-covered New Year's packages.

Could he know I had gotten him *Treasure Island*?

17

Bobby opened his McGuffey's Reader to Daniel Webster's speech for the prosecution of a murderer. He ran his finger along the words as he read.

"*This bloody drama exhibited no suddenly excited, ungovernable rage. The actors in it were not surprised by any lion-like temptation springing upon their virtue and overcoming it before resistance could begin. Nor did they do the deed to glut savage vengeance, or* ... uh ..."

"The word is 'satiate,' " I said. "It means 'to satisfy completely.' "

"*Or say-she-ate long-settled and deadly hate. It was all 'hire and salary, not revenge.' It was a cool, calculating, money-making murder. Whoever shall hereafter draw the portrait of murder, let him not give it the grim visage of Moloch, the brow knitted by revenge, the face black with settled hate. Let him draw, rather, a decorous, smooth-faced, bloodless demon—*"

Our lesson ended with Rags gently rapping at the front door. "Let me in, please."

Chapter Four

Bobby opened the door and Rags stepped through. He wore a black suit and a black necktie. In his arms, Rags carried a large package in red paper. He set it on the table in front of me. "You're looking fine today, Nell."

My pulse raced. Rags has told me the same any number of times, but this time I wondered what he meant by it. "You look rather handsome in your new suit."

A crooked smile broke out on his freckled face, a face that pleased me more that day than ever before.

"Please unwrap the present. It's for you, it is."

My hands shook. I untied the ribbon and unfolded the paper. Inside was the expensive Chinese silk dress I had admired in Yong Liao's shop a few days ago. Rags and I had celebrated the Chinese New Year for many years, but he had never given me such an expensive New Year's gift.

"Oh, my. It's so beautiful." I stood and held the dress up to me. The red silk was so much softer than anything I'd worn before. "I love the blue and white flowers and embroidered butterflies." I rushed around the table, and hugged him. "Thank you, Rags, thank you. But you shouldn't have spent so much money."

"Don't thank me. 'Tis from me mother."

My heart sank and I released him from my embrace. I had so wanted the dress to be a gift from Rags, a gift proving his feelings for me. To hide my disappointment, I shot him my schoolmarm glower. "*Me* Mother?"

"Blast. I mean, 'tis from *my* mother. 'Tis for teaching her sons to read and write and do our figures."

The light of his eyes kindled warmth in my chest.

"There's no one else deserves such a fine gift as yourself."

What should I make of Bobby's remark that Rags was in love? Had Rags told his mother? Is that why she had given me the gift, because I was the one he loved?

"I must thank your mother. Where is she?"

"She's downstairs minding the store for Yong Liao. If you'd like to wear the dress tonight, she said she'll help you put it on."

"Oh, yes. I'd love to wear it tonight." Maybe I could learn the truth from Mrs. Wu.

"I'll go and take her place in the store." Rags opened the front door and left the apartment.

A few minutes later, Mrs. Wu came up from the mercantile shop. She wore a green Chinese silk dress with designs of peacocks and lotus flowers in gold brocade which complemented her wavy red hair. As always, we greeted each other with a hug. Did her thin arms hold onto me a bit longer than usual?

"'Tis wonderful to see you, Nell."

"Mrs. Wu, the dress is just so beautiful, but really, you shouldn't have."

"Eh. A small kindness, it is, in repayment for your teachin' me boys these three years."

"Thank you, too, for inviting me to celebrate the New Year with you and your sons."

"And why wouldn't I? You're practically family."

Did she mean what I hoped she did?

"I admire you, girl. You've never been scairt of what the womenfolk of Bodie might say about you consortin' with Celestials. Now, let's see how well the dress fits."

I followed Mrs. Wu into her small bedroom. She helped me undo the buttons of my blue dress. She's always been pleasant and kind. Were I to marry Rags, I would face prejudice from most everyone in town, a lot more than I did being a supposed cripple. Why should love between two people cause others to hate them, or to call their love 'unnatural'? If only they knew Rags like I knew him, his kindness and understanding. He'd never pitied me. Despite all the obstacles he faced being of mixed blood, he kept an even temper. He would make a wonderful husband. And having his mother to talk to would be a saving grace, like "living in God's pocket" as she says.

"What's it like being the lone white woman in town who'd married a Chinese man?"

Mrs. Wu stood behind me and held up the red dress. I put an arm into each of the wide sleeves.

"Me life's had its difficulties, it has. I've suffered the chill of many a charity lady's glance, been jeered at and cheated out of money due. It's been especially rough on the boys, as you know, not bein' allowed in school. But I loved Mr. Wu from the moment I seen him. And three foine boys come of it." She turned me around. "How'd we get so serious, then?"

I folded the left side of the dress over the right. Mrs. Wu helped me fasten the buttons. I turned right and left and gazed at myself in the swing-glass above Mrs. Wu's bureau. *If I had two legs and wore a dress like this every day, all the boys would be cracked about me.*

"Turn about, now, and let me get me eyeful."

I pirouetted awkwardly in front of Mrs. Wu, in four ninety-degree turns.

"You're a fair pretty colleen, Nell."

21

"It's the dress." Except for Mama and Papa, no one tells me I'm pretty.

"Sure'n the charm is your own, me dear. Now, run on down and show yourself to Chao," she said, using Rag's given name.

Was Mrs. Wu looking at me differently? What would Rags think?

I hastened down the back stairs as fast as my leg would allow. I lifted the skirt to keep it above the slushy snow and crossed over to the boardwalk.

Several dozen Chinese men in padded blue jackets stood in the street in front of the store: among them drummers, cymbal players, flute players, and a man on stilts. Six men held the poles supporting an undulating thirty-foot-long paper dragon painted red, yellow, and green. Two pairs of men costumed as four-legged lions bobbed and weaved back and forth across the street. Marchers held red signs on poles with inscriptions in Chinese that Rags once told me were wishes for health, wealth, and longevity. Buddha-bellied Yong Liao, leader of Bodie's Chinese community, stood in front of the parade formation shouting commands.

I entered Yong Liao's store.

Rags stood behind the counter haggling in Cantonese with an older Chinese man over the price of a pocket watch in Rags's hand. Rags and his customer turned their heads and looked at me.

"Very pretty," Rags said. "You make a good Chinese."

Did he mean I'd make a good Chinese wife? "My mother would not approve."

"But you put the dress on anyway."

I didn't enjoy upsetting Mama, but I wanted more than to sit at home, dignified, but alone. I was meant to be a detective and, hopefully, a wife, too, not merely a sad, one-legged spinster.

The customer rapped his knuckles on the glass counter and spoke gruffly in Cantonese. Rags put the first watch back under the countertop and picked up another one. The two continued to dicker back and forth. After a couple of minutes, Rags shook his head. The customer grunted and left the store without the watch.

I didn't know how long we might be alone and my curiosity got the better of my prudence. "Rags, is there something you wanted to tell me?"

He looked confused, or maybe embarrassed. Before he could answer, his sixteen-year-old brother Jiang entered the shop wearing the bottom half of a lion costume. Why couldn't Jiang have waited a bit longer to show up? Over his trousers, held up by suspenders, Jiang wore leggings of what looked like golden fur. A short golden tail stuck out near his bottom.

"Hey, elder brother," Jiang said, "Yong Liao says close up shop. Parade's about to start. Hey, Nell, nice dress you're wearin'. See ya." He rushed back out to join Mr. Ren, the front half of his lion dancer pair.

Outside, someone struck a gong.

Chapter Five

Despite the late afternoon chill, several hundred men, women, and children, mostly white, lined Main Street to watch the Chinese New Year parade. Rags and I stood in front of the Carsonian Restaurant. Bobby Wu led the marchers. Every minute or so, he struck a match, lit a string of firecrackers, and tossed it into the rutted street. A lone Chinese man wearing a wide, cone-shaped straw hat followed next, hammering a gong with a mallet. The sinewy red, yellow, and green dragon held up on poles wound its way across the slushy street, chasing a gold ball, the pearl of wisdom, held by a single marcher.

An old miner standing next to me on the boardwalk covered his ears with his mittened hands. "Bless me. That's the tune kil't the old cow."

I agreed. The flutes and cymbals and drums produced a loud and unpleasant music. "Rags, do you think the fireworks and the gong and drums will really scare away evil spirits?"

"Sure'n it can do no harm."

Jiang Wu and Mr. Ren, the fore and aft of their gold- and red-colored lion swayed side to side and up and down as they approached. I patted the three-foot-wide head of the fierce beast.

Rags placed a red envelope in the lion's mouth, and Mr. Ren opened and closed the lion's jaws as if chewing. As the pair reached the center of the wide avenue, a snow ball struck the lion's left ear. A second snow ball struck Jiang Wu's golden tail. Rags and several other men raced toward a narrow opening between two buildings a short distance down Main Street. I hitched behind Rags as fast as I could.

Bill Hoffman emerged from the alley, followed by Baron Catlow, a handsome gentleman with broad shoulders. Catlow owned the recently reopened and renamed Second Chance Mine. If Mrs. Taylor was right, Catlow's mine might bring renewed prosperity to Bodie, giving the town and the mine a second chance.

Catlow held Bill by his coat collar. Bill flapped his arms. He reeked of alcohol.

"Let go 'a me, Catlow." Bill said. He giggled. "Let go, Catlow, let go. Catlow, Catlow. Let go."

Catlow shook Bill again, then he spoke briefly to Rags. Rags called out to his brother and Mr. Ren, who turned and danced toward the alley.

"Apologize, you miserable wretch," Catlow said.

"Whatch fer?"

Catlow reached back with his gold-topped cane and smacked Bill on his behind. Bill yelped.

"Give it to 'im good," yelled one of the small crowd that had formed at the mouth of the alley. Another shouted, "Let 'im go. He didn't do no harm."

Catlow pointed at the lion dancers. "Apologize to these men, or you're going to hurt a lot worse in a minute."

Bill wiped snot from his lip with his sleeve. "Why sh-should I?"

Catlow knocked Bill's hat off. "Do it because you've assaulted these good people."

"Good people? They's Chinks."

Catlow poked his cane into Bill's back.

Bill jerked up straight. "Okay, already. I's sorry."

Catlow let go of Bill. He wobbled a moment, picked up his hat, and staggered back into the shadow of the alley. Mr. Ren, the front half of the lion, bowed to Catlow. The lion rejoined the parade and the small crowd melted away.

"Mr. Catlow," I said, "thank you for humiliating Bill Hoffman."

Baron Catlow tipped his Stetson to me. "My pleasure, Miss Doherty."

"Yes," Rags said. "Sure'n it's a fine thing you did, bringing him down a peg." He held out his hand and Catlow shook it. Not many white men would have done so.

"Can't have buffoons like him spoiling a parade. It's uncivilized." Catlow stared at me for a few seconds. "You know, um, you're looking very pretty today, Miss Doherty."

I blushed under my bonnet. "Thank you, Mr. Catlow." Papa liked him. I, too, felt kindly toward him. Catlow was the only man, other than Papa, to ask me to dance at the Miners Union Hall. I had thanked him, but declined.

"Well, I wish you a good evening." Catlow sauntered south along the boardwalk, paralleling the marchers.

Down the street, the thirty-foot-long dragon undulated this way and that. A line of drummers passed, followed by two pairs of lion dancers and a man banging a gong. A short time later, the parade reversed course. The dragon, the lions, and the musicians passed us a second time before they turned onto King Street and disbanded.

At the far end of Main Street, a lone Appaloosa, saddled but riderless, stood in the middle of the roadway. The horse hadn't been there a few minutes ago. "Rags, look. Isn't that Deputy Jorgensen's horse?"

"Indeed, 'tis his. I'd know that horse among a thousand, but where's the deputy?"

"Come on."

The boardwalk ended a hundred feet from the spotted horse. Rags and I continued through the sludge. I held the dress out of the muck.

The Appaloosa backed away from us as we neared it. I held my hand up and Rags stopped. I approached the horse alone.

"It's okay, boy. It's okay." I took off my glove and held out my hand. The Appaloosa sniffed it. "You're going to be okay." I gently rubbed his neck and he bobbed his head. I ran my hand down his neck to his shoulder and took hold of his reins. "Good boy. Let's get you ... oh, my God."

A reddish-brown stain ran from the saddle down the horse's left flank. "Rags, there's blood."

Chapter Six

I walked Deputy Jorgensen's horse to the City Livery Stables. Rags ran to the marshal's office to get Papa. Twenty minutes later, in the fading dusk, I stood next to Rags at the edge of a circle of townsfolk outside the double doors of the stable, listening to Papa speak.

"You heard right," Papa said to a group of two dozen men. "It looks like blood on Vern's saddle. He may be injured." Papa glanced at the overcast sky. "It'll be dark soon. Who'll help me look for him?"

Judge Snethens returned his flask to his coat pocket. "I'll keep company with you, Marshal."

"Much obliged, Judge."

Baron Catlow raised his hand. "I'm coming, too." Catlow strode through the crowd to where Papa stood on the boardwalk. "I'll have Fergus drive my supply wagon in case Vern can't ride."

"If it's okay with you, Mr. Catlow," Doc Boyle said, "I'll join Fergus in the wagon. Just need to get my medical bag."

Several miners and merchants raised their hands to volunteer. Gideon Weed, a gaunt, bearded photographer who looked a bit like President Lincoln, stood at the back of the group. He was new to town. "I'll go, too, Marshal."

Papa pulled his watch from his pocket. "Everyone, fetch your horses and meet me back here in fifteen minutes." Several volunteers stepped inside the City Livery Stables to get their mounts. Others ran off to one or another of Bodie's other stables.

"I'll go, Papa," I said.

Papa stared at the bright red silk dress visible beneath my overcoat. "Not in that dress. 'Sides, we have enough men for the job."

"But this is like an investigation. Something a Pinkerton would do. And you said—"

"Not this time, Nell. There's no investigating to be done. We only have to comb the narrow canyon between here and Aurora."

I was disappointed, but intrigued. Papa had just told me what he'd refused to say at noon. He had sent Deputy Jorgensen to Aurora to investigate something related to the gold thefts. Had Jorgenson found the thieves in Aurora? Is that how ...? I shivered at the thought of the dried blood on the Deputy's Appaloosa.

"Be careful, Papa."

"Always am."

"Marshal," Yong Liao said. "I will send Chinese to help."

The stable's owner spit into the street. "We don't need no Chink help."

"That's enough of that," Papa said.

"Well, we don't."

Papa shook his head. Like me, he didn't understand why many white folks took a disliking to the Chinese. In fact, Yong Liao and Papa often played poker together at Yong's mercantile.

"Mr. Yong, that's very generous of you, but there's no need to interrupt your New Year's celebration."

"If you sure."

"I'm sure."

RAGS AND I WATCHED THE POSSE TROT TOWARD THE canyon north of town. Papa waved and I waved back. Then Rags and I joined the Chinese residents of Bodie at a banquet held in the old Carsonian Restaurant. Red paper lanterns, some the shape of tin cans, some like globes, and others like large mushrooms, hung from the ceiling. The smell of roast duck, garlic, ginger, and spices I didn't know caused my mouth to water.

At the back of the dining room, Yong Liao sat at the middle of a long table. Next to Yong was an empty chair reserved for Mrs. Yong. The Yong's two sons sat farther to his right. Bobby once shocked me when he told me this Mrs. Yong was Mr. Yong's 'second' wife. The first Mrs. Yong still lived back in China. According to Bobby, this wasn't unusual for a wealthy Chinese, but it seemed unnatural to me. *Customary or not, if Rags and I married, I would insist on being his only wife.*

I sat on the far left end of the head table. Between me and Yong Liao sat Mrs. Wu and her children in order of their ages: Rags, Jiang, and Bobby. The Wu family was accorded this place of honor because, twenty years earlier, Mr. Wu saved Yong Liao's life during an anti-Chinese riot in Los Angeles. The rest of Bodie's Chinese community sat at ten round tables, evenly spaced between the head table and the front door of the restaurant.

The seating arrangement meant that I could not easily speak with Rags, and could not ask him if I was the one he loved.

Rags and his mother had their heads bent toward each other. I couldn't hear what they were saying. Might they be talking about me?

Rags looked my way and winked. "Happy New Year, Nell."

"Happy New Year, Chao."

"Quite a feast, it is."

Indeed. Fish dishes, long noodles, dumplings in exotic-smelling sauces, and fat choy—something that looked like strands of black hair mixed with vegetables—all prepared and served by the few Chinese women and girls in Bodie.

As Rag's mother passed a platter of steaming vegetables and the "black hair" dish to Yong Liao, a Chinese girl served plates of dumplings at one of the round tables closest to the entrance. She wore a dress of pale blue silk and looked to be about sixteen. Her face was unusually pale and her cheeks rouged.

"Who's that girl?" I asked Bobby. I nodded in her direction. "I've not seen her before."

Bobby leaned closer. "That," he whispered, "is Huang Min. Beautiful, isn't she?"

"Why are we whispering?"

"I am not supposed to speak of her."

"Why not?"

"Oh, well, she's a hundred men's wife."

"A what?"

For a couple of seconds, Bobby scrunched up his face and squeezed his eyes shut. He whispered: "She's a fancy lady."

My head snapped back. "Don't be ridiculous. She's younger than I am."

Bobby shrugged. "She lives in a crib on Virgin Alley."

"I don't believe you. She doesn't look like the fallen women I've seen."

"I sometimes deliver Huang Min's laundry," Bobby said. "One time I heard noises in her crib. A man grunted and Huang Min moaned."

My face flushed. "That's horrible. Who would do that to such a young girl?"

"Youngest brother," Rags snapped. "What are you saying to Nell?"

"He's just teasing me again," I said. "He told me that this vegetable dish has real human hair in it, taken from someone who's cut off his queue."

Yong Liao laughed loudly. Rags and Jiang turned to watch as Huang Min placed a platter of dumplings in front of them. The girl batted her eyelashes at Jiang and he blushed. Rags frowned. Her flirting was so unseemly.

Bobby nudged me with his elbow. He stared into my eyes with an unusual intensity. "Oh, thank you. You saved my skin. You're the best."

Bobby passed the food platter my way, and I spooned pork dumplings onto my plate.

We picked up our chopsticks. I stared at Rags. A New Year, full of promise: Nell Doherty, a detective and in love. I imagined living with Rags in an apartment in Chicago. Every Sunday, on my day off from Pinkerton's, I would bake him an apple pie that he wouldn't have to share with his brothers. He would be so happy, he would sweep me off my feet and kiss me. Life would be perfect.

Pork dumplings had never tasted so good.

At all of the tables, everyone ate, drank tea or rice wine, and wished each other a healthy and prosperous New Year. Mrs. Wu spoke to Yong Liao. "I hear Vern Jorgensen's horse's come back from Aurora without 'im."

"Yes," Yong Liao said. He slurped his tea.

Mrs. Wu grabbed some of the black-hair noodles with her chopsticks. "I'n't that where the four Chinamen from Virginia City are supposed to have disappeared?"

Another mystery? Could it be related to the disappearance of Deputy Jorgensen?

Chapter Seven

A little after eleven o'clock, I left the Wu's apartment. I eased myself down each time I lowered my wooden leg onto a snow-powdered step on the back staircase. Rose-tinged snowflakes fell near the red lanterns in front of Yong Liao's mercantile. I jumped when a string of firecrackers exploded on the boardwalk a few feet behind me. The window of the Wu's apartment stood open. Bobby hung out the window. He waved his arm. "Happy New Year!"

Rags rapped Bobby on the head with his knuckles. Bobby cringed and pulled his head back into the apartment. Rags spoke softly: "Nell, are you okay?"

"Yes."

His crooked smile lit up his face. I waved and strolled on, the snow crunching under my boots. I ran my gloved fingers along the side of the building Rags called home. We hadn't had a moment alone. There'd been no chance to ask him who he loved.

Music lured customers to a nearby saloon and to Smith's Dance Hall where back doors led onto Virgin Alley, which stretched north of the mercantile, past houses of merriment and sin toward the jail. Curious, I peered from beneath my bonnet as I passed the alley's opening. A drunk banged on the door to one of the cribs that lined the opposite side of the street. Was he seeking the attentions of Huang Min? Hard to believe such a young girl could be a harlot. Surely, she was too young to have chosen that way of life. *I have to ask Rags about her. Even though he's my age, he knows more of the ways of the world than I do.*

Oh, Rags. Is it me that you truly love?

As I reached Main Street, I met the returning posse led by Odysseus Superbus Snethens. Papa's horse was tied up in front of the Dance Hall. That struck me as strange, but I was more interested in the fate of Deputy Jorgensen. I called to Judge Snethens and he pulled up. The other riders continued on. In the light that spilled out of a saloon's large windows, the judge's cheeks glowed as red as his nose.

"Did you find him?" I asked.

"I'm afraid to say that Providence failed us, my dear. We saw not the least sign of him."

The judge's Palomino, reddish-gold with a white mane, shivered beneath him. Snethens leaned forward and the snow that covered his shoulders and the brim of his Stetson fell as he patted his horse's flank. "There, there, Arion. We will reach the stables anon."

Poor Deputy Jorgensen. Could he survive if he was outdoors in this snowstorm overnight? The judge leaned down farther from his saddle and put his gloved hand on my shoulder.

"Now, don't worry yourself, my dear. In the war, I and my troops often slept in the snow and survived. The posse will be out searching again at first light. Your father told half our party to stay the night in Aurora, where they're making inquiries to ascertain if anyone knows the whereabouts of our deputy. At dawn, they will advance westward from Aurora while your father and I and the others who returned to Bodie will once more maneuver eastward. We'll find him."

"Thank you, Judge."

"Adieu." The judge turned his horse toward the stable.

I thought of the blood on Deputy Jorgensen's horse and of the cold. Could he really survive until morning?

Papa's bay was still tied up in front of Smith's, so I trod down the boardwalk until I stood in front of the dance hall. I looked through the glass doors. A band consisting of a piano, violin, mandolin, and banjo played a spritely tune. Miners and dance-hall girls crowded onto the sawdust-covered floor. Some pairs barely swayed right and left, the miner's head resting on the girl's shoulder. One miner high-stepped, as if he wanted to kick the ceiling. His female partner held his right hand and did her best to stay away from her partner's boots.

My jaw dropped open. In the middle of the floor, Irene Lockhart danced with Papa. He held one of Mrs. Lockhart's hands in his, his other lay against the back of her short dress. They spun about, talking cheek-to-cheek, smiling, happy as larks. I glared at them.

How could Papa do this to Mama? Had he forgotten Deputy Jorgensen? My face burned. It was below freezing, but sweat broke out on my forehead.

The music ceased, and Papa and Mrs. Lockhart stopped twirling. Mrs. Lockhart faced the two glass doors. I pulled my face away and hastened toward home.

I stomped down Main Street, kicking frozen tufts of snow that dared to stand in my path. My thoughts swirled like the snowflakes in the yellowish lights of a saloon I passed. Was this what the troubles were between Mama and Papa? In front of our house, I covered my face with my hands and wept.

It wouldn't do to let Mama see me like this. I took a deep breath of the frigid night air and wiped the tears from my cheeks. Two more deep breaths cooled my fears.

I entered the house. Mama sat on the couch darning Papa's

socks. Tears came to my eyes again. I pretended to sneeze to hide them.

"'Bout time you got home," Mama said, looking at the sock she was mending. "Did you enjoy yourself?"

"Very much." I took off my overcoat and hung it on a peg by the door.

Mama looked up. Her eyes were red-rimmed. "What on earth are you wearing?"

"It's my new dress. Mrs. Wu gave it to me. Do you like it?"

Mama's hands dropped into her lap. "What's got into you? Respectable women don't sashay about in red. It shouts 'Look at me. Look at me.'"

"Mama, it's for the Chinese New Year. Red is supposed to bring good luck."

"Good luck comes only from hard work and prayer."

"Have you heard that Vern Jorgensen is missing?"

Mama pulled the wooden darning egg from one sock and put it inside another. "Your father mentioned it before he left to search. I went over and helped Ingrid put her little ones to bed and then sat with her a while. We shared a good long cry." That explained her red-rimmed eyes. Mama shook her head. "Ingrid's beside herself with fear. The little ones, God bless 'em, are too young to know what's what."

Should I tell Mama the posse had returned without finding Vern? If I did, she might ask about Papa. My thoughts about him were still unsettled. What did his dancing with Mrs. Lockhart mean for Mama? My stomach tied itself in knots. It took all my energy not to wrap my arms around my middle.

Mama yawned. I sat down next to her.

"Mama, I'm too wound up to go to sleep now. Why don't you go to bed? I'll finish darning the socks."

"All right." She handed me the needle and the sock she was working on, then kissed me on the cheek.

She got up, turned, and stared at my Chinese dress again. "It is a pretty dress—I like the butterflies. But red, that will attract the wrong kind of man, my dear."

Rags isn't the wrong sort for me. Mama would not be pleased, though, if I were to marry a Chinese, even one who was half Irish.

Mama put on her overcoat and went out back to the privy. I tried to concentrate on the sewing. I couldn't. I was bothered by visions of Papa and Mrs. Lockhart dancing. Mrs. Lockhart in her knee-length ruffled satin dress, her head craned next to Papa's neck, both of them laughing gaily. That shouldn't be.

"Good night, Nell," Mama said when she came back inside.

"Sleep well, Mama."

Soon thereafter, I heard her gentle snoring. I made my own visit to the privy and brought in firewood from our padlocked shed. As I added wood to the stove, Papa and Patrick came in the front door. Patrick mumbled: "Rosy said she luffs me, she did. She luffs me, Pa." Papa rolled his eyes. I smelled whiskey on Patrick's breath. Papa supported him as they shuffled into the bedroom I shared with my brother.

A few seconds later Papa came back into the parlor and sagged onto the couch. "How was the New Year's celebration?"

I looked down and stabbed the needle into the sock I was stitching. "It was, uh, marvelous," I said. I couldn't sit next to him. "Can I get you something to eat?"

"Not just yet." He let out a big sigh. "Miss Lockhart saw you."

"What?"

"She saw you looking through the window at Smith's. You saw us dancing, didn't you?"

"Yes." Where was this going?

I grabbed the end of the couch, hauled myself to my feet, and hitched to the kitchen end of the room. He followed me.

"Nell, it's not what you think," he whispered. "I can't say more than that."

"But Papa ..."

"Trust me, girl," he said. "Trust me."

He pulled my head against his broad shoulder, where Mrs. Lockhart's head had lain, where I could smell her lavender perfume.

Chapter Eight

Papa released me from his embrace. "This will have to be our little secret."

He looked so serious I had to accept his non-explanation. But what explanation could there be, other than that he was unfaithful to Mama? I wanted to believe him, but ...

He yawned and stretched. "Now, I could use some food. How about you?"

Mama had left stew in a pot inside the oven's warming closet, next to a pan of fresh-baked biscuits. I laid this out on the dining table along with some butter. While Papa tucked into his stew, I took a baked apple pie Mama had left on the counter under a cloth and put it into the warmer. I set the coffee pot on the stove and stood there not knowing what to do.

"You going to watch the pot boil?"

I bit my lip and shook my head.

"Come, darlin', sit down."

I took the chair across the table from Papa, chewing my thumbnail to avoid looking at him. I couldn't just sit there ignoring him. I bounced my real leg nervously under the table. Maybe he'd told me the truth. Maybe he was the same Papa I'd always known and loved. There must be something we could talk about, other than his dancing with Mrs. Lockhart. Something normal. Something safe.

"Papa, do you think Deputy Jorgensen will be all right?"

"I sure hope so." He stood, ladled more stew onto his plate, and returned to the table.

"Why were you only looking for Deputy Jorgensen between here and Aurora? Had you sent him to Aurora? Is that where you believe the stolen gold is?"

"Like Sherlock Holmes, daughter, I keep my theories to myself until I have established all the facts."

"But you must have a suspect?"

"You will not draw any more out of me tonight, young lady. I won't go accusing someone based on supposings. I need evidence I can bring to court."

"You can't give me a hint?"

Papa chewed his lamb for a minute. A roguish gleam entered his eye. "You know what a real detective would do? A real detective would look at the facts and draw conclusions."

"Very well. Give me your pipe."

"My pipe?"

I held my hand out across the table. "Come, come, Watson, I've no time for foolishness."

"It's in my coat pocket."

I retrieved the curved pipe, put the ashy-tasting stem, unlit, into my mouth, and paced between the stove and the dining table. Holding the bowl of the pipe as I spoke around its stem, and in a feigned English accent, I said: "We know that on October 14th and again a week ago, the stage between Bodie and Hawthorne was robbed of gold bullion belonging to the Standard Mine. We know the thieves are clever."

"Excuse me, Holmes," Papa said, "but how did you deduce their cleverness?"

"It's plain as day, old chap. One of the most difficult aspects of stealing these bullion shipments was the ability to make off with the ingots on horseback, since they weighed over 100 pounds apiece. These thieves eliminated this problem by stealing the stagecoach along with the gold. The fact that they forced the driver to go with them also indicates cunning greater than that of the average criminal, for it is no mean thing to make one's way along the snow-covered Bodie Creek trail in the dark."

"Very good, Holmes," Papa said, "but wasn't the stagecoach found a few miles down the trail with its unconscious driver inside? How would the thieves have carried the gold from that point?"

I stopped pacing and frowned around the pipe. "A good question."

Papa got up from the table and took the warmed apple pie from the oven. He sliced a piece for himself and a second piece for me. He poured coffee into his tin cup. He put two plates with pie on the table, retrieved his coffee and sat back down. "Well, Holmes?"

"Well, obviously, the thieves transferred the gold to a wagon. They did that because they would have raised suspicions if they had ridden the stage into Aurora, or passed by Five Mile House on the way to Hawthorne."

I puffed out my chest, pleased with my deduction.

"So, Holmes, where is the gold?"

Papa apparently thought the gold was in Aurora, but why? I paced some more. Someone in a wagon could go anywhere. Why stay in Aurora?

"The gold is in Aurora, because even in a wagon they'd still be conspicuous driving at night right after the holdup. So they'd want to travel only a short distance to avoid being seen. And they'd want to lay low for a while, too, in case a posse was out looking for anyone travelling on the Bodie Creek Road."

"Sounds very logical."

"So, am I right?"

"Sherlock Holmes is never wrong."

"Papa."

He took his dishes to the sink. "I have to make my rounds. And you should get to bed."

I yanked the pipe from my mouth and stamped my good foot on the floor. "You're not being fair."

"Darlin', I told you, I'm not going to say any more until I have all the facts."

In the distance, fireworks exploded or someone fired a gun.

Papa shook his head. "Someone's celebrating Chinese New Year a little late." He hugged me again and kissed my forehead. "Off to bed with you."

On the other side of our bedroom, Patrick babbled in his sleep: "Rosy ... Rosy, girl." Tonight at least, he wasn't snoring.

I put my new dress in the bottom drawer of my dresser and pulled on my nightgown. Sitting on the edge of my bed, I loosened the cinches holding the wooden leg to my thigh then took off the short stocking I wear over the stump and rubbed liniment on my skin. It had only hurt a little that day.

I slipped under the covers, rolled onto my side, and thought of the day's mysteries.

What had happened to Deputy Jorgensen, and would he be found alive? Would things be okay between Mama and Papa? Despite what Papa said, he shouldn't have been dancing with Mrs. Lockhart.

I drifted to sleep wondering if it was me Rags loved.

THE SOUND OF MAMA AND PAPA QUARRELLING IN THEIR bedroom woke me. I put my ear to the wall. Mama was sobbing.

"Don't touch me," she said. "Go back to your lavender-scented harlot."

Mama must have smelled Mrs. Lockhart's perfume and

concluded Papa was seeing another woman. If it wasn't what it seemed like, why didn't Papa tell Mama the truth?

"I'm sorry, Mother, really. I never meant to hurt you."

"Go. Just ... leave me alone." She blew her nose, then added, "And don't you go near my babies."

A minute later I heard Papa, the love of Mama's life, open the front door and step into the bitter night. I threw the blankets over my head, bit down hard on my pillow, and bawled.

Chapter Nine

Not long after drifting back to sleep, I awoke to someone knocking on our front door. I heard Mama shuffle across our parlor. The front door creaked open and Mama said, "What are you doing here?" After a muffled response, Mama wailed, "Noooo!"

I threw off my covers, hopped on my good leg, and opened my bedroom door. The big room was lit by a kerosene lamp that Mama had apparently set on the floor. She was sobbing. Judge Snethens held her hands in his. He looked at me, his bloodshot eyes moist. "Your father's been shot."

It couldn't be. Surely I'd heard wrong, but the judge wore the truth on his haggard face. I felt as woozy as if I'd closed my eyes and spun in circles. I clutched the door jamb to keep from falling. "Will Papa be all right?"

"I don't know. Doc Boyle's tending to him."

"Oh, God."

"Nell," the judge said, "Get yourself dressed. Wake your brother."

Judge Snethens led Mama to the couch. She rocked back and

forth, her hands balled into fists. Tears ran down her cheeks. "He's dying, isn't he, Judge?"

"Mama," I said, "don't say that. Papa's going to be okay." He had to be okay. He was my hero, my ally, my protector.

"Now, now, Molly," the judge said, "Sam's in good hands. The doc saved hundreds of men with gunshot wounds in the war, and dozens more since." He looked at me. "Nell, don't tarry."

I closed the door, hopped across the bedroom, and lit the candle on my dresser. I shook Patrick. "Wake up. Wake up."

He raised himself up on his elbows. "What's goin' on? Are you crying?"

I sniffled and shook my head. "It's Papa. He's been shot."

"Shot?" Patrick threw off his covers and leapt from his bed. "Jesus. Is he hurt bad?"

"Judge Snethens is here." I bit my lip to keep from blubbering. "Papa must be in a bad way."

"Do you know who done it then?"

"No. Just get dressed."

Patrick threw on his trousers and shirt while I cinched up my wooden leg and pulled on my petticoat and my everyday dress. My fingers trembled as I fumbled with the buttons.

Minutes later, Judge Snethens took Mama's arm and led us out into the chilly night. Large wet snowflakes were falling. We hurried through fresh snow as we made our way to Main Street, the only sound the continuous hammering of the gold mills. I struggled to keep up with the others. Running was not something I did well, or safely.

We ascended the stairs to Doc Boyle's surgery and opened the door to a sharp, sweet medicinal odor. Papa lay on Doc's leather examination table beneath a bare electric bulb. Mama and Patrick rushed forward, but I paused and bent over, pushing against the pain in my ribs.

A blood-stained sheet covered Papa from his waist to the tops of his socks. Doc Boyle and his wife hunched over Papa. The doctor was sewing up the skin around an oozing hole in his stomach. Mama gasped. She tentatively took Papa's hand. "Oh, Sam."

Papa's pale body bled from two wounds, the jagged hole Doc was sewing up and a smaller inflamed circle the size of a nickel in his shoulder. Two wounds, but his chest rose and fell. He was alive. I released the breath I'd been holding and the stitch in my side stabbed again. Fear and relief hammered my heart.

Patrick pulled at his hair. "He's gonna be all right, isn't he Doc?"

"Let him finish, son," Judge Snethens said.

Mrs. Boyle held a brown bottle in her left hand, and she released drops of a clear liquid onto a mask of wire and cloth which covered Papa's nose and mouth. Bloody rags filled a bucket at Doc Boyle's feet. Blood speckled his shirt front and cuffs. His fingers were red.

"How bad is he?" Mama asked.

Doc paused his stitching. He looked at Mama, his eyes weary and sad. "Sam was shot twice. I extracted one bullet. The second went clear through him. I've stanched the bleeding."

Mama grabbed Patrick's arm. Tears cascaded down her cheeks. "Will he live, Doc?"

"He has a chance."

Only a chance? Oh, God, please help Papa. How would we survive without him? What would happen to Mama? And me? Would I lose the chance to go to Chicago and become a detective? I scolded myself and put that selfish thought out of my mind.

Doc added two more stitches and tied a knot. "Done."

Mrs. Boyle picked up scissors and cut the excess thread sticking out of Papa's stomach. She handed Doc another threaded needle. He stuck it into Papa's shoulder and I cringed. Mama collapsed to the floor. Patrick and Justice Snethens picked her up and helped her into a chair in the dark corner of the room.

"Who shot Papa?" Patrick demanded. "I'm going to kill him."

Justice Snethens cast a cold eye on Patrick. "Why don't we say a prayer for your Papa?" The judge removed his wide-brimmed Stetson and lowered his eyes.

"Dear Lord, hear us, please. We pray on behalf of a kind man, Marshal Sam Doherty, a good friend, husband, and father. Please heal his wounds and return him to us, full of life and health. Amen."

"Amen," Mama, Patrick, and I said together.

Mrs. Boyle crossed herself. Mama pulled a handkerchief from her sleeve and sopped up her tears.

Doc Boyle remained bent over Papa, slipping the needle in and out of his shoulder. Each time he stuck Papa, I jerked as if I too had been stabbed. Finally, he tied a knot and Mrs. Boyle cut the thread with her scissors.

"You can stop the ether now," he said.

His wife removed the mask from Papa's face. After cleaning his chest with a damp cloth, Doc pulled the sheet up to Papa's chin.

Mama lifted herself from the chair and staggered to the table. She combed Papa's thinning hair with her fingers. Her lips trembled before she managed to ask: "Doc, please, I have to know ... will he live?"

"The good news is, neither bullet hit a major organ. He lost a fair amount of blood, but he should survive that. What worries me is that bullet wounds cause infection. If the infection's not too bad, he'll pull through. We won't know for several days."

Mama stared at Papa lying on the table. Her lips trembled again.

Fresh tears streaked my cheeks.

Doc put his hand on Mama's shoulder. "Molly, I've done all I can. Go home and get some sleep. I'll let you know if there's a change."

Mama stood frozen in place.

"Patrick, you should take your mother home."

"Come on, Mama." My brother took her arm.

"Mama," I said, "I'm going to stay a little longer."

She patted my shoulder. "Okay."

Patrick led Mama out the door of the surgery.

Hot fear and cold anger battled inside me. The anger won. I wiped the tears from my face. I had questions. "Judge, who shot Papa?"

"Micah Pettibone."

"Micah Pettibone? That's ridiculous. Everybody knows Mr. Pettibone has no use for anything other than liquor. If he found a pistol, he'd have sold it to buy whiskey."

"He was found dead drunk, lying in the snow a few feet from your Papa, with the gun at his side. According to Bill Hoffman, Pettibone was celebrating Chinese New Year and shot your Papa by accident."

I looked up at the judge. "Bill Hoffman is Bodie's biggest liar. He says Pettibone shot Papa by accident—twice—and you believe him?"

"He says he witnessed the shooting."

"I want to talk to Pettibone."

"Not possible now. He's in jail sleeping off his drunk."

"I want to see where it happened."

"For heaven's sake, what for?"

"To find clues to who really shot Papa. It's what Sherlock Holmes would do. It's what Papa would do if someone else had been shot."

Judge Snethens closed his eyes and shook his head. "Let's wait till morning."

"We can't. It's snowing. If we don't look now, marks in the snow will get covered up. There may be evidence that proves Bill Hoffman's story, or disproves it, but it will disappear by morning."

"Nell—"

"There's no law left in Bodie. There's no one else to investigate Papa's shooting. I'm going to do it, even if you won't help."

The judge pulled on his gloves. "All right. But we're going to my hotel first. I need a drink, and we need a lantern."

Papa slept peacefully on the table. I leaned over him. His face was so pale. *Don't leave me, Papa. Please, not yet.*

Mrs. Boyle brought over a pair of blankets. As she covered Papa's feet, I noticed his socks were mismatched. On his left foot was a gray sock I'd mended recently. I could tell by the imperfect line of stitches. His right foot was covered by a sock of a different shade of gray. I'd never seen that sock before. Maybe Mama bought him some new socks, but this one looked too large.

"Hiram," Mrs. Boyle said. "I'll go home now and come back first thing tomorrow. Nell, don't stay up too late." She gave me a hug. "Your Mama will need your help tomorrow." Mrs. Boyle pulled on her coat. She kissed Doc and left the surgery.

Doc Boyle added wood to his potbellied stove and pulled a chair up beside Papa.

"Judge, before we go, I have a couple of questions for Doc." I held my hands up to the stove. "Doc, why are the holes in Papa from the two bullets ..." I gulped. "Why are they different sizes?"

"Nell, I know you want to be a detective, but are you sure you have the stomach to discuss such things?"

I sniffed. "I don't have any choice." If I wanted to be a Pinkerton operative, I'd have to get used to violence.

"All right. About the bullets, one of them entered your father's body from the front and one from behind. I assume the first shot spun your father around and that's why the one bullet entered his body from the front and another from the back. Bullets often leave a bigger hole when they leave the body than when they enter it."

I imagined Papa being struck by each bullet in turn. Anger boiled inside me. I didn't know how, but I was going to figure out who shot Papa and see that he was punished.

Chapter Ten

M inutes later, the judge and I set out for Virgin Alley where Papa had been shot. Except for the light of the lantern the judge carried, Main Street was dark. Snow flurries whirled around us, some landing on my nose and eyelashes. In the gold mills on the hill, dozens of thundering iron hammers continued to pulverize ore.

"Hurry, Judge, before the snow covers the tracks."

"You're as determined as your father."

I stopped in my tracks. "Oh, Papa."

The judge put an arm around me. "You don't have to do this, Nell."

Was I a future Pinkerton detective, or a little girl? I could walk away. No one would expect me to do otherwise. No one except Mr. Pinkerton, and me.

"Show me where it happened."

The judge and I passed through an empty Chinatown. The now dark New Year's lanterns swayed in the slight breeze. In front of Yong Liao's mercantile, we turned up Virgin Alley. The door of one of the nearby brothels opened and a man stepped outside.

Inside, a woman giggled. The man turned around. He blew a kiss toward the door and it closed.

Judge Snethens cleared his throat. Like a startled rabbit, the man's head snapped toward us. A second later, he ran off.

"You really shouldn't be here," the judge said.

"I didn't see anything."

"Yes, well ..."

"Come on, Judge."

We continued north. I rubbed my gloved hands together to warm them.

The other cribs and brothels remained unlit and quiet. Ahead, a wide swath of snow lay at the back of the businesses on Main Street. Judge Snethens and I stopped abruptly near an outhouse. At my feet, a brownish stain covered an area as big across as Papa's chest. My breath caught. Part of Papa, part of his life's blood, had spilled here.

So much blood. I wanted this to be a bad dream. I wanted to feel Papa's arms around me, feel him stroke the back of my head, and hear him sing "Polly Wolly Doodle" like he used to do.

Fare-thee-well,
Fare-thee-well,
Mister gloom be on your way,
If you think you're gonna worry,
You can stop it in a hurry,
Singin' Polly Wolly Doodle all the day!

Tears welled in my eyes. Stop it, I told myself. I remembered what Papa said to me a short time ago. "A real detective looks at the facts and draws conclusions." I wouldn't be able to see clues through eyes full of tears.

Maybe I couldn't be as dispassionate as Sherlock Holmes, not after seeing Papa's terrible wounds, but I could search for the Son of Belial that shot him and cry later.

In *A Study in Scarlet*, Holmes read footprints made on an old carpet. Surely, I could read footprints in the snow. In the light of the judge's lantern, I looked at the ground and stared in disbelief. Unlike the scene in *A Study in Scarlet*, here there were many different sets of footprints. Men attracted by the gunfire, men who carried Papa to Doc Boyle's, and the would-be assassin. Only rarely could I glean the shape of a particular boot or its heel.

"Look at these overlapping footprints. They've all been trampled by other feet. This isn't fair!"

"Steady, child. Steady."

"Judge, how am I supposed to trace the steps of the snake that shot Papa? It's impossible to read anything in this mess."

"Difficult, yes, but not impossible." The judge pointed to my left. "Look. Those footprints with a small heel are a woman's. Calm yourself, my dear, and see what can be seen. Here." The judge put the lantern on the ground. He removed the flask from his coat pocket. "Take two sips of these medicinal spirits."

I shook my head.

"I insist." He unscrewed the silver cap and filled it from the flask. He handed me the cap. I turned up my nose at the pungent smell.

"Sometimes a person needs a bit of liquid courage. A little bit can trick the brain, suppressing the myriad demons of thoughts and allowing you to focus on the singular consequential one. Now, go on, imbibe."

My first-ever sip of alcohol burned my tongue and throat. I choked. It tasted like tar and reminded me of a patent medicine Mama gave me once that contained turpentine. "This tastes awful."

"One more sip."

The whiskey tasted just as bad the second time. I coughed for half a minute.

Judge Snethens took a long pull from the flask and then

screwed the cap back on. He didn't wince or cough. He winked conspiratorially.

How could the judge drink this rot gut all day and night? What could make it worthwhile? A pleasant warming sensation spread inside my stomach and chest. I wasn't on the verge of crying anymore.

"Feeling better?"

"A little. It's foul-tasting, but thanks."

"Okay, then," the judge said. He lifted the lantern above his head. "Tell me what you can see."

The snow was coming down harder than before. I needed to hurry. I took a deep breath and inched around the circle of light, bent, studying the ground. One set of footprints left the scene of the shooting and led to the gap between Magee's Saloon and a long-closed bootmaker's shop, both of which fronted Main Street. They ran in a straight line initially, and then, between the two buildings, the footprints zigzagged wildly. Strange. The impressions disappeared as soon as they reached the boardwalk along Main.

I returned to the spot where Papa's blood had turned the snow a brownish red. I followed the small footprints that Judge Snethens had pointed out earlier, the ones with small heel impressions that looked like a woman's boot prints. They came and went from the backdoor of Smith's Dance Hall. Could they belong to Irene Lockhart, the woman I'd met just yesterday, the woman I'd seen dancing with Papa?

"Judge, these footprints must belong to one of the dance-hall girls. We should talk to them."

The judge pursed his lips. "That's a job for the county sheriff."

I tilted my head up at him. "But he's on his honeymoon in San Francisco."

I looked at the blood-stained snow, at the last boot prints left by Papa's feet. Despite the snow flurries and the myriad other boot prints, I could tell he had been facing south, in the direction of the Chinese quarter, when he fell. His footprints appeared to come from the north end of Virgin Alley, where the jail was located. He had probably just left the jail to make his rounds when ... Tears welled in my eyes again. I bit my lip.

"Have you completed your perscrutation?"

"My what?"

"Your search."

"Why do you use big words no one else understands?"

He chuckled. "People expect a judge to be not only intelligent, but also to be ..." He paused. "... pansophic."

"What?"

"To be pansophic is to be wise and all-knowing. I reinforce my sage image by using sesquipedalians, or, as you call them, big words." Judge Snethens lowered the lantern. "Let's go home, my dear."

Something in the snow caught the light. Something shiny. A few feet from where Papa's head had fallen, I picked up a gold lapel pin depicting a knight's helmet on top of a shield bearing three letters: F and C at the top, and the letter B at the bottom.

"Do you know what this is, Judge?"

"A pin for the Knights of Pythias."

"Was Pettibone a member?"

"Heaven forbid. We accept drinkers, but we do not countenance drunks."

"We? I thought you belonged to the Masons."

"So I do. I have memberships in most of the clubs here in Bodie. I've even been granted an honorary membership in the miners' union. I enjoy the good fellowship of all of these organizations, and the votes of their members at election time."

I put the pin in my pocket. "Can you find out who may have lost the pin? The devil that shot Papa must have dropped it."

We had taken two steps away from the red stain in the snow when I saw them. A line of small, perfectly round holes punctured the snow beyond the trampled area. Evenly spaced, about four feet apart, the circular indentations paralleled a set of men's boot prints that headed south toward King Street. The man whose round-toed boots made these prints walked with a cane. I knew who did it.

"Judge, look." I pointed at the little holes. "Erastus Kohl was here. He shot Papa."

"Erastus Kohl isn't the only man in Bodie who walks with the assistance of a cane. And, besides, Bill Hoffman said Pettibone shot your father."

"I don't care what Bill Hoffman says. Erastus Kohl promised to get even with Papa for sending him to prison. We should arrest him."

"Arrest him?"

"I know it's Kohl. I know he shot Papa. We can't let him get away."

The judge lifted the lantern level with his head, trod past where Papa had been shot, and circled the outhouse. "It appears from the prints in the snow that the man with the cane crossed your father's path. The two of them may have ambulated by at different times. Still, let's go have a talk with Kohl. Not just because of your suspicions, Nell, but because he's a member of the Knights of Pythias."

"That's another proof that Kohl did it." I stomped off toward Main Street as fast as I could go, elated in my conviction that we were about to arrest the devil who'd shot Papa.

"Nell, slow down," Judge Snethens said. "It's late. Somnus beckons."

We trudged clear across town, keeping to the boardwalk until we reached Green Street, where we turned up the hill. There were no lights except the judge's lantern. Other than the stamp mills, the only sounds we heard in the quarter-hour walk were the creak and clap of a privy door.

Reaching narrow, snow-covered Wood Street, we passed St.

John the Baptist Catholic Church with its simple wooden cross at the peak of its roof. I blessed myself, put my gloved hands together, and prayed, "Jesus, please, please, help Papa get well."

A minute later, we reached the door of Erastus Kohl's white-painted house. A picket fence separated Kohl's place from his sole neighbor in this most southerly part of town.

In the snow at the corner of the small clapboard house lay the red and blue remains of a string of firecrackers.

"Looks like someone's been celebrating Chinese New Year," Judge Snethens said. He knocked on the door. "Nell, let me do the talking."

I waited maybe ten seconds, then pounded on the door with my fist.

The judge grabbed my arm. "Enough."

From inside, a woman's voice said, "I'm comin'. I'm comin'."

The door opened. Rachel Kohl stood in the doorway wearing an overcoat over her night gown. She was a stout woman, with a pair of thick blonde ponytails falling midway down her back. "Is he dead?"

"No," I screamed, "but thanks to your husband, he may die."

"Vat you yellin' 'bout?"

The judge put his hand on my shoulder. "I'm supposed to do the talking, remember?" He stepped between me and Mrs. Kohl. "Rachel, the marshal's been shot. I'd like to have a word with Erastus."

"Rat Face?" Mrs. Kohl spat on the floor. "Rat Face no here. You vant to talk to him, find da whore he sleepin' vith."

Judge Snethens glanced back at me, apparently worried about what I'd just heard. The word "whore" didn't surprise me, but her anger did. How terribly sad, to hate your husband, but be forced to live with him because you had no other choice. Was that how Mama felt when she told Papa to leave the house? She couldn't hate him. If she did, she wouldn't have cried over him or touched his face so tenderly. I hoped to marry a good man. I thought Rags

56

was a good man, but how do you know for certain? Mrs. Kohl hadn't known.

"Rachel," the judge said, "when you see your husband, tell him he needs to come talk to me."

"You goin' to arrest him? Good. I sock him on da head and wrap him up like roast of beef, let you carry to yail."

"Just let him know he needs to talk to me."

"Yah. For sure." She closed the door.

The judge turned around. "Don't get any ideas about searching for Kohl among the bordellos and cribs on Virgin Alley. I'm going to escort you home."

"But—"

He held up his hand. "We both need sleep."

"But he could get away."

"We've only uncovered circumstantial evidence. We don't know Kohl's guilty."

How could the judge say that? "I do."

"Well, I don't, and I'm the law."

Chapter Eleven

Fifteen minutes later we turned onto Park Street and approached my front door. "Thank you for accompanying me, Judge."

"It appears that your mother is still up."

The light was on in our parlor.

"Would you like to come in? I could fix you a cup of coffee."

"No, thank you. I'm off to the jail to check on Mr. Pettibone. I'll check on your father a little later. Have faith."

"Goodnight, Judge."

"'Night."

I paused, hand on the doorknob and braced myself for angry words. I took a deep breath and opened the door.

Mama knelt, scrubbing the wooden floor with a brush and a bucket of steaming soapy water. Tears trickled down her cheeks.

"Mama, what are you doing?"

"I couldn't sleep for worry."

Her worry reawakened my own fears.

"Oh, child, come here."

Mama stood and took me in her arms.

"Are you afraid Papa's going to die?"

"Shush." She hugged me tighter. "Judge Snethens is right. We must hope for the best."

"Then why were you crying?"

"'Tis the shock of it. A reminder of how short life can be—not just your father's, but all of our lives, mine included. I've been reminded of my duties here on Earth: to be kind, to be loving. And most of all," she took a shuddering breath, "to be forgiving."

Did she feel guilty about her argument with Papa and sending him away? Should I tell her what Papa said, that his dancing with Mrs. Lockhart wasn't what it looked like? No. She wouldn't want me to know about their troubles, or to worry over them. Telling her would only cause her additional concern.

"How was your father when you left him?"

"He looked peaceful."

We held each other in silence for a moment.

"Nell, get yourself to bed. It will be light soon."

"I'll go if you will."

THREE HOURS LATER, IN A GRAY DAWN LIGHT, MAMA and I made our way to Doc Boyle's. Snow crunched under our boots. Mama said she had tried but hadn't slept a wink. I had slept fitfully. We met Mrs. Boyle at the bottom of the stairs leading to the surgery. She carried a bundle of wood. "Good morning, Molly, Nell."

"How is he? How's my Sam?" Mama asked.

"Both he and Hiram are asleep, bless their hearts."

I took half the logs from Mrs. Boyle and followed her and Mama up the stairs.

Doc, head on chest, slept in his chair next to the examination table. He was covered by a wool shawl. Papa still lay on the padded table under blankets, his face a ghostly white. I put the logs in a wooden box inside the door, grabbed Mama's arm and we hurried to Papa's side. She leaned down next to his ear and whispered, "Can you hear me, darling?"

Papa remained silent. I gave Mama a hug.

We shouldn't have to be going through this. Mama shouldn't be suffering. And Papa shouldn't have been shot. I'd be *damned* —I could use that word in my head, at least—if I was going to let Erastus Kohl get away with this. Earlier that morning, during one of my spells of wakefulness in bed, I swore that the devil who shot Papa would not get away with it. Erastus Kohl was going back to prison.

I fought back being angry, realizing Mama must be exhausted. Three leather-padded wooden chairs sat against the wall next to the surgery's door. I dragged one over and had Mama sit. She caressed Papa's cheek.

Mrs. Boyle added wood to the potbellied stove and set a tin pot on it. The aroma of coffee soon filled the surgery and Doc stirred in his chair. He opened his eyes and looked about, then stretched and yawned.

"Mornin', ladies."

He pulled his watch from his vest pocket and checked the time. "My, my, these old bones demand their rest."

"How's my husband?" Mama asked.

Doc removed the shawl and stood. He rewound his pocket watch and squeezed Papa's wrist while watching the time. "His pulse rate is high, his breathing, too, but that is to be expected."

Doc put a hand on Papa's forehead. "Hmm."

"What is it?" Mama said. "Tell me."

"His fever is up a bit, Molly. But don't get upset. I told you this was likely. This is how things progress sometimes. The fever comes and it goes. We just have to wait it out. Talk to him. Hold his hand. Let him know you're here."

Mama pulled Papa's left hand from under the blankets and held it. "I'm here, darling. So is Nell."

Mrs. Boyle poured coffee into a cup. "Two teaspoons of sugar, dear?"

Doc rubbed his whiskered chin. "Three, please."

She raised her eyebrows, but added the requested amount of sugar and brought him the cup. She kissed him on the cheek. "Would anyone else like coffee?"

Mama and I declined. Mama laid her head on Papa's chest. She closed her eyes and clung to his hand. She was so gentle. Not like during the previous night's argument. *She loves him so much. I love them both so much it hurts.*

"I love you, Mama."

She'd fallen to sleep. Lucky for me.

"Doc," I whispered. "Can you tell me who carried Papa here? I'd like to find out if any of them saw the shooting." ... and could confirm Erastus Kohl's guilt.

"Still investigating, eh?" He took a sip of his coffee. "I remember Henry Lewis and Buck Thompson. That new photographer, Gideon Weed, he was one of them, too. The others—" He shook his head. "I don't recollect. I was too concerned with caring for your father."

The door burst open and Albert Reeves, sour-faced editor of *The Bodie Miner*, rushed into the surgery. "Quick, Doc! Judge Snethens wants you. A mob's set to hang Micah Pettibone for killing the marshal."

"Hush," Mrs. Boyle said. She pointed at my sleeping parents.

"What mob?" Doc asked softly.

"More'n a hundred ne'er-do-wells carrying as many uncorked bottles and a single rope. They're threatening to storm the jail."

"This early in the morning?"

"I saw them with my own eyes."

"You're seeing double, triple, and whatever comes after that. You sure you're not the one with the uncorked bottle?"

"Mr. Reeves," I said. "Mr. Pettibone isn't guilty."

Reeves snarled at me in a low voice. "Not guilty? How would you know, young lady?

"Well, he's certainly not guilty of murder," Doc said. "The marshal's still alive."

"That's what the judge said, but nobody believed him. That's why he sent me here. He needs you at the jail. So it's true then, the marshal's still alive?"

"See for yourself."

Reeves approached Papa's prostrate body. "Mercy."

"Keep your voice down," Mrs. Boyle whispered.

Reeves grimaced, but obeyed. "The mob aims to hang Petti-bone. It'll be a travesty. A travesty of justice." The editor strode to Doc's desk, pushed magazines and the microscope aside, and put pencil to paper. "A mob numbering upwards of a hundred men stormed the Bodie jail and ..."

"Calm yourself, Albert," Doc said. He laid his arm on Reeves's shoulder. "Go to the jail and enlighten those inebriated fools. Tell them what you've seen."

"They won't believe me."

"Hiram," Mrs. Boyle said, "Maybe you should go with Mr. Reeves and explain things to the mob. Nell and I'll stay here with Sam and Molly."

Chapter Twelve

I couldn't let a mob hang Micah Pettibone. He might be able to provide the evidence I needed to convince Judge Snethens that Kohl shot Papa. Unless I could find lyin' Bill Hoffman, Mr. Pettibone might be the only witness to the shooting.

Doc pulled on his overcoat and hat.

Even though Mama was sleeping, I whispered in her ear. "I need to go with Doc. I'll be back shortly."

She didn't stir.

Mrs. Boyle said, "You go on. I'll watch your parents."

"Thank you." Lucky me, I'd be able to escape without an argument with Mama.

I followed editor Reeves and Doc Boyle out the door. A brisk, ten-minute trot across snow-crusted streets took us past the silent cribs of Virgin Alley to the unpainted clapboard building that housed the marshal's office and the jail. My worst fears were allayed. Judge Snethens stood inside the front door. He faced a rag-tag group of two dozen men, many with bandanas covering their faces. Several carried handguns. Men in the back row passed a bottle of whiskey amongst themselves. Several members of the Vigilance Committee shouted demands.

"Stop yer stalling, Judge."

"Release the murderer."

"We wants justice," Skinny Davis yelled. He held a Winchester rifle over his head.

"Stop yer ditherin' and hand 'im over."

Pudgy Bill Hoffman staggered up to the much taller judge. Hoffman wore a red bandana over his nose and mouth, but the torn right pocket of his brown canvas jacket gave him away. He tried to look Judge Snethens in the face, but had to catch himself from falling backward. "Give 'im up, your honor, and let jestice be done." His bandana slipped off his nose. He grabbed it and held it in place. "Well, Judge?"

Snethens shook his head. He poked his short-barreled shotgun into Hoffman's chest. "When I look at you, I understand the lament of Shakespeare's *King Lear.* 'When we are born, we cry that we are come to this great stage of fools.' "

One of the bandana-masked men waved his hand dismissively. "Quit cher palaverin'."

The one with the rope lifted it up and shook it. "Yeah, bring out the prisoner. We gots committee business to attend to."

"Hold on, boys," Doc Boyle shouted as we mounted the boardwalk in front of the jail. "The marshal's still alive."

A few men in the crowd looked confused. Perhaps they were less intoxicated. "Are you sure, Doc?" one of them asked. "We was told the marshal was killed."

"I just came from tending to him. He's in a bad way, but he's definitely alive. Who told you the marshal was dead?"

"Bill Hoffman."

Bill stood on the boardwalk between Mr. Reeves and me—so close I could smell the whiskey on his breath. At the mention of his name, he tried to slip away. I grabbed his ear.

"Ow, ow, ow. Cut it out."

Raucous laughter broke out among the mob.

"Yer in fer it now, Bill," said one.

Bill shook his head, trying to break free, but I held tight. He lifted an arm as if to strike me.

I shoved my fist in front of his face. "You want more of this?"

Bill lowered his arm. "Let go, Pencil-Leg."

I yanked his ear and swung his head around. "What's my name?"

"Pen—"

I yanked his ear again, harder. "What's my name?"

"Nell."

The crowd snorted and chuckled. One of the bandana-wearing mob shoved the man next to him. "Seems Bill cain't handle his likker or his women."

More laughter followed this remark.

I kept my fist in Bill's face. "I've got some questions to ask you."

"Supposin' I don't feel like answerin'?"

"Then the judge will arrest you for disturbing the peace. Solitary confinement and no alcohol for a month."

Bill looked at the judge. "You can't do that. That ain't right."

Judge Snethens scratched his chin. "A proper sentence would be ninety days in jail. Ninety days without liquor."

Bill's shoulders sagged. Still clutching his ear, I hauled Bill into the marshal's office.

"Sit in Papa's chair behind the desk." I let go of his ear.

"You're a devil, Pen—, er, Nell."

The mounted posse sent to search for Deputy Jorgensen rode up in front of the jail, their pistols drawn.

"Looks like we got here just in time," Baron Catlow said. "You want us to arrest these varmints?" He cocked his revolver.

The mob took one look at the determined expressions on the faces of the posse and shuffled away.

Catlow and seven others dismounted and hitched up their horses. They crowded into the wall-papered office behind me, Doc Boyle, Mr. Reeves, and Judge Snethens.

Catlow's kind eyes fixed on me. He had always been gracious to me. "I'm sorry to hear about your father."

His comment reopened the wound in my heart. I took a deep breath and swallowed.

"Don't you worry, Miss Doherty," Catlow said, "your father's a tough fellow. I'm sure he'll pull through."

"Salutations, gentlemen," Judge Snethens said. "Since the marshal has been wounded, it is incumbent upon us to shoulder his responsibilities. Firstly, I suggest we choose someone among us to act as temporary marshal. We can't have everyone believing there are no officers of the law in town. Payday's fast-approaching. We'll need someone to handle the inebriants. Secondly, today's misguided Vigilance Committee was easily swayed. Tomorrow's might not be. So before we set out again to find Deputy Jorgensen, I believe we need to remove Micah Pettibone from Bodie, on the slight chance—" He glanced my way. "The very slight chance, the marshal does not recover."

The judge scanned the faces of the men. "Who'll be our temporary marshal?" The men looked back and forth at one another. "Come, come," the judge said. "We need to have at least one sworn lawman in town."

"Someone needs to arrest the filthy bushwhacker who shot my father," I said. "I've already discovered several clues to his identity. Erastus Kohl—"

"Nell," the judge snapped. "Don't go jumping the gun. Kohl is only someone we want to talk to."

I gritted my teeth and groaned. "Well, I will help the new marshal find enough evidence to jail whichever skunk shot Papa."

My determination was met with guffaws from most of the men in the room. Only Judge Snethens and Doc Boyle appeared to be considering it.

"Maybe," Doc said, "we should give Miss Doherty a chance and appoint her a special deputy to investigate her father's shooting."

Me a special deputy?

"Doc, we may be in a black need of some law in Bodie, but you're being ridiculous." This from Vincent Bardwell, apothecary. "She's a girl. And she's only got one leg."

"At least she's willing to do the job," Doc said. "Are you?"

Doc and Bardwell glared at each other for several seconds until Bardwell looked away.

Baron Catlow shook his head. "No woman has what it takes to be a lawman in Bodie."

I clenched my fists. Why couldn't they be as enlightened as Mr. Pinkerton? I obeyed Papa's dictum and counted to ten.

"What about Calamity Jane?" Doc asked.

"Never met her," Catlow said, "but I heard rumors she was really a man."

Doc cocked his head to the side. "I met her in Virginia City. She's a woman all right."

"How could ya tell?" Mr. Bardwell asked.

"She consulted me professionally." Doc turned from Bardwell to the judge. "Well, Odysseus, what do you say? Can Miss Doherty do the job?"

All eyes turned toward the tall jurist.

Will he do it? Pinkertons would have to hire me if I had experience as a deputy. I crossed my fingers.

"Well," Judge Snethens said, "I know for a fact Nell's already been looking into the shooting. As she said, she's already discovered several clues that may help locate the villain. She has a passion for the task, for obvious reasons." He looked down at Bill Hoffman who was picking a loose thread from his jacket cuff. "Mr. Hoffman's presence here is additional testimony to Nell's abilities."

"Ha!" Doc Boyle exclaimed. "You didn't see it, Mr. Catlow, but Nell pulled Bill Hoffman into jail right handily with just her thumb and forefinger."

"That may be," Catlow said, "but this town will never accept a girl deputy."

"Well," Doc said, "today they don't seem to have much choice."

The judge rapped his knuckles on Papa's desk. "Answer me this, gentlemen: which of you want the man who shot the marshal to get away scot free?"

Judge Snethens looked at each of the men in turn. No one spoke. Several nodded or shrugged their acceptance.

"A fine group of men you are. You leave me no choice at the moment," the judge said. He opened a desk drawer, pulled out two badges, and handed them to me. "Here, Nell, take these. I hereby appoint you a provisional deputy."

"Really?" My mouth opened and closed several times on its own, as if I were exercising my jaw. Me a deputy? Could I do the job? I'd read about how Mr. Pinkerton and Sherlock Holmes solved crimes. I already knew who did it. It should be easy to uncover the clues I needed to put Erastus Kohl behind bars.

"Well, Nell?"

"I'll do it, Judge."

Several of the men objected, but the judge just shook his head. "You had your chance. Nell, the proviso to your appointment as deputy is that you first get yourself a partner who knows how to use a shotgun. Raise your right hand."

My spirits lifted as my arm went up. *Yippee! I'm sure to be hired by the Pinkertons.*

"Nell Doherty, do you swear to uphold the laws of the State of California and of Mono County?"

"Yes, your honor."

The judge handed me his shotgun. "You still have to acquire a partner that can use this before your appointment as deputy takes effect. Maybe ask your brother."

"Thank you, your honor." I flushed with pride and pinned the badge to my coat.

"Remember, your assignment is limited to investigating your father's shooting."

"Judge, I take it you haven't talked to Kohl."

"No. His wife told me he's gone to one of the ranches near Mono Lake to get more meat. She said he'll be back this afternoon."

"You've given Kohl a chance to escape."

"What's all this talk about Erastus Kohl?" Catlow asked.

I gritted my teeth. Under Judge Snethens's stern glare, I had no choice but to keep my thoughts to myself. He still wanted more proof. As if we needed any more.

"I want to talk to Kohl is all," Judge Snethens said. "I believe he may have seen the shooting." The judge took me aside and whispered. "Nell, I want you to start by interrogating Hoffman and Pettibone. See if Hoffman will point the finger at Kohl, or if Pettibone can remember seeing Kohl shoot your pa. If we get a witness that says Kohl did it, we'll go after him."

"All right, your honor."

Judge Snethens turned to the others in the room. "Now, which of you stalwart burghers will assume the mantle of temporary marshal?"

Another long silence ensued. Usually, Bodie men jumped at the chance to help their fellow citizens. Why not this time?

"If that is too difficult a decision for you, can I get two volunteers to take Micah Pettibone to the county jail?"

Five hands went up.

Judge Snethens grunted. "Charlie Prentiss and Silas Tribble, please escort Mr. Pettibone to Bridgeport. I'll excuse Doc Boyle. The rest of you have had a few additional seconds to consider your civic obligations. Will one of you take the marshal's job?"

One by one the others offered excuses, some feeble, some legitimate.

"I canna lose another shift at the mill, yer honor."

"I'm needed at the shop."

"My wife is feeling a mite poorly, Judge."

"It'd ruin my business, wearin' a badge would. None of the boys'd be comfortable drinking with the law watchin' on. 'Sides, if'n they got drunk, I could hardly leave the bar to jail 'em, could I?"

Baron Catlow rubbed his chin. "I have the mine to run, but I could serve as an assistant deputy, in the evenings perhaps."

"This is most unsatisfactory," Judge Snethens said. "However, we should not delay our search for Vern Jorgensen any longer." He waved his arm toward the door with a flourish. "*Exeunt omnes.*"

"We'll be back to collect Pettibone," Charlie Prentiss said. "As soon as we saddle another horse."

After the posse left, Bill Hoffman bit his forefinger. He slapped the desk top several times. "Hee-hee ... hee-hee-hee."

"What's the matter with you?" I said.

"Don'tcha see? They's left you as the only law in town. Bodie's got itself a girl marshal, a peg-leg one to boot."

Chapter Thirteen

Me, the only law in town? I looked at the badge pinned to my coat. Deputy Marshal Nell Doherty. Well, really just Special Deputy. The judge would strongarm one of the posse to take Papa's place by the time they returned. My position as the only law in Bodie would no doubt be short-lived.

Papa would be proud. Mama would not. She would be as angry as a cornered rattlesnake. But someone needed to track down the godless cur who shot Papa. Since no one else volunteered, wasn't it, as the judge said, my civic duty? Of course, no argument would hold water with Mama, so I had to conduct my investigation quickly. Step one: interview the known witnesses—a drunk and a liar. I started with Pettibone, the drunk, since he was leaving soon for Bridgeport.

"Bill Hoffman, you stay put while I talk to Micah Pettibone."

I grabbed the large iron key from the hook behind Papa's desk and hitched to the cell at the end of the narrow hall. I peered through the small barred opening in the solid wooden door to see Pettibone hunched on the bed, fingering rosary beads with jittery hands, and whispering. "Hail Mary, full o' grace, the Lord is with thee—"

He looked up as I unlocked the door. Though his clothes were dry, Pettibone smelled like three-week old urine. I waved at the air in front of my face. It didn't help.

"Are you saying the rosary because you feel guilty, Mr. Pettibone?"

"No more'n usual, Miss Nell. My wife, Ailene, rest her soul, made me promise to start each day with me prayers. I do it still in her memory."

"Tell me about last night."

"Last night?" Pettibone dabbed at the side of his head. "Don't 'member last night, Miss. It's a fact I don't 'member most nights by the next morning."

How could he not remember? He was there. He had to recall. I wanted to cry but Sherlock Holmes wouldn't cry. I took a breath. "So, you don't remember why you're here?"

"I suppose I drank too much last night, like always, and your pa drug me in to sober up. Is your pa coming soon with breakfast?"

"Do you remember shooting someone last night?"

"If someone were shot, it weren't me that done it. Did you say yer pa's gonna let me out soon? I'm parched."

I bit my lip. "He won't be letting you out, Mr. Pettibone, because he's the one who was shot last night. Your friend Bill Hoffman says you did it."

Pettibone leapt from the bed. "He said what? Where is that miserable polecat? Where is he? Jest wait'll I get my hands on 'im." Pettibone wobbled and sat back down. "I'll skin him alive."

"Take it easy, Mr. Pettibone."

He looked at me through red-rimmed eyes. "I's everyone's friend, miss. You know that. Bill Hoffman, he's the lyingest mongrel in all o' Bodie. He's jest tryin' to puff hisself up, make like he's got a big story to tell. Thinks others'll buy 'im a beer to hear it. Miss, I never shot nobody. I don't even own a gun."

I believed Pettibone but decided to test him in case Bill Hoffman was telling the truth for what might have been the first time in his life. I hitched back to the front office to get the revolver that had been found in the snow next to Pettibone.

Bill Hoffman, blast him, had disappeared. I counted to ten and returned to Pettibone's cell with the pistol.

"Here is the gun that shot Papa. It was found lying next to you. Do you remember this gun? Or where you got it?"

"I never, miss. Never owned no pistol."

His sorrowful eyes touched my heart. "I believe you." Bill Hoffman was such a liar. I couldn't wait to get my hands on him. "Mr. Pettibone, did you see someone else shoot the marshal? Erastus Kohl, perhaps?"

"No, miss."

"Are you certain? Try to remember, Mr. Pettibone, try. Do you remember anything from last night?"

"I'm so sorry, miss, but I don't. Not exactly, anyway." Pettibone pulled his battered Union Army cap from his head. Only a few gray hairs sprouted on his age-spotted skull. Above his left ear was a raised purplish bruise the size of a silver dollar. "It's not so much 'membering from last night, but this morning. I've a frightful headache from this lump. I thought yer pa walloped me for some reason."

"Has Papa ever hit you before?"

"No, miss. He's always been kind. Is your papa going to be all right?"

"Doc Boyle isn't sure." The tears wanted to come again. I squeezed my eyes shut and pushed them back.

"I'm right sorry to hear that."

"I wish you could remember something from last night, something that would help me figure out who did it." I turned to leave the cell.

"Well, there's this one thing."

73

I spun around on my wooden leg so fast I wobbled. "Yes?"

"When I first touched this bump on my head this morning, it were like I 'membered somethin' in a dream—a smell I 'member 'cause Ailene hated it so, the stinky-sweet smell of Oriental toilet water."

Chapter Fourteen

I stood in the jail cell, staring at Pettibone. Had he offered me a solid clue or a figment of his whiskey-fueled imagination? Amber, or Oriental toilet water, was not something a man would wear. I knew its musky, honey-sweet scent. Two months earlier, Rags had asked me to sample perfumes a girl would like. He said Yong Liao wanted to know the best fragrances to order for his store. I wondered at the time why Rags hadn't asked his mother. Perhaps he'd been thinking of buying me a gift. If so, why hadn't he said so?

"Pardon, Miss, but the hunger is gnawing at me somethin' fierce. Could you get me a drink?"

"Sorry, Mr. Pettibone. Maybe Mr. Prentiss can get you a beer before they take you to Bridgeport."

"Thank'e."

I locked the cell door and returned to the front office. Bill Hoffman hadn't miraculously returned on his own. *Dang him.*

Judge Snethens's short-barreled shotgun lay on Papa's desk. Carrying the shotgun around town was sure to breed taunts, but I'd have to carry it until someone agreed to be my side-partner. Who'd be willing to do that?

My brother wouldn't do. Patrick had his own job working in the Standard Mine, and he was too hot tempered. The name of the most likely candidate popped into my head. I grinned. Rags, my best friend, might accept the job. But a Chinese deputy? The good citizens of Bodie would be horrified. There would be angry words directed at me and Rags. Judge Snethens might even take my badge if I chose Rags. Still, who besides Rags would agree to work with a provisional special deputy—and a young lady at that? Besides, if Rags and I worked together as deputies, maybe he'd share his heart with me.

From the jail, I trudged toward Yong Liao's mercantile. The two-story clapboard building sat on King Street and faced Virgin Alley. I entered the mercantile and found Rags bent over an open wooden crate, brushing straw off a pale green teapot. "*Nay hoh*," I said.

He looked at the shotgun. "Hello, Nell." He placed the teapot on the glass counter. "Sorry I was to hear about your pa."

"Thank you."

"If you're wantin' to sell the shotgun, I'll have to ask Yong Liao to come down to tell you what price he'd give you." Rags did a double-take. "What's that you're wearin' on your coat?"

"It's my badge. Judge Snethens made me a deputy marshal."

"The devil you say." He folded his arms in front of him.

"I'm not teasing. No one else would look into who shot Papa. I couldn't let that pass. I insisted that there be an investigation, and the judge appointed me a deputy."

"Bullheaded Nell Doherty insisted, did she, and the judge bowed to her wishes?"

"Doc Boyle supported me, too."

"All of two men out of five hundred, was it?"

"There's a catch, though. I have to find a partner who knows how to use a shotgun." I pulled the second badge from my coat pocket. "Will you be my partner? It comes with this."

Rags's Irish half reacted first. He shook his head several times.

"Sure'n the town will be lovin' this. A girl and a Chinese wearing badges in Bodie."

I waited. He closed his eyes and shook his head twice more.

We were friends, at the least. There were obligations his Chinese half would contemplate. Offering to make him a deputy, I had bestowed a major honor upon him, an honor which carried its own obligations.

Rags pulled on his ear. "Confucius said, 'to see what's right and not do it, 'tis cowardice.' Honoring your father by searching out the man who shot him 'tis the right thing to do. Still, I must ask Yong Liao."

"Of course." I hefted the shotgun. "I'll make sure no one steals anything while you're gone."

"Sure'n you don't know how to shoot it."

I stood up straighter. "I do so. You just point and pull the trigger."

Rags shook his head. "You must cock the hammers first."

"Oh."

Rags put on his coat and hat and left to talk to his employer. I sat on a black lacquer drum stool with carved flowers and dragon's heads on its sides. I massaged my thigh just above my stump. It hurt from all the extra walking I'd done.

God, I know it's crazy for me and Rags to be deputies, but how else will I find the evidence to prove Kohl shot Papa? Please let Yong Liao give his permission for Rags to be my partner.

The door opened and portly Yong Liao entered the store, followed by Rags. Mr. Yong wore a dark-blue quilted jacket over a knee-length cassock-like gown, and pants.

I stood and bowed as he approached.

"Good morning, Miss Doherty. Would you have tea?"

"Nay hoh, Uncle," I said, in what I hoped was passable Cantonese. In English, I added, "Tea would be nice. Thank you."

Rags moved a rocking chair from the corner of the shop and set it next to the potbellied stove. He then left to fetch tea.

Yong Liao pointed at the lacquered drum stool next to his chair. "Please sit."

He sat in the rocking chair and laced his fingers together on his rotund belly. "Tell me please, how your father is."

"Papa looked very pale when I saw him. Doc Boyle doesn't know if he'll live." I lowered my head. I was not going to cry.

Yong Liao reached over and patted my hand. "This news brings much sorrow. Your father good to Chinese. If I may do something, let me know."

Rags reentered the shop carrying a teapot and cups on a bronze tray. He set the tray on the glass case, poured tea into two China cups, and gave one to me and one to Yong Liao.

I inhaled the tea's smoky scent and brought the cup to my lips. "It's very good. Oolong is my favorite."

Rags winked. I must have been right about the tea.

Yong Liao set his cup on the stove top. "Is good that you like it." He pulled Rags's badge from his pocket and held it in his hand. "You and Wu Chao very young. This is allowed?"

He didn't say no. He didn't say no.

I took a deep breath. "Judge Snethens offered me a position as deputy marshal as long as I get a partner who can use a shotgun." Remembering to use Rags's Chinese name, I continued. "Wu Chao has hunted ducks with you at Mono Lake."

Yong Liao put the badge on the edge of the stove and picked up his cup. Between pauses, he took sips of tea. Rags shifted his weight from his right foot to his left foot and back again. My stomach tightened like the cinch around my thigh. *What will I do if he says no?*

I counted to ten four times before Yong Liao leaned forward in the rocker and put his cup back on the stove. "Hunting ducks not like hunting man. You do this for vengeance?"

"No, Uncle, for justice. If I can arrest the person who shot my papa, it'll be up to the courts to decide what happens to him." Since I didn't have enough proof for Judge Snethens, I didn't mention Kohl to Yong Liao. He might have thought acting solely on my belief would be equivalent to acting out of revenge.

Yong Liao tilted back in the rocker. He fixed his gaze above my head.

Oh, God, he doesn't want to look me in the eye when he says no. What am I going to do?

Rags pointed at the ceiling. "I see it, too, Uncle."

Above my head, near the ceiling, a small spider dangled from a single thread.

"This spider's an omen," Rags said. "It brings good luck to Nell, it does, and to her search."

Yong Liao tapped his lips with a pointer finger. "Sometimes, spider only spider." He leaned forward and took the badge off the stove. "My decision this: Wu Chao, you be Miss Doherty's second eyes and ears—for time being. Carry shotgun as judge asked. Also put pistol from store in pocket."

"Oh, thank you, thank you," I said.

Rags bowed deeply. "Thank you, Uncle.

"Decision may change. We see how long good luck last."

Rags went behind the counter. He opened a drawer, fetched out a revolver, opened the magazine and closed it. He put the pistol in his coat pocket. "All set. What do we do now?"

"Find that good-for-nothing, Bill Hoffman. Who hopefully will recant his testimony against Mr. Pettibone and implicate the real villain." Who I knew to be Erastus Kohl.

"Suggestion," Yong Liao said. "Gold Brick Saloon open early."

Chapter Fifteen

"Why are we looking for Bill Hoffman?" Rags asked, as we left Yong Liao's mercantile.

"Because Hoffman supposedly saw Papa get shot. He told others that Micah Pettibone did it, but I don't believe that. I think Erastus Kohl shot Papa. Kohl dropped his Knights of Pythias pin in the snow near where Papa was shot, but Judge Snethens won't let me arrest him until I get more evidence."

"What's Kohl have to say for himself?"

I huffed. "I haven't been able to talk to Kohl yet. According to his wife, he spent time with a, um, soiled dove last night. That would put him near the Virgin Alley spot where Papa was gunned down. The judge tried to talk to him this morning, but Kohl had gone to a ranch at Mono Lake to get more beef. He's due back this afternoon, and I want to talk to him as soon as he's back. Assuming he hasn't skedaddled. For now, we'll have to settle for talking to lying Bill Hoffman."

"I'm up for bein' a help, I am, as much as I can, but you know they won't let me in the Gold Brick Saloon. How'm I supposed to keep me eye on you?"

" 'My' eye, not 'me' eye." I dodged a patch of ice on the board-walk. "You can watch through the window."

On Main Street, miners and mill workers were leaving hotels, boarding houses, and restaurants for work. They carried their tin lunch pails and trudged up the snow-covered hill to start their twelve-hour shift for the mine companies. The barber shop and meat market were closed, as was the Bodie Bank. Next door, however, the Gold Brick Saloon did a brisk business from miners thirsting for what Papa called 'a wee drop' before work. Three miners in dunga-rees left the bar as Rags and I approached the entrance.

"Well, by gum, if Bill weren't tellin' the truth," said George Crawford, a barrel-chested miner. He leaned toward me and stared at my badge. His breath smelled like the foul liquor in Judge Snethens's flask. "Can't believe my eyes, a girl deputy. Hey, deputy, ain't ya got washin' and ironin' to do?"

"I'm here on official business, looking for Bill Hoffman. Step aside."

"Git on home, little girl, and leave poor Bill alone."

No miner was going to question my authority. "It's against the law to interfere with a deputy in the performance of her duties. You could be arrested."

Crawford's glance changed from glassy to mean. Maybe I'd pushed too hard. Sweat broke out on my forehead.

Crawford set his lunch pail on the boardwalk. "Think you can threaten' me, do ya? You need to see what's what and I aim to show ya. I'll bend ya over my knee and spank your behind."

Papa had taught me how to throw a punch, but I was no match for these burly ruffians. I couldn't have Rags shoot these morons. How was I to avoid a monumental embarrassment?

Crawford's friends snickered. "Tan her good," one of them said.

The other added, "Take this, George." He pulled his denim jacket up and unbuckled his belt.

Rags cleared his throat. "Top of the morning to you, gentlemen."

All heads turned toward Rags. The miner who'd unbuckled his belt said, "Whatcha doin' with that shotgun, boy?" Then he shouted, "My God, this Chinaman got a badge, too."

Crawford stared, bug-eyed, at the badge on Rags's coat. "No!"

"It's all official," I said. "Judge Snethens gave us the badges."

Rags shot me a look as I stretched the truth. Judge Snethens hadn't given him his badge.

"Must have been drunker'n usual," Crawford said. "So, it don't count fer nothin'."

Rags bowed his head slightly toward Crawford. "I spoke with Miss Polly yesterday and she told me she's missed you these last few weeks, but she bears you no ill will. She sends her compliments to your wife."

Crawford's face turned bright red and his nostrils flared. He poked Rags in the chest. "You yellow weasel. You'll say nothin' to my wife if you know what's good fer ya." With his forefinger, Crawford flicked the badge on Rags's coat. "We'll see about this."

Crawford grabbed the wood handle of his lunch pail, and he and the other miners moved up Main Street. They grumbled and shot us dirty looks as they clomped along the boardwalk.

"Thanks," I said.

"Just doin' my job, Deputy."

"I'm glad you're my partner." I turned toward the Gold Brick's double doors. "I'll be right back with Bill."

Bill Hoffman sat at one of the round tables. A half-dozen miners wearing metal hats with lanterns stood around him, apparently enthralled by something Bill was saying. All of the miners laughed and shook their heads, then headed for the door. They gave me dirty looks. Only one of them spoke. He shook his head and asked, "Are you crazy?"

Bill Hoffman had become the saloon's only customer. He got up from the table and wobbled to the bar. "Another beer, Toby."

The bartender, Tobias Hurlbutt, filled a glass from a wooden keg.

"None o' that foam, now. Fill 'er to the top, my man. I got a thirsh-t."

The saloon's air, fouled by tobacco smoke and the vapors of drink, stung my lungs. I coughed.

Mr. Hurlbutt handed Bill his beer. He turned to me. "Get outa here. We don't allow women or children."

"They're pesh-ts, Toby. One-legged one's the worsh-t."

"I'm a deputy marshal and I'm here on official business."

"I don't care. We don't allow women, ever."

If I spent all of my energy convincing people of my position, I wouldn't have any left to investigate Papa's shooting. That I couldn't allow.

"Mr. Hurlbutt, I'm not leaving until Bill Hoffman agrees to accompany me to the jail to be interviewed."

"She's like a horsh-fly. All-ays bzzz bzzz bzzz."

I looked at the clock on the wall behind the bar. "Bill Hoffman, I'll give you one minute to finish your beer."

"And if I don't want to go from here?"

"I'll drag you out by the ear like I did before."

Mr. Hurlbutt snorted. "She drug you about by the ear? I'd like to have seen that."

"Got a grip like a vice. Ruined me ear."

Hurlbutt picked up a rag and wiped down the bar. "You best drink up, Bill, before your wife here gets any madder."

"I wouldn't marry her if she was the lash-t woman on earth."

I shivered at the thought.

Bill upended his glass and finished his beer. "I'll be goin', Pencil-Leg."

"You're going with me."

Bill turned and ran toward the back door.

I gave chase. "Come back here!" My right foot slipped on the sawdust. My thigh twisted inside the leather cinch and my wooden leg flew away from me as I fell. My stump hit the floor like a hammer. Pain shot through my leg as if it had exploded into a million screaming pieces.

"Lordy, Lordy, Lordy."

Mr. Hurlbutt snickered.

Rags flew in the door.

"Hey, we don't allow no Chinks in here. Get out."

Rags ignored him and rushed to my side. "Nell, are you all right?"

Black spots appeared before my eyes. I gritted my teeth and took a deep breath. "Fine. Just catch that son-of-a-gun. He went out the back."

"You sure?"

"Yes. Go."

Rags ran after Bill.

I rolled onto my side and took a deep breath. My right leg throbbed from the stump to the hip. Pain or no pain, I had a job to do. I crawled to my wooden leg, grabbed it, and sat against the bar. My face burned from anger and humiliation. Mama would have fainted if she'd seen me, but right there in sight of Mr. Hurlbutt, I lifted my skirt and petticoat to expose my still throbbing stump. Gingerly, I tightened the stocking over the stump and re-cinched the wooden leg in place. Walking was going to be a lot more unpleasant than usual.

Cigar ash dropped onto my left shoulder. Mr. Hurlbutt leaned over the bar, seeing a lot more than my ankles. I threw my skirt over my legs. My face got hotter. Thank God no one else was in the bar.

"Give you a quarter if you show me the stump."

It was going to hurt like hell to get to my feet, but if I stood, I'd be able to smash the cigar into Hurlbutt's face with my fist. In the sweetest voice I could muster, I said, "Mr. Hurlbutt, would you help me up?"

"Help yourself. You ain't supposed to be in here in the first place."

Rags reentered the saloon, alone.

"Where's Bill?"

Rags lowered his head. "Disappeared, dang it. Let me help you up."

He set the shotgun on the bar, leaned down, and took my hands. To keep most of my weight off my wooden leg, I bent my left leg under me. Rags pulled me onto my feet.

"Ah, ah, ah. Oh, Lord have mercy."

When I'd adjusted to the new level of pain in my stump, I noticed Rags staring at me intensely.

"How do you feel?"

Bill Hoffman, so far the only potential witness to Papa's shooting, had gotten away. A common drunk had eluded me. Pinkerton will never hire me. I wanted to scream "I'm a failure." But I wouldn't give Mr. Hurlbutt the pleasure of seeing my distress.

"I'm going to need my crutches."

Mr. Hurlbutt removed the cigar from his mouth and blew smoke in Rag's direction. "You two make a fine pair of deputies. Now that the young lady's on her foot, get the heck out of my saloon."

I hopped toward the front door, leaning on Rags's arm. As Rags opened the door, Mr. Hurlbutt shouted, "When the posse gets back, I'm gonna see to it the judge takes back those badges."

Chapter Sixteen

Rags left me on the bench outside the saloon and ran to my house to get my crutches. I massaged my thigh as best I could through my dress, flinching when my fingers touched a sore spot on my stump. "Lordy be." I rocked forward and back until the pain subsided.

Sun Lee, carrying a basket of clean laundry, stopped in front of me. He bowed. "You okay, Miss Nell?"

"Yes, thank you. My leg's a bit sore is all."

Sun Lee continued up Main. Three workers for the Bulwer Mine exited the Delmonico Restaurant carrying their lunch buckets. They glowered at me as they passed. Could they have heard I'd been made a deputy? I hoped Rags hurried.

Clouds still obscured the sun, but the air seemed a bit warmer than the day before. Maybe that would help keep Deputy Jorgensen alive until the posse found him. Though the sooner the posse returned, the shorter the time I would have to prove Kohl shot Papa. Where was that wretch of a scapegrace, Bill Hoffman? Why had he been afraid to talk to me?

Rags slipped between a pair of freight wagons as he crossed Main with my crutches. "Do you need help standing?"

"I've got to do it myself."

I grabbed the crutches, gritted my teeth, and pushed up with my left foot to keep the weight off my stump. The crutches made me look more like a cripple, which I hated, but I could also get around more quickly on them. "Bill Hoffman's not likely to show his face for a while, until he needs a drink, so let's stop at Doc Boyle's and see Papa."

Rags and I drew stares as we made our way to the surgery, as if we were marching down Main Street in our underclothes. Mr. Bonner started to wave to me from inside his dry goods store, but his hand froze midway. Dean Howells moved past us in his buckboard. He turned his head to follow Rags and me as we crossed the muddy sludge of the street. Maybe he saw our deputy badges, or maybe it was Rags's shotgun he found curious, or that Rags and I proceeded side by side, Rags walking and me swinging my crutches. I'd been made a freak by my accident six years earlier, and becoming deputy made me a curiosity all over again.

"How ya feeling?" Rags asked.

"I want to smash something."

"'Cuz Bill Hoffman got away?"

"Not because he got away, because of why he got away—because I can't run. What good am I as a deputy if I can't even catch Bill Hoffman? How can I pretend I have what it takes to succeed as a Pinkerton?"

Rags smiled his lopsided smile. "You'll succeed. You will. Like Mr. Pinkerton, you'll outsmart 'em."

I stopped my three-legged lumbering and faced Rags. His gaze kindled warmth in my breast. My heart fluttered.

A gruff bellow broke the spell. "Get the hell outta the road!"

A freight wagon bore down on us. "Whoa, Thunder. Whoa, Lightning," the driver shouted.

Rags grabbed my shoulders and pulled me out of the horses' path.

The wagon driver leaned backward hauling hard on the reins.

His two grays slowed to a stop just ahead of where Rags and I had been standing. "Daggum it! The road's no place to be napping."

"Sorry," I said.

Rags bowed to the wagon driver. "Me apologies, sir." He turned to me. "Me apologies to you, too, Nell. I should have seen the wagon coming."

"We both should have."

A few minutes later, we reached the stairs to Doc Boyle's office. The prospect of climbing stairs made me uneasy. It had been over a year since I'd used crutches. "Rags, would you follow me up the stairs in case I fall?"

"Sure."

I wobbled on the top step. Rags's hand on my back steadied me. We reached the landing and I opened the door to the surgery.

Doc was standing over Papa as we entered. Mama still slept, resting her head on the examination table next to Papa's chest. She held his hand.

"Hi, Doc." I whispered. "How's Papa?"

"Still unconscious. How come you're on crutches?"

"I fell and bruised my stump."

"Want me to take a look at it?"

I shook my head.

"Very well. How are you, Wu Chao?"

"Fine, sir, thank you."

Mama stirred a bit, then sat up. I hobbled over to her, set my right crutch against the table and embraced her.

"How are you, Mama?"

"About what you'd expect." Mama pushed me back and studied my face with bloodshot eyes. "How are you, darlin'? I see your leg's bothering you again." Her gaze dropped to the badge on my coat. "What in tarnation is that?"

"Judge Snethens said I could help find who shot Papa. He made me a special deputy."

"He what?" Mama's face flushed. She glared. "Listen to me

now, Nell, and listen good. You give that badge back to the judge this instant. You hear me? This instant. The old fool should know better than to put a girl in such an unwomanly position, and in harm's way to boot."

Why didn't she ever see things the same as I did? I'd have to put the best face on it I could, and not mention how difficult the job had been. "Mama, I'm just asking questions, same as I might as a Pinkerton agent. And I have help. The judge insisted I get a partner, one who could use a shotgun to look after me."

Mama looked at Rags.

He bowed his head. "Good day to you, Mrs. Doherty."

She pointed her finger at him. "You. You should know better than to be helping her in this foolishness." She frowned. "Nell, what's become of your good sense? Having Rags work with you just compounds the impropriety. Go find the judge and return the badge."

"No one else has time to investigate who shot Papa. If I don't do it, the gunman may go free. I already have a suspect."

"I don't care. It's not the place of a young lady to be a police-man. There's a reason there's no such word as policewoman."

"But Mama ..."

She stood. "Take the badge back, Nell. Now."

"Mama ..." *No, don't make it worse. Count to ten first. She's overly worried and doesn't understand I'm the only one who can catch the varmint who shot Papa.*

I took a deep breath. "I can't quit. I'd be letting Papa down."

Mama stomped her foot. "You've always been a stubborn, willful child, and we pampered your whims because of your leg. Not this time. Nell Doherty, take that badge back right now or find yourself someplace else to sleep."

I wobbled as if my other leg had been swept out from under me. She couldn't be serious.

"I mean it. Take that badge back this instant."

If I returned the badge, I'd lose the opportunity to show the

Pinkertons that I could do the job. I'd never prove Kohl shot Papa. He'd go free. I couldn't allow that. How could Mama make me choose between her and what I wanted most in life?

I picked up my right crutch, bent over, and kissed Papa's cheek, then hitched toward the door. Rags opened it, but instead of walking through it, I turned. "Mama, I can't quit now. On top of everything else, Rags and I are the only law in town."

Mama's eyes grew moist. "I'll let your brother know you've left home."

Her words stung as if I'd been slapped. She surely didn't mean what she said.

Rags scowled as I swung past him into the cold air. He closed the door behind him.

"Nell, you should go back and apologize to your mother."

"Apologize?"

"'Tis the duty of children to obey their parents."

"Just what a proper Chinese son would say. Criminy, you sound like my mother. What does your Irish half think?"

"The same."

I gritted my teeth. Maybe I should have asked someone else to help me.

"Nell, are you—"

"Don't talk to me right now." I squeezed the crutch handles and let my anger flow through my fists into the wood. I put the ends of the crutches on the step below the landing and swung my good foot out. My arms wobbled. Panic made my heart race. If I tumbled to the ground, Mama would win. My foot landed on the step. After three deep breaths, I teetered down the remaining steps ahead of Rags, too angry to ask him to walk in front of me. If I fell, I fell.

Chapter Seventeen

As I swung down the boardwalk, my wooden leg got heavier by the minute. Holding it off the ground tuckered me out. My irritation with Mama and Rags subsided a little.

"Mr. Pettibone might still be at the jail," Rags said. "He might know Bill Hoffman's hiding place."

Given my luck so far today, Pettibone was probably long gone. Still, Rags's idea was a good one. Though I was still too angry to praise him for it. "Fine. We'll check the jail."

We got more stares and several snickers as we proceeded north on Main Street. We passed Dean Howells carrying a milk can into the Delmonico Restaurant. "It's all over town, how you two couldn't catch that drunk, Bill Hoffman."

Wonderful. "It's early yet. We'll catch him."

"Tobias Hurlbutt at the Gold Brick Saloon is giving three-to-one odds that you don't catch Hoffman."

"Yeah, well you can tell Tobias Hurlbutt he can stick his tiny head in a spittoon."

Dean Howells climbed into his wagon.

Rags shot a disapproving look my way. "Rather colorful language for a young lady."

"I'm not feeling particularly ladylike right now." Rags and I trudged on toward the jail. "We're going to catch Bill Hoffman," I said.

"That we are. So, 'twould be a good idea to return to the Gold Brick and make a bet."

The idea of Tobias Hurlbutt paying money to me and Rags brought a smile to my face, but I wasn't as confident of success as I'd suggested. "Let's see if Pettibone can tell us where Bill Hoffman's holed up first."

We found both the marshal's office and the jail cells empty. I wasn't surprised that Pettibone had already left for Bridgeport. Everything that could go wrong seemed to go wrong for me. Mama stood against me. The town stood against me. I dropped into Papa's chair behind the desk and picked up a pencil. I tapped it on the desktop for several seconds, thinking. But my thoughts refused to slow down and clear. I slammed down the pencil. "Dag nab it."

"I could use some tea," Rags said. "Would you like some?"

"Tea? That's the best—" A wounded look flashed in his eyes. "I'm sorry. Tea would at least warm us up a bit. Thank you."

Rags added wood to the stove in the corner, then left for Yong Liao's mercantile. He returned a few minutes later and brewed the tea. We sat across the desk from each other sipping in silence.

Papa never told me how hard police work was.

The front door opened and Mrs. Lockhart entered. She wore no coat over her pale blue dress. Her shoulders and blonde hair were covered only by a dark-blue shawl. Rags's stare told me he noticed her beauty, the same, I guess, as Papa had noticed. Could she steal Rags's heart, too?

Mrs. Lockhart uncovered her head. "Good day, Miss Doherty."

Rags jumped up. He bowed. "My name's Wu Chao, but most folks call me Rags. Would you like some tea?"

"Thank you, Mr. Chao. My name is Irene Lockhart. A cup of

tea would be wonderful." She removed her gloves. "Miss Doherty, I was very sorry to hear about your father. When I saw you enter the jail, I just had to come and ask about him. How is he?"

Remembering Papa and Mrs. Lockhart dancing together, I bristled, but she might have been in Virgin Alley near the time Papa was shot. She might have seen something. She might have even been in the alley to see him. I pushed that thought away. "He hasn't woken up yet. The doctor doesn't know if he'll survive."

"Oh, no." Mrs. Lockhart blanched and covered her mouth with her hands. Maybe she had real feelings for Papa. But that would be wrong.

"Perhaps you should sit down," Rags said.

Mrs. Lockhart lowered herself onto the chair in front of Papa's desk. I noticed she wore small boots. They could have made the marks in the snow I'd seen.

"Were you in Virgin Alley last night? Did you see what happened to Papa?"

"I didn't see anything, but I heard a burst of firecrackers. They were followed by two shots close together. A few seconds later, I heard a third shot. Several of us rushed out of the dance hall to see what was going on."

"You say you heard three shots. Are you sure?"

"I'm certain."

Papa had one bit of luck. When Kohl shot at him, he missed once.

"Did you see Erastus Kohl? He's a butcher. Walks with a cane."

"I don't know him, but I didn't see anyone with a cane."

Rags handed Mrs. Lockhart a cup of tea. She held the cup in both hands.

I took a sip of tea. "When you spoke with my father last night, did he say anything that might suggest who shot him?"

"No."

"What did Papa say to you?"

Mrs. Lockhart set her cup on the desk but kept her hands wrapped around it. She leaned toward me, staring intently, her head tilted to the side. "He talked about you. He's very proud of you. He told me he thinks you'll make a good Pinkerton agent. And, by the way, congratulations on being appointed deputy marshal."

Papa thought I'd be a good detective? The knowledge should have warmed me, but hearing it from Mrs. Lockhart's lips stole the sweetness from it. Papa had shared family things with Mrs. Lockhart, personal things.

"Miss Doherty, I also came to tell you about a rumor. It's being said that your father's shooting was related to the recent gold robberies. Have you heard about that?"

"No. Who told you?"

"I overheard one miner telling another at the dance hall."

Gold? Kohl couldn't be one of the gold thieves, could he? The first gold shipment was stolen before he'd gotten out of prison. Was Papa close to unmasking the thieves and did they know? If only he'd told me his suspicions the other night.

"I'll keep the gold in mind. Did you see or hear anything else that might help me determine who shot Papa?"

Mrs. Lockhart sipped her tea. "There was one other thing. I noticed a young Chinese girl staring out the window of a crib. When she saw me looking, she yanked the window blind down and turned out her lamp. It seemed odd that she'd turn out her lamp."

"Do you know the girl's name?"

"One of the miners called her Min."

"Huang Min?" Rags asked.

"The miner just said Min."

Mrs. Lockhart had provided what could be important information, but I still couldn't thank her.

Rags waited several seconds for me to show my gratitude, then said, "Thank you, Mrs. Lockhart."

She pulled on her gloves. At the door, she turned. "I hope your father recovers quickly."

"I wish you had left Papa alone. We could have been friends."

Mrs. Lockhart winced. "I am your friend."

I didn't believe her. How could Mrs. Lockhart be my friend if she was causing problems between Mama and Papa?

She said goodbye to Rags and left.

"Um," Rags said. "Do you want to tell me what that was about?"

"No." I pushed myself out of Papa's chair. "Let's go talk to this Huang Min."

The color drained from Rags's face. "Uh, that wouldn't be proper. She's ..."

"A fancy lady. Yes, I know. Even though she's only a girl. But she may have seen something last night." So, I was going to a prostitute's den. To do this deputy work, I would have to offend my mother at every step. "Do you know which crib is hers?"

"Well, yes." Rags blushed. "I've made deliveries to her, I have."

"Good." I put my weight on the crutches and swung toward the door. "Let's go."

"But, um, she won't be awake yet."

"I don't care. When the posse gets back, Judge Snethens might take our badges. We may only have a few hours to prove who shot Papa."

"Huang Min probably didn't see anything until after the shooting was all over."

"We'll find out."

"She doesn't speak much English."

I cocked my head and stared at Rags. "Are you afraid to speak to her?"

"Of course not." He looked hurt, as if I'd misjudged him. "I'm only trying to protect you."

"If you're trying to protect my reputation, I'm afraid it's too late."

Chapter Eighteen

Rags and I stepped out of the jail. The clouds had lifted and the sun shone for the first time in a week. Each icicle along the building's eaves dribbled onto the melting snow on the ground. Rags and I cut along the side of the jail and passed through Virgin Alley, the backs of Main Street's shops on our left and Bodie's bordellos and cribs on our right. As a proper young woman, I shouldn't know that such things existed, but I was the daughter of the marshal. I'd heard talk. I'd never spoken with a fancy lady, of course. How could I when I wasn't allowed on Virgin Alley? Likewise, I wasn't allowed to shop on Monday afternoons, because that was when the scarlet women did their shopping and respectable women stayed home.

Rags pointed at one of the small boxy wooden cribs on the west side of the lane. It hardly looked big enough for anything but a bed.

"Huang Min's is that one. I'll run ahead and try to wake her up."

Hobbling on crutches strained my arms. I slowed my pace. So far, no one else was out and about in the alley.

Rags knocked on the crib door and spoke in Cantonese. After a few seconds, he knocked and shouted. He put his ear against the door and then turned my way.

"I hear movement."

As I swung up to the left of Rags, the crib door opened half an inch. Huang Min screamed at Rags in Cantonese.

"Tell her to quiet down."

He shook his head. "She'll be more awake. Better at answering questions."

The stream of invective continued for ten seconds or so, until Rags pointed at the badge on his coat. He pointed toward me and spoke to her in her native language. The door opened a fraction wider, enough for me to see one bloodshot eye.

"What want?"

"Tell her we want to know everything she heard or saw last night."

Rags translated my request.

She uttered a curt response and Rags spoke to her with greater force. The door slammed shut.

"Well?"

"She says she didn't see or hear anything. I told her she was lying, that we knew better."

Rags pounded on the door. He shouted, "Hoi mun!"

Huang Min giggled inside the crib.

Rags scratched his head. "Do you want me to break down the door?"

"Let me think." I paced through the slush, swinging my crutches and then my left foot. A few paces back and forth. "Who does she work for? Can we get her employer to force her out?"

"She's owned by Yong Liao and ah, and … um, well, he might be afraid of where our questions may go."

"Yong Liao owns her? Like a slave? How can that be?"

"Chinese custom."

"But we don't have slaves in America. Not anymore. Owning people is wrong."

I'd never given much thought to fancy ladies. Why they did what they did. For that matter, I didn't know *what* they did, other than it had something to do with sex, a topic about which Mama had told me nothing.

What little I knew, I'd learned from my friend Lucy Barnes. "It's sort of like when a bull jumps up on the cow's back and pokes her in the nethers," she'd said. "But people do it face to face, and lying down."

I understood face to face, but the "doing" and the "it" parts remained a mystery.

The giggling inside Huang Min's crib grew louder. Her door opened two inches. She spoke this time in a sing-song voice. "Irish boy, Irish boy, you like Min? You want? You want?"

Rags looked quickly away and as he turned his head, I caught sight of Min. She gyrated back and forth, back and forth, her robe open to her waist. My mouth dropped open. She had nothing on under the robe. I turned my head away. If a man saw me naked, I'd be embarrassed to death. Why wasn't she?

"Two dollar, Irish boy. Two dollar."

Before I could get over the shock, the crib door slammed shut again. Inside, Huang Min laughed raucously. Rags stood frozen in place.

"Are you all right?" I asked.

He shivered back to life. "Excuse me. I'll be right back."

He sidled away from me as if he didn't want to face me.

"Where're you going?"

He ignored me and ran toward the outhouse across the lane. The outhouse near where Papa had been shot. My confusion over Rags's sudden actions faded when I thought of Papa. I paced through the slush in front of Huang Min's crib. *She saw something of what happened last night, at least after the shooting. Why would she deny that? Could she be afraid to speak?*

Huang Min. What would her life have been like? A young foreigner in a strange world, and a fancy lady, she could easily have fears about which I had no clue. No clues. *What would Sherlock Holmes do? My only sources, Bill Hoffman and Huang Min, weren't talking.*

I turned around to make another pass in front of the crib and saw something colorful in the melting snow at the corner of the little wooden structure. I pawed at the slush with one of my crutches. Blackened bits of red and blue paper lay in the snow, the remains of a string of firecrackers, the same kind I'd seen outside Kohl's house.

These could be the firecrackers Mrs. Lockhart mentioned, the ones that went off just before someone gunned Papa down. If so, Huang Min might have looked outside to see who set them off. She might have seen who shot Papa. She might have seen Kohl.

I swung twice on my crutches. That brought me in front of the crib door. I banged on it with a crutch. "Open up."

"Go 'way."

I attacked the door with my crutch.

"Go 'way."

I planted the crutches in the wet snow, swung my left leg back a bit and then swung my body forward, kicking the door near the jamb as hard as I could.

The door flew open.

I landed on my back, in the slush.

Huang Min screamed in Cantonese. She swooped toward me, a brass teapot raised over her head.

The ridiculousness of being attacked with a teapot, and the fact I was lying in muddy sludge, made me laugh. Huang Min soon joined me.

"You crazy."

"I think you're right." I reached toward her. "Help me?"

She stepped outside and offered me her hand. She pulled on my arm and I rose. Without my asking, she picked up my crutches and handed them to me. She was being much nicer to me than to Rags.

"Thank you, Huang Min."

"Come." She motioned for me to join her inside. "Get warm."

Did she want to talk?

Chapter Nineteen

Min's crib was aptly named. Half of its area was devoted to the narrow bed which took up most of one side of the single room. Beneath the bed lay a chamber pot, a porcelain bowl, and pitcher, and three pairs of embroidered slip-on shoes. One pair, oddly enough, had the heel in the middle. None of the shoes looked sturdy enough to last an hour outdoors in winter.

Min had closed her robe and bound it with a sash. She helped me out of my wet coat and then, with a hand gesture, invited me to stand next to the stove at the back of the room. Careful to avoid hitting my stump, I swung through the narrow space between her bed and a two-foot square table set against the opposite wall. I turned my back to the stove and leaned on my crutches.

Min placed her teapot on a small bureau at the foot of her bed. We stood and stared at each other. Min had traces of white powder on her face and rouge on her cheeks. She didn't need the powder or the rouge. Her creamy skin didn't have a single blemish. She had pulled her hair into a long, lustrous black ponytail. She was very pretty.

"How old you?" she asked.

"Eighteen."

"Min sixteen. Sixteen is two dollar. I charge man two dollar. Two bit, four bit, six bit, then dollar is eight." She showed me her hands, folding back the thumbs. "This many finger, two time, is sixteen. How many finger eighteen?"

I held my hands up, folding back just the right thumb. "Eighteen is this many fingers two times."

Min considered that a minute.

"How did you come to America?"

She looked down. "Sorry. Wish better, but English bad."

"You know more English than I know Cantonese."

A musky honey scent hung in the air—Oriental toilet water. Before I could consider what this meant, a mewling sound greeted me from near Min's feet. She bent down and pulled a wood crate out from under the foot of the bed. In the crate, curled into a ball on a blanket, lay a little calico cat. Min laid the crate on her bed. She shushed the cat while stroking its spine.

If I start slow, maybe I can make friends with her and then maybe she'll talk. "I'm Nell Doherty. You," I pointed at Min, "are Huang Min." I pointed at the cat. "What is your cat's name?"

"Lao fu. Big cat."

"Hello, Lao fu."

"Why you show strong?"

"Show strong?"

Rags knocked on the door. "Nell, are you in there?" He sounded nervous, no doubt worrying about my reputation again.

"Yes."

"You're both, um, decent, are you?"

"Yes, silly."

Huang Min said something in Cantonese.

Rags opened the door and slowly peeked around it. His gaze flitted around the room, never focusing on either me or Min's. "What have you been talking about?"

"You."

"Me?" He turned bright red.

My, he's behaving oddly. Have I made him uncomfortable? "I was just teasing. We've only been talking about Huang Min's cat."

He closed the door and leaned against it. His face returned to its normal pale brown.

"Min and I seem to be getting along okay, so maybe she'll answer my questions about what she saw last night."

Finally, he met my gaze. "'Twould be polite to chat a bit first, ask about her family and such."

"Okay. Ask her about her family."

Rags spoke in Cantonese. Huang Min had her back to Rags. She stroked her cat. Only I could see a smile that shone briefly on her lips before she turned her head and responded to Rags's question.

"She says a month ago she received a letter from her mother in Canton. Chong Wen, the letter-writer, read it to her. Her older brother is to be married to a housemaid."

Huang Min teared up. She stood and approached Rags. She wept intermittently as she spoke.

"She says she's very unhappy that she won't be able to attend the wedding. She's also afraid she will never see her parents again."

Min fell against Rags, her face pressed to his shoulder. He stood still as a post while she talked and cried. He continued to translate.

"Why I not free? Why no one protect Min?"

She pushed herself away from Rags and sniffed. She spoke. Rags translated. "Why doesn't anyone help me?"

"Tell her we'll talk to Yong Liao. He's got to let her go. Slaves aren't allowed in America."

Rags froze again. He bit his lip.

"What is wrong with you today?"

"Um, I's um, still tryin' to get over the shock of, um, you know, what I saw."

"Tell Min what I said."

Rags spoke a few words.

Min grunted. She spoke angrily to Rags, but this time she didn't shout. When she was done, she wiped her eyes, sat on her bed, and picked up her cat.

I wished I spoke Cantonese. "What'd she say?"

"She doesn't believe we'll help her. Lots of her customers promise the same. They none of 'em deliver."

"Tell her I promise I'll talk to Yong Liao."

Rags repeated my promise.

Min shook her head. She stroked her cat's belly.

"Can I ask her about the shooting now?"

"I guess. Just don't ask anything that'll make her cry."

"Ask if she remembers hearing firecrackers right outside her door last night."

Rags translated.

"She remembers."

"Right after that, when she looked out the window, what did she see?"

Huang Min scowled. She spoke angrily.

"She says she didn't look out the window."

Why won't she admit that? "Ask her how long it was between when she heard the firecrackers and when she heard the gunshots."

"She wants to know what a gun sounds like.'"

"Go outside and fire two shots from your uncle's pistol into the ground, then come back."

"You're crazy, you are. People will come running from all over town."

"Please, just do it. There's no other way."

Rags went out and fired his pistol twice in a row. When he reentered the crib, I asked him to ask her again about how much time passed between the firecrackers and the shots.

"She's not sure, maybe a few seconds."

Will she confirm what Mrs. Lockhart said? "How long afterwards did she hear the third shot?"

Rags turned his head my way. "She says about ten seconds."

Rags pulled two long brass cartridges from his coat pocket. "Found these in the snow, I did, just outside the crib. In the same spot where someone tossed some firecrackers. These came from a rifle."

"Now we're getting somewhere," I said, "maybe. If the bullets that hit Papa were fired from just outside the crib, it couldn't have been Pettibone that did it. He was drunk. He couldn't have shot Papa from here and then staggered to where Papa lay before people ran outside to see what was going on.

"So it has to be someone else. Someone like Erastus Kohl. He could have fired a rifle from just outside here and then slipped behind Min's crib before anyone else came outside. He could have waited in the dark until Papa had been taken to Doc Boyle's surgery. Then he could have walked home unseen." I hadn't seen any of Kohl's cane prints near the crib. Perhaps they had been covered by the previous night's snow.

"Wonderin,' I am, if Mr. Kohl owns a rifle."

"We'll ask him as soon as we see him. For now, ask Huang Min again about who she saw, and tell her she'd been seen staring out the window."

Huang Min shook her head violently in response.

"Ask her if she was with someone at the time of the shooting, someone she's afraid of."

Min spoke, then started sobbing.

"She's always afraid. Doesn't know what'll happen to her. Whether she'll ever see her family again."

She stood and flung herself at Rags, crying. Rags hesitated. He patted her back and said something soothing in Cantonese.

Min winked at me. Then she pushed Rags away from her and wiped the tears from her cheeks. "Go, Irish boy. Tell Yong Liao, Min sad." She dismissed him with a backhanded wave. "Go." She pushed him toward the door.

"I'll be right outside," Rags said. He closed the door behind him.

Min pointed to a tear on her cheek. "Nell. Not be crazy. With man, *Be* strong, *Show* weak. You learn."

"What did you see?"

Huang Min looked at the floor. "Not see. You go now."

Chapter Twenty

I pushed the crib door open. Two women, a dark-haired soiled dove and her red-headed madam, stood in the slush just outside. They had come from The Mother Lode, the bordello next to Huang Min's crib. Both wore knee-length coats over muslin night gowns. Their boots were unbuttoned.

The madam, almost as tall as Papa, looked down at Rags with a contemptuous scowl. "You slant-eyed buffoon," she said. "My girls need their sleep."

Rags bowed his head to the woman. "I apologize, I do. I was trying to kill a rat that's been botherin' Huang Min."

The madam's jaw dropped. "A rat? With a pistol?"

A dozen or so men had run our way, drawn by the gunfire. The group included Bob Hooper, attorney-at-law, and Sean Finney, a blacksmith. Finney carried a shotgun. Mr. Chen and Yong Liao approached from the mercantile shop at a more considered pace appropriate to Yong Liao's lord-like status.

Bob Hooper looked about. He examined the madam and the soiled dove from head to foot. "What's goin' on?"

"You won't believe it," the madam said. "This imbecilic half-breed Chink says he was shooting at a rat. The fool should know better."

Rags bowed again to the madam, more deeply than before. "Perfection is something one strives toward, but rarely achieves."

Rags amazed me with how calmly he took the woman's insults. The temptation to lash out at her in Rag's defense was strong, but I held back. *She or her "girls" might have heard or seen something last night. I can't afford to alienate them.*

The small crowd of men shook their heads, rolled their eyes. Most of them walked away. On the way back to doing what they'd been doing, they muttered. "Chucklehead." "Idiot." "Whatya expect from a crazy Chinaman."

After receiving a wink from Bob Hooper, the madam turned to leave. I swung toward her on my crutches. "Pardon me, ma'am. Shooting at rats isn't why we're here. We're here to investigate the shooting of my father, Marshal Doherty. It happened last night near the outhouse there. I wonder if you saw or heard anything."

She looked down her nose at me. "We were attending to our own business last night. We didn't see anything. And we couldn't hear anything over the piano in the parlor."

"You didn't hear the fireworks?"

She focused her haughty stare at Rags and then me. "You and —*Rags* isn't it? You of all people should know it was Chinese New Year. One more string of firecrackers wouldn't have meant anything to us last night."

"You didn't hear gunshots?" I asked.

"Slow-witted, are you? I already said the piano would have drowned out any noise from the alley. Anything else, dearie?"

Would you mind, dearie, if I broke your nose? I counted to ten. Did Papa have to do that all day, too? I took a deep breath. *Focus on finding the gunman. If I solve this case, I'm sure to get a job with the Pinkertons. I have to solve this case.*

I would like to ask the names of last night's customers, but I'm sure the madam won't divulge them. "No more questions at the moment, thank you. I'm sorry if we disturbed you and your girls."

The madam spun around and, followed by the young prostitute, stomped into the brothel.

Yong Liao had not left. He raised a finger and Rags approached him. They traded a few words in Cantonese. *Please don't say that Rags can't be a deputy.*

Rags turned to me. "Yong Liao wishes to speak with us when convenient. By 'when convenient' he means now."

"Tell him that's fine. No, wait. Tell him: I would much enjoy his hospitality."

Rags tipped his head. "You're learning." He said a few words to Yong Liao and then bowed.

Yong Liao, head held high, ambled back to his mercantile at the end of Virgin Alley. Rags and I followed behind.

"One thing, Nell," Rags whispered, "don't go telling Yong Liao what you think about him owning Huang Min. At least, not now."

"Why not?"

"Yong Liao doesn't need another reason to be angry. Probably best to avoid mention of Min altogether."

"Will he let you continue to be a deputy?"

He shrugged. "We'll see."

The photographer, Gideon Weed, approached. He looked to be about thirty. He had a long thin nose, hungry eyes, and an Abe Lincoln beard. Weed greeted Yong Liao and joined Rags and me. He doffed his fedora. "Hello, Miss Doherty. You and your friend are making quite a name for yourselves. I wonder if the two of you would sit for a portrait. No charge."

He wants a portrait of the soon-to-be famous Nell Doherty and Wu Chao. Papa had told me that everyone who came to Bodie searched for gold, but people did so in different ways. Some dug in the mines. Some sold miners tools, food, or clothing. Some cheated miners at cards. Others sold them whiskey, opium, or photographs of the queer or the fantastic.

"Perhaps another time, Mr. Weed. I'm afraid we have an appointment to keep."

"Stop by any time." The photographer doffed his hat again.

Rags and I hastened along the slush-covered alley toward the mercantile shop. We passed a few feet from the outhouse where Papa had been shot. The boot prints had disappeared. I could no longer see the bloody patch of snow where Papa fell, but I'd never forget it. *Just wait until I get my hands on you, Erastus Kohl.*

Inside the mercantile shop, Rags and I sat on matching black-lacquer stools. Yong Liao sat in his rocker near the potbellied stove. He did not offer us tea. He sat quietly for two or three minutes with his hands in his lap. Finally, he spoke to Rags in Cantonese. Rags hung his head.

"Miss Doherty, I speak to Wu Chao about his responsibilities as a Chinese. Remind him of laws like Chinese Exclusion Act, like Scott Act. Remind him of Chinese hung by neck for no reason. Many Americans not accept us here, want us go back to China. We must, especially Rags must, take care in actions, not stir troubles. Chinese deputy make some Bodie men afraid. Men afraid are dangerous."

"If I may speak, Uncle?" I said.

"Proceed." He rocked back in his chair.

"Rags, I mean Wu Chao, has been very helpful to me. He has been treated badly by a number of people here in Bodie, but has always ignored their insults. He has shown great patience and has treated everyone we have spoken to with great respect. I would hope that you would be proud of his actions."

Rags lifted his head.

"Rags's good actions as expected. Shooting gun in town no reason, not expected." Yong Liao stroked his chin. "You spoke to Huang Min. What she say?"

Why is Yong Liao bringing up Huang Min? Rags told me not

to ask about her. "She heard shots. She may have seen who shot Papa, but she wouldn't talk about it. Maybe if you spoke to her, told her she doesn't need to be afraid, maybe then she would talk to us."

"I will consider suggestion."

"Thank you, Uncle. Of course, talking to Huang Min will only be helpful if I can continue the investigation. To do so, I need Wu Chao's help. A few minutes ago, I stood where Papa had been shot. The footprints which Judge Snethens and I saw last night have melted away. If I must stop my search for the man who shot Papa, other clues may melt away."

"If Wu Chao succeed as deputy, may be good thing for Chinese. If only stir troubles, will be very bad for Chinese."

I glanced at Rags. "We understand."

"Perhaps yes. Perhaps no."

"I promise we'll be more careful."

"Understand, Miss Doherty, if troubles stir once more, Wu Chao no more allowed to be deputy."

I bowed. "Thank you, Uncle."

I'd escaped the worst possible consequences.

Or so I thought.

Chapter Twenty-One

As Rags and I stepped onto the boardwalk in front of the mercantile, two Chinamen on horseback rode by us. Mr. Zhao and Mr. Ren led a dozen mules laden with firewood. Old Zhao removed the clay pipe from between his tobacco-stained teeth and greeted us.

Rags and I bowed our heads and replied, "Nay hoh, Uncle."

The train of mules trudged on through the muddy lane.

A moment later, the newspaper editor, Albert Reeves, turned the corner from Main Street at a dead run. He waved his hand and shouted. "Miss Doherty!"

Mr. Reeves halted in front of me, bent over, and gasped for breath. "So exciting." A deep breath. "Your being a deputy." Another deep breath. "Front page story." The editor straightened himself. He pulled a piece of paper from his hat and a pencil from his coat pocket.

"Mr. Reeves," I said, "you're just the man I was looking for. You know most everything that goes on in Bodie. What have you heard about Papa's shooting? Have you heard any rumors?"

"I haven't heard a thing," he said. "No time to dilly-dally." He licked his pencil. "Deadlines to meet. Tell me about being anointed a deputy."

"Do you know where I might find Bill Hoffman?"

He looked up from the piece of paper. "Last time I saw him, he was in the jail, with you. Please, just let me ask the questions. How did it happen that you became a deputy?"

Begrudgingly, I related the proceedings in the jail. "And then I asked Rags, Wu Chao, to help me."

"You deputized a Chinese?"

"I'm half Irish," Rags said.

Mr. Reeves squinted at Rags. "You don't look it. Back to you, Miss Doherty. A female deputy is unheard of. One might even say it's unnatural for a woman to be a deputy. What made you, a young lady, and a cripple to boot, accept such a position?"

"I wanted to make sure whoever shot Papa was caught."

"I don't think you get my point. Why would you think a woman could do the job?"

"Why wouldn't I be capable enough?"

"Really, Miss Doherty." Mr. Reeves laughed. "It goes without saying. You're a woman."

"And women are weak."

"That's the way the good Lord chose to make them."

My fists clenched. Out of Mr. Reeves' sight, Rags held up his ten fingers, took a deep breath, and slowly exhaled

I counted to ten, twice. The urge to strike Mr. Reeves remained.

Mr. Reeves scribbled a line on his paper. "You've always been unconventional, Miss Doherty, running with Chinese boys, dragged out of an opium den by your father when you were four-teen. Do you understand that you're breaking social taboos in unprecedented ways? Hiring a Chinese as a deputy. Breaking into a prostitute's crib. Spending time there, behind closed doors, in the company, not only of the, uh, lady in question, but also a young man, who's Chinese to boot. How would you respond to those townspeople who think your behavior borders on the immoral?"

"It's immoral for a woman to bring a villain to justice?"

"Many will think so."

I sagged onto my crutches. If this is what he printed in the newspaper, not only would Mama kick me out of the house, but I would only be able to shop on Monday afternoons, along with the ladies of the evening.

"You're not going to print all that, are you?"

Mr. Reeves stopped his scribbling. His head jerked up, and he looked at me as if I were a two-headed donkey. "Not print it? Of course, I'm going to print it. This is the best story to come my way in years. Why, the articles I'll write about you represent a veritable news gold mine. I'm assured of being able to syndicate these stories—nationwide. I'll be famous!"

"Series of stories?"

"Why, certainly. To begin with, your background and appointment as deputy. That will be followed by your performance in your brief and disastrous career. Hiring the Chinese, failing to capture a drunk in a saloon because you were so drunk you fell down, ordering your Chinese to disturb the peace and fire his pistol in the air. Why, it will take me days just to decide on fitting headlines."

"But you have your facts wrong. I wasn't drunk."

"I have a witness who says you were so drunk you couldn't even get up off the floor."

"I have a wooden leg, for gosh sakes. It's difficult for me to get up after a fall."

"Hmm. I'll have to make something of that wooden leg. A symbol of something. Got it! Your leg symbolizes your folly. Your hubris. That's it. You exhibit a two-fold hubris, not only taking on a man's job, but, being a cripple, you should have known better than to assume such responsibilities. That's rather brilliant." He put pencil to paper again.

Something inside me snapped. "Rags, give me the shotgun."

Rags shook his head. "I don't care for that look in your eye. Crazy, it is."

I swung toward him on my crutches. "Give it to me."

"'Tis best if I keep it." He stepped back out of my reach.

"Rags, I just need the gun for a second. I want to make Mr. Reeves a symbol."

Mr. Reeves's head popped up from his paper. "I think I'll be going." He stuffed his pencil and paper into his coat pocket and ran toward Main Street. Over his shoulder he shouted, "One last question: How much did you drink before you fell down in the Gold Brick Saloon, or don't you remember?"

"You look pleased with yourself," Rags said.

"I may only be a girl with a wooden leg, but I scared Mr. Reeves."

"And me the same. Wonderin', I am, if you had that drink."

Mr. Reeves turned onto Main and disappeared.

A sharp pain shot up my leg. I gritted my teeth and swung my crutches in the direction Mr. Reeves had taken.

Rags fell into step with me. "Where to?"

"I aim to search every saloon in town until I find Bill Hoffman. Who knows? We may even run into Erastus Kohl."

Chapter Twenty-Two

Rags and I hitched up King Street and turned onto Main. The posse rode by us at a mournful pace, Judge Snethens in the lead. He slouched in the saddle. He wore a mask of weariness and despair. Before I could ask, he shook his head to indicate that they had not found Deputy Jorgensen. The posse continued on, the horses' heads low, their legs and bellies splattered with mud.

"God help him," Rags said. He crossed himself.

Poor Mrs. Jorgensen and her little ones. God help them, too. "Rags, let's start our search at Smith's Dance Hall."

We entered through the windowed double doors to find the dance hall nearly empty. The piano player sang and pounded out a sprightly "Oh, My Darling Clementine," for two dance hall girls and their customers. The owner, Harold Gant, poured brown liquor from a large bottle into one of several pint-sized bottles on the bar. Irene Lockhart stood behind the bar, at the far end of the dance hall, washing glasses in a tin tub filled with soapy water. She smiled at me, as if we might still be friends. I remained stone-faced. She shrugged and continued to clean the glasses.

Mr. Gant studied Rags a moment, then grunted. He shot me a cold look. "Whatcha want, girl?"

I swung forward on my crutches until I stood opposite him. "We're looking for Bill Hoffman. Have you seen him today?"

Gant picked up a cork and pushed it into the top of one of the pint bottles on the bar. Mrs. Lockhart looked at Gant and then shook her head.

I was tired of people mistreating me. *Dang it. As an officer of the law, I deserved respect. I will get it from Gant, or else.* "Well, have you seen him or not?"

Gant picked up another cork. I swung my right crutch up and over. As hard as I could, I slammed it on the bar, rattling the bottles. The piano player stopped singing and playing. The dancers froze and looked my way.

"Hey," Gant said. "You almost spilled my whiskey."

"Just getting started." I inched the crutch along the bar toward the bottles.

Gant's mustache twitched. "Ain't seen 'im."

"Well, if you do ..."

"Oh, I'll be sure to tell 'im you're lookin' for 'im."

I had half a mind to arrest Gant out of spite.

"We're grateful for the help of law-abiding citizens like yourself," Rags said.

"Eat dirt, yellow man."

Rags lowered his head briefly, then he stared at Gant and began to laugh hysterically.

Gant's face grew dark. "Whatcha laughing about?"

"I imagined, I did, this splendid dirt you mentioned served up at one of your tables here. And you sitting across from me, ladling that fine dish onto your plate, insisting on the first bite."

"Get your crazy ass outa my saloon."

"Harold," Mrs. Lockhart said. "She's deputized—"

"Hush your mouth. And wash them glasses."

I pulled my crutch from the bar and set the tip against the lip

117

of a brass spittoon on the floor. I pushed a little. Maybe half full. It would make quite a mess.

"Deputy," Rags said, to get my attention. "We're to keep the peace, we are."

I planted my crutches on the sawdust covered floor and swung toward the door. "You're no fun."

With Rags at my side, I hobbled up one side of Main and down the other. None of the other bartenders matched Gant in surliness. Except for Mr. Hurlbutt at the Gold Brick Saloon, who was openly belligerent, the others limited their hostility to sour or contemptuous looks. I grated at being a laughingstock or the subject of their incredulity.

An hour later, I gave up the search. Bill Hoffman had given us the slip.

Rags and I returned to the marshal's office. Fresh mud decorated the boot scraper to the left of the door. I tottered a bit while cleaning my left boot, then entered.

Judge Snethens sat behind the desk in Papa's chair. He appraised me with sad bloodshot eyes. He lifted a pint bottle of whiskey from the desktop and took a swallow. "We have to talk."

Chapter Twenty-Three

"Have a seat," the judge said. "Both of you."

I lowered myself into the wooden chair opposite Judge Snethens and set my crutches against the desk. Rags retrieved a stool from one of the cells, brought it into the office, and sat next to me.

The judge looked weary. "The good citizens of Bodie are not happy with the town's new deputies. They have brought certain facts to my attention."

Certain facts? Uh, oh. Had the judge spoken to Tobias Hurlbutt? Had that odious man convinced the judge to take our badges? "Judge, I was not drunk at the Gold Brick Saloon," I said. "I can explain."

"I hope so. Your mother excoriated me for sullying her daughter's reputation." He took a sip of his whiskey. "Proceed."

I relayed the events of the day and Judge Snethens nodded along until I asked him a question.

"Judge, according to Rags, Huang Min is owned by Yong Liao. That's not legal, is it? She says she wants to go home to China, but she isn't allowed to. Can't you free her?"

The judge glanced at Rags. "Different people have different traditions, different ways of life. The law in Bodie tends to make allowances—"

"You allow slavery?"

The judge straightened himself in the chair and hammered the desktop with his whiskey bottle. Liquor splashed onto the desk. "Young lady, I'm not about to be lectured by you on the law."

"But—"

The judge held up his hand. "I will talk to Yong Liao, when I get a chance. At the moment, you need to relate to me your every action as deputies."

"There's one more thing. You remember, Bill Hoffman said he heard two shots fired? Well, both Irene Lockhart, a dance hall girl at Smith's, and Huang Min heard three shots fired last night. Rags, Wu Chao, found two spent cartridges just outside Huang Min's crib."

"Where's the gun that was found in the snow next to Micah Pettibone?"

"In the center drawer of the desk," I said.

The judge pulled the revolver from the drawer and spilled the bullets onto the blotter. Only one had been fired.

Compared to me, Sherlock Holmes's Dr. Watson was a genius. I blushed. "I should have checked that earlier, Judge. I'm sorry."

"I didn't examine the gun either. No reason to berate yourself over it."

"If this pistol was fired only once, it means that Hoffman definitely lied about Pettibone shooting Papa. At most, Pettibone fired one of the three shots heard that night, and I don't believe he shot Papa at all."

"So you said." The judge took another sip from his bottle.

If two shots were fired from outside Huang Min's crib, and

one was fired from this revolver ... "Oh, my God! Judge, if three bullets were fired, and only one of them came from this pistol, it follows that Papa was shot by two different people."

"Saints preserve us," Rags said.

The judge leaned back in his chair. "That is alarming news. Well done, Nell, and you to, Wu Chao."

"Your honor," I said. "It's now more important than ever that Bill Hoffman be interviewed about what he saw last night. We spent time this afternoon searching all the saloons without luck. I'd like to try again this evening."

"I see the logic of that. However, you may not be the best person for the job. There's been a lot of talk about you and Wu Chao being made deputies."

Not the best person? He's going to take our badges. "Judge, you have to keep us on as deputies. There's no one else. Taking our badges would be the end of any investigation into who shot Papa. He deserves better. You can't take our badges. You can't."

"It's critical that the law be respected. I'm sorry, Nell. This situation is all my fault, and I apologize for getting you into this mess."

"Your honor," Rags said, "What if I resign? Nell could get someone else to help her, she could. A white man."

"Rags, you can't quit." Becoming a deputy meant a lot to him. His offer to resign warmed my heart. But if he deserted me, who could I find as a replacement? "Judge, think of my Papa. If you take our badges, who will track down the low-down bushwhackers that shot him?"

At that moment, the front door to the marshal's office opened and Baron Catlow strolled in. "Hello, everyone." He looked at each of us in turn. "Why're you all looking so sad?"

"Even though Wu Chao and I found important evidence about who shot Papa," I said, "the judge is about to take our badges from us."

Catlow lifted his Stetson from his head, smoothed his hair, and replaced his hat. "Oh, I doubt he'll want to do that."

"Baron," the judge said, "have you decided to accept the appointment as temporary marshal?"

"Only if I can choose my own deputies, and I choose Miss Doherty and Mr. Wu."

"Oh, my gosh." I blurted. Did Catlow mean it?

The judge crossed his arms. "You can't be serious."

"Completely serious. No deputies, no marshal. Which is it to be, Judge?"

"*Filius canis!*" the judge shouted. He slammed his fist onto the desk. "This is blackmail."

"Nevertheless ..."

Judge Snethens looked at me and Rags, then at Catlow. "I will agree to make Nell and Wu Chao *temporary* deputies, whose appointments expire as soon as I can find replacements. And the earlier restrictions apply—they are only to investigate Sam's shooting."

"Agreed." Catlow unbuttoned his overcoat.

Mentally I crossed my fingers. "So, are Rags and I still deputies?"

"You bet," the new marshal said.

"Thank you."

The judge stood, reached into his vest pocket, and tossed the marshal's badge to Catlow. "Raise your right hand.... Do you solemnly swear to uphold the laws of the state of California and Mono County?"

"I do."

The judge came around to the front of the desk. "If you will excuse me, I have to go and put a bottle between me and the more angry members of the town's populace." He shook hands with Catlow. "Good luck, sir. May you have a quiet tenure as marshal."

The judge left. Catlow took Papa's chair and then pinned Papa's badge onto his purple waistcoat. Marshal Catlow. It didn't sit right with me that someone other than Papa would be called marshal. That he would sit in Papa's chair. But if it had to be someone else, at least Catlow wanted to keep me and Rags as deputies.

"Nell," Rags said, "I'd like to ask Yong Liao if he can help find Bill Hoffman. He can put the word out to the Chinese to be on the watch for him."

"That sounds good to me," I said. "What do you think, Marshal?"

"An excellent idea."

As Rags left, Catlow put his hands behind his head. He was a treasure to look at. Still, he hadn't wanted me to be a deputy earlier. "Now, Deputy, tell me about this important evidence you discovered."

"First, tell me why you insisted Rags and I remain as deputies."

"I like Mr. Wu—Rags as you call him—and he's your friend."

"And me?"

Catlow dropped his hands from behind his head and sat up straight in Papa's chair. "I've seen how much you wish to bring your father's assailant to justice. And I appreciate how well you handled Bill Hoffman earlier today. You've done a remarkable job investigating your father's shooting, and I expect you'll continue to do well as a deputy."

He'd changed his mind. He thought I *could* do the job. He wasn't just trying to flatter me. And he certainly wasn't trying to get me to do something I didn't want to do. I wanted to be a deputy. I looked at Catlow with growing interest.

Catlow pulled his watch from his vest pocket. He was handsome, maybe ten years older than I, but still young. A tingle shot up my spine, like the sensation Lucy Barnes once told me she got when Tommy Watson stared at her in school.

He wound his watch, then looked up. "I need to check operations at my mine. Before I leave, I'd like to hear about the new evidence you found."

I summarized what Rags and I had discovered so far. Catlow's jaw dropped when I told him Papa had been shot by two different people.

"My God. Listen to me Miss Doherty, if two men ambushed your father, then there's much more here than meets the eye. Your investigation may put you in grave peril. Contact me first, before taking any steps other than searching for Bill Hoffman."

"I'll be safe with Wu Chao at my side. In addition to interrogating Hoffman, I need to talk to Erastus Kohl. Kohl swore to get even with Papa, and he was in Virgin Alley last night."

"All right, but be careful. I'll come back later this evening. If you need me, you know where to find me."

I stood and grabbed my crutches. Catlow came around the desk and stopped in front of me. He shook his head. "You're really something, Deputy Doherty." He smelled of the sweet orange scent of *Florida Water* cologne.

My pulse raced.

"I don't want any harm to come to you. Promise me you'll be careful."

"I promise." I raised my hand. For no reason I understood, I wanted to touch his face.

Catlow pulled his head back, then took my hand in both of his. "Miss Doherty, you are the prettiest dang deputy I've ever seen and—"

The door to the marshal's office opened and Rags stepped inside. He turned away.

My face burned. I slipped my hand out of Catlow's.

Catlow rubbed his two hands together as if warming them. "Ahem. Well, um, I'll be at the mine office if you need me." He left.

Rags stared at the closed door for a bit. "Did I interrupt something?"

"I don't know."

Rags looked puzzled. "You don't know?"

"No. I don't know." *What must Rags be thinking after seeing Catlow holding my hand?* Was he angry? Jealous? I loved Rags, but Catlow made me feel precious, like the speck of gold hidden in a ton of quartz ore. Was I a terrible person for having feelings for Catlow?

Chapter Twenty-Four

"Let's find Kohl." I swung toward the jail door on my crutches.

Rags picked up his shotgun and followed me onto Virgin Alley.

The sun had made its first appearance in a week. The warmer air brought more people outside and the boardwalks were dotted with women and children. As Rags and I approached Mrs. Talbot's Millinery Shop, a group of young girls standing out front pointed fingers at us and giggled.

One of the group, a little girl maybe six years old and wearing a purple bonnet, stepped in front of me. "Is it true you're doin' a man's job? Is you that shameless?"

Out of the mouths of babes ... come their mothers' words.

Shameless. Could have been my mother's word, too. I resisted the urge to go into the shop and give the girl's mother a piece of my mind. Instead, I spoke as sweetly as I could. "What's your name?"

"Amelia Granger."

"Hello, Amelia. I'm Nell Doherty."

She wrapped loose strands of her hair around her finger.

"Everybody knows you."

"Did you know that my Papa, the marshal, was shot?"

"I heard Papa tell Mama about it."

"Don't you think the person who shot my Papa should go to jail?"

She considered that while uncurling the hair wrapped around her finger. "I suppose."

"Well, I feel the same as you. But you see there weren't any men who had time to look for the bad man who shot my Papa. So I volunteered to look for him."

Amelia looked inward a moment. "You're going to put the bad men in jail?"

"If I can."

Two women exited the milliner's chatting amiably, until they caught sight of me and Rags.

"Amelia," said the woman wearing a new red hat trimmed with satin and feathers, "stay away from them."

The other woman, adorned by a green hat topped with cowslips, motioned to the girls with her hands, driving them like cattle down the boardwalk, away from Rags and me. The girls shot us curious looks as they skittered away. The women scowled and rushed their charges homeward.

"Goodbye, Amelia," I said, to get her mother's goat. "It was nice talking with you."

Amelia turned and waved to me. For her pains, her mother screamed at her. "Amelia, stop that."

Rags stared at the departing women and children. He looked wistful.

"Sorry," I said.

"I'm used to such."

Rags and I crossed Main Street's muck and mud and stepped onto the boardwalk in front of Kohl's Meat Market. We took turns wiping our shoes across the boot scraper outside the front door. I knocked the ends of my crutches against it, too.

I crossed my fingers. God willing, when I left his butcher shop, I'd be taking Kohl to jail.

Rags opened the door and we entered the shop. Faint odors of fresh blood and excrement greeted us. Whole chickens, a dressed pig, legs of lamb, and other cuts of meat hung from hooks along the back wall. Slabs of bacon and roasts sat in metal trays on the counter on either side of a large scale. I could see my breath in the store. Unlike other shops, the meat market wasn't heated.

Fergus Poague, a tall man as broad as the horses he smelled like, leaned up against the front of the counter talking to Erastus Kohl, who stood in the back of his shop. Poague had a dark, bushy beard. He'd been part of the posse that looked for Deputy Jorgensen.

"See ya tonight, then," Poague said. He grinned at Rags and me as he headed for the door. "Deputies."

Erastus Kohl stood at a butcher block in a ruddy apron holding a thin-bladed knife in one blood-drenched hand and a hook in the other. He had a thin, pale face and a long nose. His head was completely bald. When he caught sight of me and Rags, he stopped slicing the side of beef he was cutting up.

"Bless my soul. You's the marshal's daughter, ain't ya? I was terrible sorry to hear about the marshal bein' shot."

"You hated him," I said.

"Ain't true. Least ways, not no more." He looked from me to Rags, seeking, I thought, a sympathetic face. He didn't find one. "I's changed, I has. Honest."

"Wu Chao and I have been deputized." I glanced at the badge on my coat. "We're investigating Papa's shooting. Where's your Knights of Pythias pin?" I wanted to hear him say he'd lost his pin. I knew his was the pin I'd found in the snow next to where Papa was shot.

"Me K-o-P pin? It's at home. Why?"

"I want to see it."

"What fer?"

"Never mind, what for. I need to see it."

"Just askin'. Ya don't need to get all riled up about it." Kohl bobbed his head. "I could bring it to you after I close."

"I'd like to see all the guns you own."

He grinned, revealing a missing front tooth. "I ain't gots no gun." He put the knife and the meat hook down on the butcher block table and rubbed the front and back of his red hands on his dirty apron. He reached into his hip pocket.

Was he lying about having a gun? Did he mean to draw down on us?

Rags raised the barrel of his shotgun level with the marble front counter.

"Just gittin' this." Kohl held a small book with a black cover and gold-tinged pages. "I carries my Bible now, not no gun. Chaplain at the penitentiary convinced me to renounce sin. The Lord 'restoreth my soul: he leadeth me in the paths of righteousness.'"

Rags shot me a curious look. I hoped he wasn't falling for this hogwash.

"You've renounced sin? Really?" I rocked forward on my crutches. "Most folks wouldn't put Virgin Alley's bordellos on the path of righteousness. Your wife said you were there last night with a soiled dove."

"I was only doin' me missionary work, tryin' to get 'em to give up their evil ways."

"And the names of these angels to be?"

He scrunched up his face, creasing his long nose half way down its bridge. "Sally, or maybe Sarah, or Suzy? Wasn't interested in names. I cares only about their souls."

"Uh-huh."

Nothing in Kohl's voice or his manner suggested he was lying. But he was lying. I was sure of it. I glanced at Rags. He shrugged.

My next stop would be a bordello to see if Suzy or Sarah or Sally spent time in prayer with Kohl. Mama would die another death if she found out. "Well, even if you don't remember her name, you must know which bordello you visited last night. Which was it?"

"The Mother Lode."

Wonderful. I sagged onto my crutches. It had to be The Mother Lode, the bordello next door to Haung Min's crib. The house run by the madam Rags had angered by firing his pistol earlier that morning, at my request.

"While you were trying to save this woman's soul, did you hear the shots last night? Did you see the shooting?"

Kohl pushed his Bible back into his hip pocket. "I heard some shots. Didn't think much of 'em. Chinese New Year, ya know." He picked up the hook and the butcher knife and began cutting the meat away from a leg bone.

"Did you hear or see anything else?"

Kohl shook his head.

"Come on, Nell," Rags said.

I hadn't gotten a shred of evidence to put Kohl in jail. But I knew in my gut that he'd shot Papa.

Rags tapped my shoulder. "Come on, we'll talk to the madam of The Mother Lode."

I leaned toward him and whispered, "I don't believe a word of Kohl's saintly fairy tale. Give me one reason I shouldn't arrest him this instant."

"I don't believe him either," Rags whispered back, "but he could've run off, he could, and he didn't."

Rags was right. All my muscles tensed. I was ready to explode. "Mr. Kohl, you better bring me your Knights of Pythias pin the minute after you close shop."

"Will do, miss. And I'll be prayin' for your Papa, too."

Rags and I left the shop and headed back to Virgin Alley.

I gritted my teeth and growled. "If he doesn't bring me his Knights of Pythias pin—right after he closes—I *am* going to arrest him."

Chapter Twenty-Five

I knocked and pounded on the front door of The Mother Lode for several minutes before it swung open. We were greeted by a young woman wearing an apron over a gray gingham dress.

"'Tis early for company," the young woman said, looking at Rags. "My name's Abigail. What is it you want?"

"Excuse me," I said. "I'm Nell Doherty and this is Wu Chao. We've been deputized to investigate the shooting of the town marshal. We want to talk to one of the women here. She might be named Suzy, or Sarah, or Sally, whoever Erastus Kohl, uh, spent time with last night."

"You mean Cecilia. Mr. Kohl always asks to see Cecilia. Follow me."

Rags and I shared a glance. Kohl had lied.

Abigail led us through an open door a few paces down the carpeted hallway. Once there, she grabbed the fireplace shovel and scooped ashes from the banked fire into a large brass bucket, then added three more logs on top of the glowing coals of the previous night's fire. On her way out the door, Abigail said, "I'll tell Cecilia you're here."

The rectangular parlor had upholstered sofas set against three of its chintz-covered walls. In between the sofas, house plants drooped from brass pots sitting on stone pillars. Rags and I approached the wide fireplace that occupied much of the fourth wall. The new logs had begun to flame, and we took off our gloves and warmed our hands. A large wooden clock adorned with a carved pair of cherubs holding a heart sat in the middle of the mantelpiece. Time: a quarter to three. I hoped Cecilia was already awake and dressed.

At a quarter past three, a woman with large brown eyes entered the parlor. She was tying a bow on the sash of her silver satin robe. I stopped pacing the floor.

"Hello, I'm Cecilia." She looked askance at me and Rags. "Abigail said two deputies wanted to talk to me. You don't look like deputies."

"My papa told me that people often aren't what they seem." Her round face and dull hair weren't all that attractive for a woman in her profession. "But we are deputies." I pointed to the badge on my coat. "Duly appointed by Judge Snethens."

Cecilia covered a yawn with her hand. "What is it you want?"

"To talk to you about Erastus Kohl."

"I don't remember a Kohl. Of course, not all of my gentlemen tell me their real names." Cecilia looked Rags up and down.

"Kohl's bald," I said. "Has a bushy mustache. He owns a butcher shop on Main Street."

"Doesn't ring a bell."

Was she afraid she'd lose a good customer if she talked to us? I didn't care. "It's against the law to lie to a deputy. Maybe you need to spend some time in jail to revive your memory. Abigail said Kohl's one of your regulars."

Cecilia pouted. "Abigail should keep her mouth shut."

"So, you remember Kohl, now? He told us the two of you spent time last night praying."

Cecilia laughed. "Praying? Well, perhaps Mr. Kohl was praying for more. He didn't want to leave when his time was up.

Don't you want to sit? You look uncomfortable leaning on your crutches."

"Thanks. I'll stand."

Cecilia sat on one of the sofas and crossed her legs. The lower half of her robe opened, exposing her knee. She winked at Rags. "You're kinda cute for a Chinaman."

He blushed.

Cecilia batted her eyes at him and wiggled her foot.

She was flirting with Rags just like Huang Min had done. Not something I could do. Opening one's robe wouldn't have the same effect if one's leg was made of wood. "That's enough of that, Cecilia."

"Oh, sorry. I didn't know he was yours."

I jerked my head back. "He's not mine." Oh, might I have hurt his feelings? Rags didn't look anguished. Was someone else his true love? Who could it be?

"Is that it?" Cecilia asked. "Are we done?"

"Not yet. What time were you and Kohl together last night?"

"If you must know, we were together from midnight to one."

Papa was shot just after one. "Did you hear the gunfire?"

"Yeah, a few minutes after I pushed Kohl out of my bedroom."

Kohl, the swine, had lied about trying to save Cecilia's soul. And, he had no alibi for the time Papa was shot.

"Did you hear or see anything else last night that might help identify who shot the marshal?"

"I don't think so, unless seeing Sam go into the crib next door means anything."

"He went into a crib?" *Papa? It can't be.*

"That's right. Sam comes around all the time. All of the girls adore him."

"What?" *They call Papa by his first name? I'm not hearing what I'm hearing. Papa visits the bordello? He visited Huang Min's crib?*

Cecilia uncrossed and re-crossed her legs. The silver robe opened a bit more, revealing her thighs. "Well, sometimes customers get drunk or they get a bit rowdy. Sam comes and arrests them before any of the girls get hurt, you know. I hope he gets better soon. He's a really nice man. He's good at keeping the peace."

Whew. She meant Papa just does his job as marshal.

"Do you have any other questions? If not, it's time for me bath." Cecilia winked at Rags again.

He looked my way.

"No more questions. Thank you."

"Nice meeting you. And you, too, Mr. Wu. Don't be a stranger."

Rags and I plodded up Virgin Alley toward the jail. He was quiet. He stared at the muddy lane. Rags's little brother had said Rags was in love. When Bobby told me, I was thrilled. Rags and I were both outcasts. We'd been companions and best friends since my accident. I loved Rags. But he didn't make me tingle like Baron Catlow. Was that love, too? If it was me Rags loved, why hadn't he said so?

"Learned new respect for your pa," Rags said. "This law work is devilish hard."

"We're almost there. Kohl doesn't have an alibi, and he was in or near Virgin Alley when Papa was shot. If he fails to bring me his Knights of Pythias pin, I have him."

Rags and I entered the office. I sat behind Papa's desk and Rags put a pot on the stove to make tea. Before the water boiled, heavy footsteps on the boardwalk outside announced the arrival of the stagecoach driver, Percy Odell. His shoulders stooped abnormally. He looked from me to Rags and back to me.

"Have I heard it right, Miss Doherty? Is you two deputies?"

"That's right."

"Certain strange, that is, miss. I, uh, has bad news. I'm here to report I found Deputy Jorgensen's body."

"Body? Oh, no. He's dead?"

"Yes, miss."

"His poor little children." They loved it when he brought them to see the jail. He'd always surprise them with a wooden toy he'd carved for them. I opened the left-hand desk drawer and found partially finished wooden figures of a dog and a horse. He would never get to finish these gifts for his boys. Tears welled in my eyes. I was a deputy and needed to be tough. I couldn't cry.

"'Tis sad news you bring us, Mr. Odell," Rags said, "powerful sad." He exhaled noisily. "What happened to the deputy? Could you tell?"

"Well, he looked to have been shot. His body was in the gully below the road. His legs was covered by snow, but his upper half was clear of it. There was blood on his chest."

Not one, but two Bodie lawmen shot. Were the two shootings connected? Papa had sent Deputy Jorgensen to look for the gold robbers. Had they killed him? Had they, not Erastus Kohl, shot Papa, or was Kohl one of the gold thieves?

Odell removed his wide, flat-brimmed hat. "I's sorry for not bringing the deputy home, but, before I saw his body, I come across a Chinaman almost froze to death."

A tear escaped. I wiped it from my cheek. "A Chinaman was on the road?"

"Yes, miss, sittin' on a rock at the side of the road. On account of needin' to get the Chinaman to the doctor, I dared not stop for the deputy. I come here straight from Doc Boyle's."

"Who's the Chinaman, then?" Rags asked. "What condition's he in?"

"He were delirious, not able to talk but gibberish. Older than you. Wore a ponytail. Found him near where Bodie Creek meets Esmeralda Gulch. His teeth was chatterin' to beat the band. Doc don't think he'll make it."

Rags crossed himself again. "God have mercy on his soul."

Odell looked at me. "Did you wish to get the deputy's body?

If we leave now, there'll still be enough daylight, and I can show you where he is."

"Rags, go to Doc Boyle's. See if the Chinaman can tell you what happened to him, or if he knows anything about what happened to Deputy Jorgensen. Then meet us at The City Livery Stables."

The stable owner loaned us a horse and wagon to collect the deputy's body. The owner had just finished harnessing the horse to the wagon when Rags appeared.

He shook his head. "The Chinaman has passed."

"I'm so sorry."

"Thanks. I suggested Doc notify Yong Liao. He'll make arrangements for the burial."

Rags and Odell climbed onto the wagon. It had two seats and there was room for me, but I chose to ride Sunrise, my Palomino pony. It wasn't logical to refuse riding in the wagon. But I didn't care. The thought of riding in a wagon made my stump throb. I'd break out in a sweat. Maybe I should have risen above my fear of wagons over the course of the last six years, but I hadn't. So, I climbed the little set of stairs the stable owner had built for me and mounted Sunrise side-saddle. Sunrise and I followed the wagon.

We rode north of town, winding through Bodie Creek Canyon. Scrub brush covered with melting snow dotted the rocky slopes on either side. The west wall tended to be taller and steeper, the east wall more gently sloped. The wagon rattled along the road ahead of me.

"Mr. Odell," I yelled ahead. "Did you see anyone else on the road earlier today?"

"No, miss, not a soul."

We passed an abandoned log cabin, its roof stove in. Above, on the slope, several thick timbers pointed at the sky, the frame-work of a forsaken mine works whose walls and roof lay scattered on the slope between the large beams and the ruined cabin. Signs of another dream dashed to pieces.

Odell stopped the wagon near five fractured rocks that resembled giant rust-colored fingers. They stood in a group, ten to twenty feet tall. Deputy Jorgensen's body lay in a gully between the muddy road and the rock formation.

Rags helped me dismount and I tied Sunrise to the wagon. Rags handed me my crutches. I slung myself to the edge of the gully at the side of the road.

Deputy Jorgensen lay face up in a patch of wet snow. A brown stain spread from the center of his jacket to the tops of his trousers. My stomach clenched. There should have been something more to show for his life, but all I felt was sadness. Husband, father, and good friend, gone now, ended by a bullet. It just wasn't right.

The deputy'd been left on the ground in a ditch ... in a ditch and near a large sagebrush. I took a deep breath. Six years ago I'd been left on the ground. There hadn't been snow that day, but there had been a ditch and a sage plant. And lots of blood.

IT HAPPENED ON A WARM SUMMER'S DAY. I WAS TWELVE and my brother Patrick fourteen. We rode a borrowed wagon from Bodie to a farm near Mono Lake. The day started out well.

"Do you think Mama will peek when Papa tells her to cover her eyes?" I asked. "I hope she doesn't guess what her present is. I want to see the surprise on her face." I grabbed Patrick's arm. "It will be a big surprise, don't you think?"

"Well, I hope so, after all the trouble Papa's gone to."

Mono Lake came into view, sky-blue water with a snow-capped peak to its south. Only a few puffy clouds speckled the sky. The scent of blooming sagebrush filled the air.

We arrived at the Neely's farm about noon. Mrs. Neely served us lemonade and collected Papa's forty-five dollars while Mr. Neely and several Paiute workers loaded Mama's birthday present into the wagon. She'd wanted a piano for as long as I could remember. It was a small upright, but she wouldn't care about the size.

"Thank you for the lemonade," I said.

Patrick's chest swelled as he shook hands with Mr. Neely. My brother walked taller that day because Papa entrusted him with the responsibility of fetching Mama's piano.

"Say hello to your parents, dear," Mrs. Neely said, after Patrick and I climbed onto the buckboard.

Half way home, the wagon picked up speed on the backside of a small hill. From behind a bush twenty yards in front of us, a rattlesnake slithered onto the dusty trail. The rattler was huge, at least six feet long. It coiled its body in the middle of the road and rattled its tail. The horse's head snapped up. She bolted off the trail, running over sagebrush as she fled from the snake.

"Whoa, girl," Patrick yelled. "Slow down." He yanked on the reins.

I grabbed the seatback, holding on for dear life. "Make her stop, Patrick."

He stood and leaned backward, tugging harder on the reins. "Whoa. Dang it, stop."

The frightened horse ignored him and headed for a ditch.

"Jump, Nell," Patrick yelled.

I shook my head and held tighter to the seatback.

"Jump," Patrick yelled again.

The horse galloped toward the gully. As the buckboard's front wheels rolled into the ditch, it flipped over. I was thrown from the wagon and my body slammed into the ground. Gravel scraped my cheek. A rock as big as Papa's derby punched me in the ribs and took my breath.

Patrick screamed, "Look out."

Mama's piano cartwheeled toward me. I lay dazed and

couldn't move. The piano landed on my right leg. I cringed against the crushing blow, the pain—initially numbed by shock—was still severe. "God, oh God."

The piano rolled past me, struck a boulder, and burst apart. The strings played a mournful note that stretched on and on until everything went black.

Patrick's frightened voice woke me. "Nell. Nell. Stop it, will you?" He patted my cheek. "Stop bawling."

I was bawling? I opened my eyes.

Pain flooded my consciousness. My ribs hurt. But that was nothing compared to my leg. Oh, my God. The difference between my ribs hurting and my leg pain was like the difference between being sunburned and being scalded with boiling water.

It wasn't just pain. I couldn't move my right foot. Why couldn't I move my foot?

"You're going to be all right," Patrick said.

I lifted my head. Patrick looped his bandana around my right thigh to make a tourniquet. He used one hand and his teeth to tie the knot. "I stopped the bleeding, I think."

Blood covered the lower half of my dress. My thigh bone stuck out from the bloody pulp of my skin. I threw up.

Patrick laid a shaking hand on my shoulder. "I'm gonna get help." He stood.

"Noooo. Don't leave me alone. Take me with you."

"I can't. My arm's broken." Patrick held his arm against his chest. His wrist stuck out at an odd angle. "You're gonna be okay. I'm gonna fetch the doctor. I'll be back soon, soon as I can." He scrambled up the side of the ditch and was gone.

I lay in the dirt in the shadow of a large sagebrush, a few feet from the overturned wagon, alone. "Mama," I cried. "Get Mama." There was no response.

"Mama, where are you?" I blacked out again.

After I awoke, I turned onto my side, hoping to see Mama coming to save me. The pain in my leg exploded. An army of miners smashed my leg with ten thousand sledgehammers, all in unison, in a four-beat rhythm, ta, ta, ta, boom. Ta, ta, ta, boom. Every fourth beat stars exploded in my head. Such pain could only mean one thing—I was dying.

"Mama, help me. I don't want to die."

I drifted in and out of consciousness, in and out of pain, slipping toward oblivion. I tallied each breath I took, each a miracle, a sign I still lived. The shadows grew longer and still no one had come. "I want you to hold me, Mama. Hold me."

Somewhere beyond the wreck of the piano, between one searing ta, ta, ta, boom and the next, the poor horse moaned. I hoped she was in less pain than I was. After an hour or so, when the horse stopped moaning and the buzz of the flies swelled, I knew she was.

Later that afternoon, Papa rescued me from where I lay in the ditch next to that sagebrush. He laid me in the back of a buggy and raced for town. Tears streaked down his cheeks as he carried me up the stairs to Doc Boyle's surgery.

"I'm going to put you to sleep," Doc said. When I was out, he sawed off my leg just above the knee.

I SHUDDERED. SIX YEARS AGO. THE DAY I STOPPED riding in wagons. I had died that day, in a way. My two-legged life died. In my new life, most people saw and treated me as different. Despite what they thought, I was not a cripple. That would not be my fate. Sometimes I wanted to tell them all to go to blazes, even Mama.

"Nell," Rags said, "you all right? Do you need help getting down the slope?"

I stood at the top of the ditch that held Deputy Jorgensen's body and the snow-covered sagebrush. No smashed wagon. No dead horse. No shattered piano.

I took a deep breath to clear my head. "I'm okay."

"You were still as a statue for so long, I began to wonder."

Tentatively, I placed one crutch on the moist slope and rocked a bit to see if I had purchase. I repeated the actions, making my way slowly down the side of the trench, hoping my crutches wouldn't slide out from under me.

Rags, Odell, and I approached the deputy's body slowly. We looked for tracks, but found none in the slushy snow. If the killers had left any footprints behind, they had been obliterated by the warmer weather.

I took a pencil and a small notebook from my coat pocket and made notes. A single hole pierced the deputy's jacket, surrounded by brownish blood stains. My stomach turned and I looked away. *How horrible to be shot. First Papa, and now, Deputy Jorgensen.*

Sadness squeezed my chest. I had to let it go though. I'd need to be tough like Kate Warne, Pinkerton's first female detective, if I wanted to work for them.

I looked around and tried to focus on the details like Kate Warne would have done. The deputy had lost his hat. The skin of his frost-bitten hands had turned black as his hair. I closed my eyes for a few seconds to blot out the gruesomeness.

"Who shot you, Mr. Jorgensen?" He didn't answer. All he could do was stare at the darkening blue sky, toward the heaven I hoped was his new home.

Rags and Odell brushed the wet snow from the body. The deputy's right leg was crossed over his left. Rags tugged on the deputy's boots to straighten them.

"It's no good," Odell said. "He's still too frozen."

They wrapped the body in a blanket. Odell bent over and took the shoulders. Rags grabbed the deputy under his knees, and they carried him up to the wagon.

Unlike the place Papa had been gunned down, no blood had soaked into the ground beneath the deputy. Maybe he fell from his horse after being shot, after he bled out. Resting on my crutches, I jotted down in my notebook everything I saw.

"His gun's missing. Do either of you see the deputy's pistol?"

Odell and Rags stalked along the ditch at the side of the road in opposite directions and came back.

"Don't see it," Odell said.

Rags shrugged. "Me neither."

I used a crutch to scrape moist snow from the ground in the area where the deputy's body had been. Nothing lay hidden beneath the snow like the Knights of Pythias pin I found where Papa had been shot. No clues at all. Dang. I kicked at the snow with my good leg.

"Ready to go?" Rags said.

With Rags's help, I got into the wagon and from there mounted my pony. I stroked her neck. "Take me home, Sunrise."

The shootings of Papa and Deputy Jorgensen filled my mind. Sherlock Holmes and Allan Pinkerton didn't get angry when they witnessed murder. It made me angry. I burned with a desire to bring justice.

It was so easy to shoot someone. The only thing preventing more murders were people's consciences, which are weak. Like Daniel Webster said in the speech Bobby Wu was reading the other day, some emotions are so strong they can overcome the better promptings of our souls. Even as angry as Papa's shooting made me, I couldn't imagine feeling Webster's "savage vengeance." I couldn't imagine being so angry I would take a life.

The darkening sky leached the green from the shrubs, turning them gray. I rode alongside the wagon imagining what would happen if we should run into Mrs. Jorgensen on our return to Bodie. It would fall to me to tell her she was a widow.

Chapter Twenty-Six

We returned to Bodie just before six p.m. and went to Doc Boyle's surgery. Rags and Odell waited in the street while I went up to ask Doc if he wanted us to bring the body up. I hoped to find Papa awake and doing better. My stump was sore, but tolerable. I left the crutches in the wagon and climbed the stairs to Doc's office, leading with my good leg.

I entered the surgery winded and sweating from the exertion of climbing. Mama sat in the chair beside the examination table Papa lay on. She held his hand as she'd been doing seven hours ago. His face glowed red. Doc Boyle stood on the other side of the table from Mama. He pulled a thermometer from Papa's mouth.

"Hello, Mama," I said. "Hello, Doc."

"Have you come to your senses?" Mama asked. She didn't turn to face me.

I swallowed an exasperated reply, closed my eyes, and counted to ten. "How is Papa?"

"Still breathing. Blissfully unaware of what you've been up to."

"Mama."

"Hmm," Doc Boyle said. He shook his head while he stared at the thermometer he'd removed from Papa's mouth.

"What is it?" Mama said.

"His fever is rising. A hundred-and-five now."

Mama whimpered.

Doc Boyle came around the table and patted Mama's shoulder. "There, now, Molly. There's still hope."

I squeezed my eyes shut. *Please, God, please save Papa.* "Doc, is there anything more you can do?"

"A sponge bath should bring the fever down." Doc peeled back the blanket and sheet and exposed Papa's chest. He got a sponge and a ceramic bowl of water. He wet Papa's head and body.

"Doc, I've got some bad news."

He looked up.

"We found Vern Jorgensen. He's dead."

"Lord have mercy," Mama cried.

"How—"

"It looks like he was shot."

Mama released her grip on Papa's hand and turned my way. "Nell, stop your foolishness this instant and go home. Enough is enough. I couldn't bear it if you were hurt. I couldn't."

"I'm never alone when I'm investigating, like Papa and Vern were when they were shot. Rags and his shotgun are always with me. I need to finish what I've begun."

"You're mad, girl. Mad. And you'll not sleep under my roof while you're a deputy. Do you hear me?"

"Mama, you can't mean that."

"I most certainly do."

"But I can't quit now."

Mama put her hand on her forehead. "Doc, talk some sense into her, please."

Doc removed his glasses. Deep, dark wrinkles hung below his eyes. He wiped his glasses with a handkerchief and put them back on. "Nell," he said, "it appears that being a lawman, er, well, wearing a badge in Bodie, makes you a target."

"Doc, I'm not quitting. Not now."

"Nell, your mother's right. You're putting yourself in danger. You should be helping her now."

"I'm duly deputized. And I'm being as cautious as I can, Doc."

"Nell," Doc said, "It's not your job to put your life in danger."

I put my hands on my hips. "I have to get back to work. Did you want to see Vern's body?"

"Yeah, I better take a look."

"What happened to the Chinaman?"

"He was too far gone when he got here—a person can only stand so much cold. Yong Liao's men took the body away."

"Did they recognize him?"

"They weren't sure. Might have been one of four Chinamen missing from Virginia City."

Mama didn't say another word to me before I left. I didn't speak to her either. I didn't know where I might be sleeping that night.

But I had no choice. I needed to find the devils who shot Papa as much as I needed to breathe. Why didn't Mama feel the same?

I waited in the cold with the horses while Rags and Odell carried Deputy Jorgensen's body up to Doc's office. After taking the horses and wagon back to the stables, Odell went to his hotel. With Rags at my side, I headed to Yong Liao's mercantile, swinging on my crutches again.

"Would ya like some supper?" he said. "Me mother will've saved some food for me. We could share it, we could."

"That'd be nice. But first I'd like to talk to Yong Liao about the Chinaman that died. Do you think his death could be related to the shootings?"

"I don't see how. 'Twould be a mighty mess if it were."

Rags and I turned down Main Street. My left crutch slipped through a hole in the boardwalk and I fell backward. Rags caught me under my arms. He held on until I got back on my feet.

"You're always there when I need you. Thank you, Wu Chao. Thank you for everything."

"What're friends for?"

Rags and I were finally alone. I could ask him if I were the one he was in love with. But what if he said no? I remembered the tingling sensation that Baron Catlow gave me and wondered, what if Rags said yes, I was the one he loved? Rags had never made me tingle.

"You all right then?"

"Thanks to you."

We continued down the boardwalk past the cigar store and Annabelle's Seamstress shop. Both sat empty, closed years ago. Annabelle had made a name for herself sewing wedding gowns, symbols of love.

Love. Why would Rags tell his brother who he loved before he told me? What did it mean that Baron Catlow's presence made me tingle all over? Maybe I should wait until Rags was ready to tell me his secret. And maybe that would give me a chance to sort out my feelings toward Catlow.

Now that I have the chance to talk to Rags, I no longer want to. I laughed out loud.

"What's so funny?" Rags asked.

"Nothing."

He stared at me, but it was too dark for him to really see my face. He shook his head. "You're a wonder you are, Miss Nell Doherty."

"That's Deputy Doherty to you."

Despite the terrible day we'd had, we both laughed.

Chapter Twenty-Seven

Rags and I turned onto King Street and entered Yong Liao's brightly lit mercantile. A circular table sat in the middle of the store. Yong Liao, Mr. Zhao, Mr. Ren, and two other Chinamen I didn't know, were playing poker.

"Greetings, Uncle," Rags and I said together. We bowed. The other men at the table bowed their heads and turned back to their cards.

"Will be just minute," Yong Liao said. "Please warm yourself by stove." He tossed a silver dollar into the pile of coins in the center of the table. Mr. Ren studied Yong Liao, then he tossed a dollar into the center. The two men I didn't know threw their cards face down onto the table. Mr. Zhao grunted. He placed a silver dollar in the center and tapped it with his finger. "Call."

Yong Liao laid out his cards. Mr. Ren and Mr. Zhao laid out their hands. Zhao grunted again and spoke in Cantonese. Yong Liao raked the coins toward his large belly.

Rags and I sat on the pair of black-lacquered stools by the potbellied stove. He leaned toward me and whispered. "Zhao said 'You have all the luck tonight, Yong Liao. As every night. Only Marshal Doherty ever beats you at poker.'"

Yong Liao removed his large gold watch from his coat pocket. "Let us continue tomorrow," he said. "Maybe luck change."

The others stood, bowed to Yong Liao, and left.

Yong Liao collected his winnings, placed them in a red, embroidered, silk purse, and slipped the purse into an inner pocket of his quilted coat. He sat in his rocking chair and folded his hands together on his belly.

"Uncle, thank you for taking the time to speak with us," Rags said.

"A sad day, very sad. Li Sui-bak die of cold. I hear Deputy Jorgensen also dead." He looked at me as if asking for confirmation.

"Yes, Uncle. He was shot in the back."

Yong Liao rocked back and forth. "Not surprised."

"Do you know something about the deputy's shooting?"

"Only know marshal also shot."

I leaned forward, stretching my arms toward the stove to warm my hands. "Did you know Mr. Li?"

"He from village next mine in Guangdong. Farmer in China. Left wife and six children to find wealth on Gold Mountain. Was gold miner in Virginia City. Disappear two month ago with three others. Li work hard as two men. Bitter man. Never satisfied."

"Do you know why he might have left Virginia City?"

Yong Liao rocked back and forth a few seconds while he thought. "Li want be rich, maybe found different way."

"A different way? What do you mean, Uncle?"

Yong Liao reached inside his coat and drew out a small leather pouch closed with a drawstring. He opened the pouch and poured a small mound of bits of gold into his palm.

"This in Li's pants pocket."

"What is it worth?" I asked.

"Maybe sixty dollar."

"That's not a fortune."

Yong Liao poured the gold back into the pouch and pulled

the drawstring tight. He placed the pouch back into his jacket pocket.

"Not fortune, no, but strange. This not gold dust. Is gold leaf."

"Gold leaf? What's that?"

"Is gold pounded flat then cut in pieces. Not thing miner would dig up. Made in Denver or San Francisco. Is used like paint. Put on dish, on picture frame. Unusual that it cut into small flakes. Must consider this. But now, Miss Doherty, have advice."

Yong Liao leaned forward in the rocker and fixed his eyes on mine. "Since father not able to talk, I may speak for him. Perhaps best if you stop being deputy."

Not again.

"Do not roll eyes. You not lose face if quit. Maybe save life."

"Uncle, please—"

Yong Liao raised a hand. "Allow me finish. You quit, may also save Wu Chao life."

I had ignored the dangers to myself. I hadn't, until that moment, considered the danger to Rags. That's why Yong Liao mentioned saving face. I would not lose face if I quit, but Rags would. Men are supposed to be the ones who face danger. Rags would feel obligated to pursue the gunmen as long as I did. He would let me decide. I couldn't back down though. Not yet.

"I understand, Uncle, all of what you're saying. But I can't quit now."

Yong Liao frowned. "As expected. You much like father." He reached into an outside jacket pocket and removed a short-barreled revolver. He handed me the pistol.

"You really think I need this?"

"You refuse advice. This second choice. Gun easy to use, only need pull trigger. Keep with you all times. And, very please, be careful."

Chapter Twenty-Eight

Rags and I passed brightly lit bordellos and saloons as we made our way up Virgin Alley toward the jail. A man wearing a derby looked over his shoulder before entering one of the cribs. In several of the larger establishments, bands played lively tunes, and male and female voices sang along.

I paused, swinging my crutches, and asked Rags, "Would you like to quit? You can if you want."

"If you don't mind, I'm liking the name Deputy Wu. I am."

"Thank you, Deputy Wu. Do you think we'll find Erastus Kohl waiting for us at the jail?"

"If'n he knows what's good for him."

We found someone waiting for us at the jail, but it wasn't Kohl.

Mrs. Lockhart stood inside the marshal's office, next to the potbellied stove. "Did I hear it right? Is Vern Jorgensen truly dead?"

"Yes," I said. I let myself sink into Papa's chair and set my crutches against the wall.

Mrs. Lockhart covered her eyes with her hand. She sniffled. "That's horrible." She wiped tears from her eyes and faced me.

"The reason I came to see you was I wanted to tell you that Jack Murphy saw Bill Hoffman at the Gold Brick Saloon just thirty minutes ago. I gave Jack a dollar and asked him to join Bill and keep buying him beer until you got there."

"Thank you."

Mrs. Lockhart left to go back to work.

"C'mon, Rags. Let's go skunk hunting."

Rags picked up his shotgun. "What about Kohl?"

I grabbed my crutches. "Let's hear what Bill Hoffman has to say first. He may provide the evidence we need to convince Judge Snethens to charge Kohl."

Rags and I trudged up Main Street to the Gold Brick. I sent Rags around back. I waited a minute and entered through the front door. The saloon was crowded and smoky. Miners played faro at several tables. Others stood along the bar, vying for the attentions of two women with blue and green feathers in their hair. They wore knee-length silk dresses.

Bill Hoffman sat at a table with Jack Murphy. Despite the fact Bill was facing the front door, he didn't see me until I stood six feet from his table. The saloon went quiet.

The bartender, Tobias Hurlbutt sneered. "Hey, Bill, yer wife's come for ya."

Many of the bar patrons chuckled.

Bill lowered his beer mug. "Well, if it ain't ol' Pencil-Leg, baddest-est deputy in Bodie."

"You need to accompany me back to the jail so we can finish talking about what you saw when my Papa was shot."

Bill slapped Jack Murphy on the back. "Thank'e Jack. It's been a pleasure drinking with you. But I has to run."

"Don't do it, Bill," I said, while hoping he would run.

"You knows you cain't catch me, Pencil-Leg."

I hobbled toward him on the single crutch I'd brought into the saloon. He bolted for the back door. Exactly what I'd expected. I followed him toward the rear of the saloon, but slowly this time so I wouldn't fall.

Two miners, arms as thick as hams, blocked my path. "Whatcha bothering Bill fer?" one of them said. His eyes were bloodshot, and he tilted from side to side like a very slow metronome.

I would not fail again. "Get out of my way."

"Or whut?"

I raised my single crutch and rammed it into the right side of the fellow's chest, timing my jab to accelerate his tilt to the left. He hit the sawdust-covered floor, shaking the timbers beneath us. This job was getting easier.

His partner took a step toward me. "You done it now, missy." He raised his fists like the famous boxer, John L. Sullivan. He did not wobble. Probably less drunk than his friend. A greater threat.

Stories of this incident would no doubt be whispered to my mother afterward. I didn't care. I was red hot and impatient to catch up with Bill Hoffman.

I drew back my crutch, aimed, and jammed its narrow point as hard as I could where his legs met. His eyes bulged and he collapsed to the floor holding his crotch.

Swinging my crutch left and right, I stared down the remaining bar patrons standing between me and the back door. "Anyone else want to keep me from doing my duty?"

Anger flared in the eyes of some, but most of the men were laughing at the drunks on the floor. No one challenged me.

I exited through the saloon's back door and found Bill Hoffman lying in a heap on the frozen ground. Rags handed me my other crutch, the one I had given him to trip Bill with.

"Good job, Deputy," I said.

"'Twas a pleasure."

"Get up, Bill."

"Dag blame it, Pencil-Leg. Leave me be."

Several miners and Tobias Hurlbutt came outside. The

bartender elbowed one of the miners in the ribs. "What I tell you? It's jess another lover's quarrel a tween them two."

He and the miners laughed raucously.

I jabbed one of my crutches into Bill's stomach to get his attention.

Bill whined. "That hurts."

I poked him lower, level with his belt.

"Dang it, Pencil-Leg, cut that out."

I drew my crutch back preparing to strike him lower still.

One of the miners yelled. "Better do what she says, Bill, if'n ya want to spare yer manhood."

Bill's eyes went wide. "Okay, okay. Help me up."

I lowered my crutch to the ground.

Rags lifted Bill to his feet and the three of us headed back to the jail, followed by hoots and jeers from the crowd.

Chapter Twenty-Nine

Back at the marshal's office, I dropped into Papa's chair, exhausted and beaten down by the chase after Bill Hoffman, and by the town's hostility. My shoulders ached—my stump, too.

Bill slouched in the chair on the other side of the desk. His stale beer breath failed to mask the stench of his unclean clothes and body. His steamy breath hung in the air for a few seconds. "Kinder cold in here."

I stared into Bill's shifty eyes.

He squirmed. "Well, it's cold."

Rags stirred the ashes in the stove and added two logs. "There you go." He stood between Bill and the door with his arms crossed.

"Bill Hoffman, I want you to tell us what you saw when my father was shot. Don't leave anything out."

"Well, I come outta the saloon to take a piss, see, and I heard Micah arguin' with the marshal. Afore I could button up my pants, bang bang goes a gun and the marshal falls. Micah's just standing there holding the gun."

I shook my head. "Don't tell me Micah Pettibone did it. He's got a goose egg on his skull where someone knocked him out. How'd he get the goose egg?"

"Well, ah, it was the marshal. Yup, the marshal. He slugged ol' Micah with his gun. That's why Micah shot him."

"He shot the marshal after he'd been knocked unconscious?"

"He managed to get a shot off afore he fell."

I looked over Hoffman's shoulder at Rags. He rolled his eyes.

"You're more likely to have shot Papa than Mr. Pettibone. You admit to being there and no one had knocked you unconscious. I should arrest you for attempted murder. Ten years in prison would do you good. What do you say to that?"

"I didn't shoot nobody." He turned to look at Rags, who scowled. "Honest, I didn't."

I leaned over the desk, closer to Bill. "Everybody knows you're a liar, Bill Hoffman. Just now, you lied about Micah Pettibone being the shooter. Why would you say Pettibone did it, except to put the blame for your crime on someone else?"

Bill's eyes stared off into the corner a moment. He slapped his palms on the desktop. "Well, tellin' the truth, I jes been pullin yer leg." Bill snickered. "Get it? Pullin yer leg?"

I wasn't in the mood for stupid jokes about my leg. My right hand formed a fist. I wanted to hear the sound of it breaking Bill Hoffman's nose. "I don't want any more of your lies. Tell me everything you saw the other night, right now."

Bill leaned forward. His beer breath nearly choked me. "What would ya say if I told you a Chinaman done it? It was dark, sure, but there was a little light comin' outta the back door of the New Bonanza. I seen the fellow runnin' and he had a Chink's pigtail."

Bill stared at Rags. "Well, what does ya say about that, huh?"

"I'd say, 'tis well known, it is, that Yong Liao and Marshal Doherty were good friends, and any Chinaman in Bodie would know his life was forfeit if he should harm the marshal."

"Well—" Bill paused to lick his lips. "It seems one of yorn

didn't get the Tong boss's message." Bill pointed a finger at Rags. "It were somebody looked a lot like you, cuz it was you."

Rags took a step toward Bill. "You filthy, lying cowpie. I wasn't in Virgin Alley when the marshal was shot and you know it."

"I seen what I seen." Bill tilted his chair back as if he hadn't a care in the world. "Could I get something to drink?"

Rags took another step toward Bill, one fist raised to strike.

Bill leaned back so far his chair tipped over. He fell to the floor. "Don't hit me." The coward waved his hands in front of his face.

"Deputy," I said, "didn't Confucius say something about not acting rashly?"

Rags fist hung over Bill. "The Master said, 'He who seldom does things he regrets will get his reward.'"

"Bill has to be able to talk."

"I suppose." Rags unclenched and lowered his fist. He righted Bill's chair. "Get up, you sorry excuse for a man. Stop your lying, or I may do something I'll regret later." Rags backed up.

Keeping a wary eye on Rags, Bill got off the floor and sat. He pulled a bandana from his coat pocket and wiped sweat from his brow. "Did you say there's a reward, Pencil-Leg?"

"Ha. Not for you."

"I's been telling the truth."

"Only partly. I believe that you saw the person who shot my Papa. But it wasn't Deputy Wu. He doesn't wear a queue."

Bill scratched his cheek. "Well, maybe I got that wrong, but he still done it."

I pounded my fist on the desk. "Don't lie."

Could I trick him into revealing the truth a little at a time? "The man who shot my Papa, where exactly did he run to?"

"Hightailed it for Main Street 'tween the New Bonanza and the old bootmaker's place. Kinder wild like, zigging and zagging."

I sagged a little in my chair. One set of boot prints in the snow had followed a zigzag pattern the night Papa was shot, just like Bill said. But that couldn't have been Kohl. The marks made by his cane had not followed that wiggly path. Kohl could still have been the shooter with the rifle who fired on Papa from next to Huang Min's crib. Bill's given me a small part of the truth. Something told me he'd seen everything.

"Strange thing for a man to zigzag. Why'd he do that?"

Bill got an ugly gleam in his eye, as if he'd found a prize he didn't want to share.

"What's it to ya, Pencil-Leg?"

Rags lunged toward Bill.

Bill jumped up and cowered against the wall. "What's ya doin'?"

"Picking this up," Rags said. He bent over and picked up a red bandana like the one Bill used to sop up his sweat. It was tied into a knot. "Fell out of your pocket, it did."

"Gimme that," Bill yelled. He stuck out his hand. "It's mine. I want it back." He took a tentative step away from the wall.

Rags squeezed the bandana. "Suspicious, this is."

Bill took a second step away from the wall. Rags glanced at him, and Bill retreated. Rags set the bandana on the desk and untied it. He peeled back the four corners of cloth.

I stared in amazement. In the middle of the bandana, a small pile of gold leaf flakes sparkled. It looked just like the gold Yong Liao found in the pocket of the Chinaman who had died. "Bill," I said, "where'd you get this?"

"I, uh, I found it."

"Where?"

"Don't rightly remember."

"You stole it," I said. "Didn't you?"

"Didn't neither. I earned it." Bill clamped his hands over his mouth. He mumbled, "Give it back."

I shook my head. "Rags, how much do you think it's worth?"

Rags wrapped the handkerchief into a ball and hefted it again. "If'n it's pure gold, it'd be worth fifty dollars."

"Fifty dollars?" I said. "That's two-weeks' wages for an honest man, Bill. You're not an honest man."

"I told ya. I found it."

"Bill, before you leave this jail, you're going to have to tell me how you got this gold."

The office door flew open and Jimmy Sullivan rushed inside. The red-faced stable boy took several rapid breaths. "Miss Doherty." He spoke in a church whisper. He took his cap off and wrung it like a wet dish towel. "Mrs. Boyle sent me to fetch you. Said you should git over to Doc's surgery pronto."

"Papa? Is Papa all right?"

Jimmy wouldn't meet my eyes.

"Nooo!" I grabbed my crutches. "Rags, I mean Deputy Wu, lock Bill in a cell. Search his pockets before you lock him up."

"Sure. And I'll say a prayer for your pa."

I hightailed it across Virgin Alley to Main Street, pumping my arms and legs as fast as a locomotive. "God, no. God, no. God, no," I whispered in rhythm with my crutches. "Don't take him yet."

Pedestrians on the dimly lit boardwalk scattered as I approached, yelling for them to get out of my way. My armpits screamed with each step, but I ignored the pain. I hopped up the stairs to Doc's surgery and threw open the door.

Papa lay on the table, a blanket pulled to his chin. Mama bent over him, sobbing. Mrs. Boyle stood behind Mama, her hand on Mama's shoulder. I froze just inside the door. My eyes filled with tears.

"I'm so sorry," Mrs. Boyle said.

I bawled. "No. It can't be."

Mama turned and stretched out her arms. I rushed into her embrace.

Chapter Thirty

After Mama took the sedative Doc Boyle gave her, my brother Patrick and I put her to bed. Patrick trudged off to a saloon to drown his sorrows. I paced back and forth between the dining table and the cook stove in our big room.

Life wasn't fair. Papa was dead, but his killers were still breathing. Tears poured down my cheeks. "Oh, Papa."

I rested on my crutches next to the table, empty save for the blood-stained pile of Papa's clothes I'd brought back from the surgery. I fingered the collar of Papa's shirt and traced the pocket that had covered his heart.

As if I were about my usual washing, I sat in one of the dining chairs and, by rote, went through the pockets of Papa's coat and trousers. From an outside coat pocket, I pulled a box of matches, his tobacco pouch, and his pipe. The pouch smelled of Papa's sweet cherry tobacco. A new fit of sobbing swept over me. Just the other day, Papa had loaned me this pipe to play Sherlock Holmes. I'd never get to play with Papa again. Never get to do anything with him. Never get another hug. I brought the tobacco pouch to my nose and inhaled deeply.

Oh, Papa, did you know who shot you?

I wiped tears from my cheeks and opened Papa's coat. From the inside pocket, I pulled a piece of paper with Chinese and English writing. Papa had written all of the English words. Twenty rows of Chinese script were followed by the phrase "I agree to the transfer of my property in lieu of cash payment." Papa had signed his name below that. Several Chinese characters had been printed above Papa's signature, and another set of Chinese characters had been printed below.

At the bottom of the page, Papa had written, "The terms of the contract have been fulfilled." He had signed the paper again beneath this phrase. I'd have to ask Rags to translate it.

Someone pounded on our front door. "Hush," I said, as I opened it.

Erastus Kohl stood in the dark. "Here," he said. He threw something small at me. It bounced off my chest and clattered on the floor.

Kohl marched into the night, stabbing the ground with his cane every other step. Holding onto our sofa, I bent down and picked up Kohl's Knights of Pythias pin from the floor. He must have talked to Cecilia, the soiled dove whose company he liked to keep. He wasn't pretending to be nice anymore, or to have found religion.

Giving me the pin didn't fool me a bit though. I took a step outside and closed the door. I shouted at Kohl's back, "I know you shot Papa and I'm going to prove it."

Kohl waved his cane in the air for a second and hastened away.

FOR THE NEXT THREE DAYS, MAMA AND I TOOK TURNS wailing on each other's shoulders. *God, why did you take Papa? Why?* Sorrow haunted the house. Every little thing I saw was attached to a memory of Papa. My stomach curled in on itself, and I shook my fists and bawled when I opened a cupboard and saw Papa's tin cup.

At night, there were times I wanted to scream, but feared I'd wake Mama. Patrick killed his pain with alcohol, but I couldn't do that. While my brother snored, I tossed and turned in my bed, trying to figure out who besides Erastus Kohl had shot Papa. I vowed to get them both.

The only times Mama and I could set our agony aside were the times our neighbors stopped by to offer their condolences. They brought fried chicken, beef stew, and a ham. Three days after Papa died, we put on black dresses that Mrs. Taylor gave us and walked to the funeral service.

Papa's open casket lay on a table in the middle of the Miners Union Hall, underneath one of the crystal chandeliers. Mama, Patrick, and I stood just inside the door, greeting black-clad mourners. Mama's face was gaunt and pale. She hadn't cried that day, though she'd keened for hours on each of the last three days. Patrick swayed when anyone shook his hand. A pint bottle, the second one that day, jutted from his hip pocket.

I stood, without crutches, in my new black dress with its itchy collar, crying anew as each mourner paid his or her condolences. My tears stopped only when my anger with God surged in my breast.

Chairs sat around the periphery of the hall. Streamers of black crepe hung near the ceiling and draped across all four walls. Beyond the casket, toward the stage, other tables contained food and drink. The ladies gravitated to the coffee, chicken, pies, and cake. The men formed a line leading to the barrels of beer and casks of whiskey.

Judge Snethens doffed his Stetson to Mama. "I'm so sorry, Molly." Tears filled his red eyes. "Reminds me of when I lost Sarah. It's true, the good die too young." The judge patted Mama's hand and shook Patrick's. He bent down and whispered in my ear. "Come talk to me when you get a chance."

"What is it?"

"Later." The judge joined the line to the liquor.

He knows something, something about who killed Papa. I craved to know what it was, but I had to stay with Mama.

Mrs. Jorgensen entered the hall. When she and Mama saw each other, they both began to cry. Mrs. Jorgensen enveloped Mama in her arms. "Molly," Mrs. Jorgensen said, "I can't believe we've both lost our men."

A few minutes and several mourners later, I watched Judge Snethens mount the stage at the back of the room. A hand gripped my shoulder from behind. It reminded me of Papa's strong grasp. I whirled around.

Baron Catlow stood before me, his face blurred by my fresh tears. On my right, Mama shook another mourner's hand while she glowered at Catlow. Was she upset because he touched my shoulder?

"I'm sorry, Miss Doherty," Catlow said. "I wish there was something I could do to take away your pain. I would do anything."

I wiped my tears with my handkerchief. "Find Papa's killers."

"We'll do that together, shall we?"

With our combined energy, we would surely succeed. "Thank you, Marshal."

He bowed his head and stepped deeper into the hall. Men in line to get drinks shook Catlow's hand. Some patted him on the back.

On the stage, Judge Snethens began the first of many tributes praising Papa. He handed his wide-brimmed hat to a man at the edge of the stage. "Friends, I'm passing my hat for the grieving family. Bodieites, remember all that the marshal did for us. Be princely in your generosity."

Mrs. Lockhart appeared in the reception line. Her golden hair shone against her close-fitting black silk dress. How could she be so bold to show up here? I stiffened as she introduced herself to

Mama and paid her respects. I waited for Mama to explode, but she didn't react at all.

How could Mama remain calm in the face of this woman over whom she and Papa had argued just days before? Was I wrong? Papa had said his dancing with Mrs. Lockhart wasn't what it looked like, but Mama had chased him out of the house that night.

"My condolences," Mrs. Lockhart said. "I am truly sorry your father died."

"I, uh, thank you."

She patted my hand, then moved toward the tables of food.

Another woman took my hand. Her dress reeked of mothballs. "I'm so sorry about yer father," she said. "It was him found my Joey when the lad got lost in the tunnels of an abandoned mine. I'll always remember him for that." We shared a tear, and she stepped aside to be followed by more than a hundred others.

By noon, mourners had packed the hall. I had trouble hearing Mama over the din. "Let's sit down." She and I retreated to a table in the corner set aside for the family. Patrick went off to get himself a beer.

Mama scanned the room. "It's turned out to be a splendid send-off for your father." Her lips puckered as if she was about to sob.

I squeezed Mama's hand. "Can I get you something to eat or drink?"

"Coffee would be nice, dear."

I stood and turned toward the food tables. Across the room, Baron Catlow stood talking to Mrs. Lockhart. They stood very close together. Half under my breath, I said, "Why is he talking to her?" I hadn't spoken quietly enough.

Mama followed my gaze to Catlow and Mrs. Lockhart. "Why would you care?"

Why did I care? "Just, well, just curiosity, I guess." I blushed.

Mama had the decency not to say, "I don't believe you," though her stern look expressed that very thought.

"I'll be right back with your coffee." I wove my way through the crowd and approached Papa's open coffin. Drunken huzzahs rang out from a group of men who encircled it. The men held playing cards. Patrick stuck his hand out and several men put money into it. He caught my eye and pointed at the coffin. He shouted, "He won." There, atop Papa's cold, crossed hands, lay four Jacks. Despite having seen such frivolity at other wakes, it disgusted me at that moment.

I pushed on through the crowd, receiving hugs from several of Mama's friends. Accompanied by the band, a tenor began singing, "The Vacant Chair." The crowd quieted.

"We shall meet but we shall miss him.
There will be one vacant chair...."

Dozens of handkerchiefs appeared, and both men and women paused to shed a tear for Papa. I cried, too.

Judge Snethens offered me his handkerchief. "I have seen too much death." He had been a major in the Union Army during the war. "Each new death rips the scab off the scar of my grief. I ... forgive me, Nell, I've become maudlin."

"That's all right, Judge. What did you want to tell me earlier? Is it about who killed Papa?"

"Possibly. I believe I know who lost the Knights of Pythias pin you found in the snow near where your father was shot. At last night's meeting, Fergus Poague bought a new pin. He said he'd lost his recently."

"Of course. Poague could be the second gunman. He and Kohl knew each other. I saw the two of them together at Kohl's butcher shop. They did it together. We should arrest them immediately. Where's Mr. Catlow?" I stretched to make myself as tall as I could. "Judge, can you see him?"

"I believe our temporary marshal left the wake some time ago. At any rate, Nell, we mustn't prejudge Mr. Poague any more than we should prejudge Erastus Kohl. It's possible Poague lost his K-o-P pin while passing through the alley hours, or even days, before your father was shot."

"Judge, Poague drove both stagecoaches that got robbed."

"That's not proof. According to Doc Boyle, Poague nearly died the second time when knocked unconscious by the thieves."

I shook my head. "Judge, Poague's as guilty as Kohl. They just had different reasons for shooting Papa. Kohl hated Papa. I'll bet Papa suspected Poague of stealing the gold, and Poague was scared he'd be found out. We should arrest them both."

"Young lady, the law requires more than mere hypothecation. The law requires corroborating evidence to establish a man's guilt."

"I know where I can find some."

Chapter Thirty-One

"What evidence?" Judge Snethens asked me.

I looked around the crowded Miners Union Hall to make sure my whispered conversation with Judge Snethens remained private. Gideon Weed stood directly behind the judge. He leaned toward us. I pointed over the judge's shoulder. "Behind you."

He turned around.

Weed straightened up. "Hello, your honor."

"Were you eavesdropping, Mr. Weed?"

"Oh, no, sir. I was only waiting for you to finish your conversation with Miss Doherty." Weed lifted up the judge's wide-brimmed hat filled with dollar bills. "I have the collection."

"Judge," I said, "why don't we meet at the jail after the wake?"

"Very well."

The judge took the hat from Mr. Weed. He frowned. "Feels light. Pardon me, Nell, I wish to speak to some of the town fathers." The judge waded into the crowd.

Mr. Weed tipped his hat. Biscuit crumbs peppered his Abe Lincoln beard. "Again, my deepest sympathies, Miss Doherty. I didn't know your father very long, but I knew him to be a good man."

"Thank you."

He whispered in my ear. "I hope you are close to catching his killer."

What an odd thing to say. If it was an invitation for me to share information with him, he was out of luck. Papa wouldn't share his suspicions with me. I wasn't going to share mine with a photographer.

"Mr. Weed, I must get back to my mother."

"Of course." He took a step backward and bumped into one of Mama's friends. "So sorry. Clumsy of me."

I picked up a coffee pot from the refreshments table. I poured a cup for Mama and one for myself, and returned to Mama. She stood next to Mrs. Jorgensen.

The deputy's wife daubed tears with a black handkerchief. "Oh, Molly, without our menfolk, what's to become of us?"

"We can only hope that God will provide," Mama said.

"And that God will punish," I added under my breath.

"Will you sit and have coffee with us?" Mama asked Mrs. Jorgensen.

"Thank you, no. I must get back to the little ones." She hugged Mama and left the crowded hall.

Judge Snethens approached, holding a stack of greenbacks. "Molly, the good citizens of Bodie have contributed two hundred twenty-seven dollars and seventy-five cents to help see you and your family through this time of difficulty." The judge placed the stack of bills in front of Mama. From his pants pocket, he added three quarters. "More will donate when they get their paychecks. It's only been a few days since they contributed funds to help the Jorgensen family."

Mama hugged the judge. "Thank you, Odysseus. Please thank everyone for me."

"Certainly. I anticipate that others, not currently in the hall, will increase the size of this donative in the days ahead."

The judge made his way to the stage. The crowd quieted when he raised his hands. "Mrs. Doherty thanks you all for your generosity. Please suggest to your neighbors who aren't here that they also make a contribution."

Mama and I sat down. She laid her head on the table. "What'll we do? Two hundred dollars, that won't last four months. And we have to pay for the wake and the funeral."

I rubbed Mama's back. "Patrick's still working at the mine," I said, though I knew his wages were only about half of what Papa made as marshal.

"Nell, you and I are going to have to find work."

"I have a job."

Mama narrowed her eyes. Slowly, she said, "We will discuss that later."

Then or later, I had no intention of giving up my dream of becoming a detective. And before I did anything else, I had to jail Papa's killers.

Behind us, the band played, the mourners in their dreary suits and dresses ate, drank, and smoked the clay pipes Mama had provided. For the rest of the afternoon and into the evening, men and women stopped at the table and reminded Mama of the time Papa caught a petty thief, or settled an argument with a joke, or what a fine example Papa was to children.

When the dancing started, Mama got up. "I'm ready to go home, after we say goodbye to your Papa."

The crowd around the coffin parted as Mama and I approached. Mama opened her chatelaine purse, pulled out her rosary, and laid it in Papa's hands. "God be with you, Sam."

God, why weren't you with Papa here on Earth?

I looked at Papa's closed eyes and wiped away my tears. "I will track down your killers, Papa, and bring them to justice."

Several men smirked.

"Come, Nell," Mama said, and we left the hall.

Most of the snow had melted. Still, my breath turned to vapor in the cold air. On the way home, Mama didn't walk, she stomped. As soon as she stepped into our big room, she turned on me. "I'm not going to argue with you anymore about being a deputy. It's not safe. As long as you keep that badge, I won't be able to sleep."

"Mama, I thought you understood."

"You must quit." She dropped onto the couch. Her stern look no longer scared me like it used to. "Nell, it's time you gave up childish notions. Women have no business being deputies. It's not natural."

"Women have been detectives. That's practically the same thing."

"Fallen women. Women with two legs."

My hands clenched. "Mama, I can't quit now. I know who shot Papa. I need more time to prove it."

"Mr. Catlow can track them down."

"He asked me to help him find Papa's killers."

"I saw you at the wake, mooning after him. Do you have feelings for him?"

"Maybe."

I did have feelings for him. He cared for me, too. He said I was the prettiest dang deputy he'd ever seen. But I didn't want to tell Mama.

Mama shook her head. "Forget all this investigation nonsense. And forget this Mr. Catlow. He looks like trouble." She stood. "Hand me the badge. I'll return it to Judge Snethens."

"I'm not a child to be told what to do." I counted to ten, but a touch of fury remained in my voice. "I'm not giving up my badge. I have a job to do."

"Don't talk to me that way, young lady. March yourself into your bedroom this instant."

I'd had it.

"Mama, I refuse to be ordered around." I opened the front door and stepped outside.

"Come back here."

I closed the door.

Pain stabbed me behind the eyes. I missed Papa. He always let me take a chance on what Mama called my crazy, unladylike notions. Without him, I felt penned in, I lacked the air I needed to breathe.

I'm sorry, Mama, but I'm not going to let you prevent me from becoming a Pinkerton. That will be guaranteed as soon as I discover one more bit of evidence against Kohl and Poague. I smiled. All I had to do was trick Bill Hoffman. I could do that in my sleep.

RAGS SAT BEHIND PAPA'S DESK AS I STRAGGLED INTO the office. He peeked around the newspaper in his hands.

Bill Hoffman shouted from his cell. "Hey, out there. I needs more wood for the stove."

Rags got up from his seat. "I'll take care of it." He carried an armful of logs down the hallway, opened Bill's cell, and gave him the wood.

Back in the office, Rags said, "Didn't expect to see you here tonight, I didn't."

"Mama and I had a fight."

"Sorry to hear that."

"I don't care."

Rags looked at me askance. "Of course you care."

I cared, but I didn't want to admit it.

Rags pointed at the newspaper he'd left on the desk. "Have you seen this?"

"I haven't had time. Is it terrible?"

"The story about you could've been worse, it could, but Mr.

Reeves had bigger news."

I sat in Papa's chair and picked up *The Bodie Miner*. The headline read "Bodie's Second Chance!" The article gushed over a gold shipment Baron Catlow's mine would be sending to the mint in San Francisco, that there was more gold to come, and Bodie was on the edge of a revival. A side article said the stock of the Second Chance Mine had risen in value from $1.50 to over $7.00 per share. At least something good had happened in Bodie.

The article on Papa's death occupied the middle of the front page. I shook my head to prevent tearing up. That didn't work. Would thoughts of Papa always hurt now? I took a deep breath.

Mr. Reeves's article on my outrageous behavior was squeezed between a report on Vern Jorgensen's death and a summary of the Chinese New Year parade. "It's hard to be thankful for this small mercy, seeing as how such tragedies were needed to nearly push me off the front page."

I beckoned to Rags to come closer. So that Bill Hoffman wouldn't hear, I whispered what Judge Snethens said about Fergus Poague losing his Knights of Pythias pin. "I have a scheme in mind. Please fetch the judge and Mr. Catlow."

"Quick as I can."

———

BARON CATLOW ARRIVED BEFORE RAGS AND THE JUDGE. "Have you heard? We've hit a vein. The Second Chance Mine's first big shipment is goin' out. I'm gonna be rich. I'm so excited, I can't sit still. Can you dance?"

"What?"

He grabbed my hands and pulled me from the chair. "Can you dance a bit?"

"Maybe."

He twirled me around in circles between the desk and the

171

potbellied stove. His eyes sparkled. He sang, "Ta dum, ta dum, ta dum, dump dum ..."

I spun on my good leg, faster and faster. My head grew dizzy. I didn't know how long my wooden leg would stay fastened to my stump. "Stop, stop."

"Oh, I got carried away. I forgot about your wooden leg. I hope that wasn't too much for it."

It warmed my heart that he had forgotten my wooden leg. "It's okay."

I was flushed and winded, breathing deeply. Our faces were inches apart. I pulled him closer and closed my eyes. Catlow's lips melded into mine. Frantic warmth rushed through me, a wild bliss.

Should I be kissing a man ten years older than I? Should I be kissing him now, when I should be thinking only of Papa and catching his murderers? What would Mama say? I didn't care. A man was kissing me because he wanted to. Me, a girl with one leg. He must have feelings for me. Was this bliss? It must be, because I wanted to go on pressing my lips against Catlow's forever.

"Hey, out there," Bill Hoffman yelled from his cell. "I needs me somethin' ta drink."

I jerked my head back and opened my eyes. Catlow gently kissed each of my palms. I held his glance, not wanting to break the spell.

Bill pounded on the wooden door of his cell. "Are you asleep out there? I'm parched, I tell ya."

"Just a minute," Catlow said. He helped me hop back to Papa's chair. He kissed my cheek.

"I'm coming," Catlow said.

"That's more like it."

I held my hand to my cheek, against the spot where the warmth of Catlow's lips still lingered.

Chapter Thirty-Two

Rags and Judge Snethens entered the marshal's office. That was close. What would Rags have thought if he'd seen me kissing Catlow? Would he have been hurt?

I put my finger to my lips to keep him and the judge quiet. I didn't want Bill Hoffman to know who all was there.

Catlow filled a tin cup with water and strolled down the narrow hall to Bill's cell. He unlocked the door and handed Bill the cup.

"Water? I don't want no water. I wants a drink."

"This is a jail, you varmint, not a saloon."

Rags pulled a pint of whiskey from his coat pocket. He whispered, "I was thinkin' we might trade Bill this for the truth."

"I don't think we'll need it," I said. I moved toward the cells.

Catlow backed up against the wall, and I squeezed past him sideways. We were face-to-face in the narrow hallway, our clothes brushing. I nearly stopped to stare at his soft lips. Instead, I again put my finger to my lips. Then I waved at Rags and the judge to join Catlow in the hall. I stood in the doorway to the cell.

Bill sat on his narrow bunk. "What do you want, Pencil-Leg?"

"I have some bad news for you, Bill. You're going to hang."

"You're drunker'n I ever was."

I shook my head. "We tried to arrest Fergus Poague for the murder of my Papa, but he decided to shoot it out. He was mortally wounded in the conflict, but before he died, he said that you were the second gunman who shot Papa."

"Second gunman? What're you talkin' about? I didn't shoot nobody. Fergus's the only one shot yer pa."

Fergus Poague, you murdering scum, wait till I get my hands on you.

I counted to ten, like Papa taught me. I rested my chin in my hand, imitating a pose I'd seen illustrated in a Sherlock Holmes story. I pretended to consider what Bill had said. Judge Snethens nodded and Rags winked. Catlow looked shocked. I'd won the first round with Bill, but there was one more I wanted.

"The only thing that might save you from the noose, Bill, is if you make a clean breast of it. You'd have to tell the jury everything you saw, the *whole* truth. You'd have to explain that Poague gave you the gold to insure your silence."

Rags winked at me twice. Both the judge and Catlow stood open-mouthed.

Bill hung his head. "I didn't shoot nobody."

"You only blackmailed Poague."

"Why do ya hav'ta be so harsh all the time? I just asked Fergus for a stake, ya know, somethin' would keep me in drink a while."

"So, he gave you the gold."

"Yeah."

"Bill, you're pathetic." He hadn't shot Papa. No, he'd only used Papa's death to suck blood money out of Poague.

"Now, tell me about the second shooter."

"I didn't see no second shooter."

"You're lying."

"I tell ya, I didn't see no second shooter."

Dang it. Bill hadn't seen Kohl. But maybe Poague would implicate him after he was arrested.

"How about that drink, Pencil-Leg?"

"Rags," I yelled as if he were in the office. "Bring the whiskey."

I had Poague dead to rights. He would give up his partner, Kohl. Then Papa would be avenged. And I would be good as hired by the Pinkertons.

As Rags passed me in the hall, he said, "Well done, that was." He tossed Bill the pint, locked the cell door, and joined the rest of us in the office. I sat in Papa's chair, Judge Snethens sat in the other chair, and Catlow perched on the edge of the desk.

"Well, Baron," the judge said, "what do you make of Hoffman's story?"

"I can't believe it. Poague shooting the marshal?" Catlow shook his head. "He suckered me good with his story about wanting to quit the stagecoach business after being attacked twice. Can't believe I gave the varmint a job. The curious thing is the pouch of gold flakes he gave Hoffman. Where did Poague get it? Miss Doherty, if you knew all this, why didn't you tell me?"

Catlow's last sentence struck me as accusatory and I blushed. "I only figured it out a short time ago, after talking to the judge at the wake. I meant to tell you."

"I'm sorry, I didn't mean to scold. It's my fault. When I got here, I was so excited about the mine, I hardly let you get a word in."

Thinking of our few minutes together, and that first kiss, especially that kiss, I blushed again. Rags raised an eyebrow, but said nothing.

The judge looked at Catlow. "We need to arrest Poague. Do you know where he might be?"

Catlow pulled his watch from the pocket of his purple and gold vest. "It's going on seven, so he won't be at the mine yet. He's either at his house on Wood Street or in a saloon."

Judge Snethens removed a revolver from his coat pocket. He

checked to see if it was fully loaded. "Mr. Wu, do you really know how to use that shotgun?"

"Yes, sir."

"Then, Marshal, I think the three of us can take him. Nell, you stay here and guard Mr. Hoffman."

"I'm a deputy, too. I'm going with you."

"You will not," the judge said.

I stood up. "I will, too."

"*Filius canis!*" Judge Snethens roared. He knew I could, and would, tag along behind them after they left. "You will promise me this instant that you will stand thirty paces behind us and will not approach Poague's house, or by thunder I will lock you up in a jail cell this very minute."

"I promise."

The judge took several deep breaths. He half grunted, half growled, and turned to the door.

We left the jail in pairs. Rags crept ahead with Judge Snethens because the judge wanted the shotgun up front. He told Catlow to protect me first, then worry about catching Poague.

Being assigned a protector upset me, but that was nothing compared to the exhilaration of joining the arrest party, or of walking beside Catlow on this starlit evening.

When the judge and Rags turned the corner onto Main and were momentarily out of sight, Catlow took my hand in his and squeezed. It was all I could do not to throw my arms around his neck and kiss him.

Poague's house sat two blocks east of Main on Wood Street, a small shack whose wood siding had been covered with rusty, flattened tin cans.

The judge and Rags tiptoed up to the house while Catlow and I stood back. My mouth went dry. I leaned forward, trying to catch the slightest noise from inside Poague's house. Catlow and I drew our pistols from our pockets.

The judge drew his revolver, knocked on Poague's door, and

entered. Rags followed right behind him. Seconds later, they emerged from the house and trudged over to where I stood with Catlow.

"He must be in a saloon," the judge said.

I'd been a deputy for only a week, and this would be my third search of Bodie's saloons. How much of his time had Papa spent looking for miscreants in the same places over and over? *Oh, Papa.*

Catlow glanced at me and Rags. "Judge, if all four of us walk into a saloon, it will create quite a stir. Word might get around that somethin's up before we catch up with Fergus. If it's just you and me that enter the saloons, we won't raise any suspicions."

I didn't want the Judge to send us home. "Deputy Wu and I will search Poague's house. We'll look for clues."

"That's not a good idea," Catlow said. "Poague might return any time."

"Well, Mr. Marshal, just what are we allowed to do?" I crossed my arms and scowled.

Catlow lowered his head to his breast for a second. He looked at me with a pained expression. "Miss Doherty, it's my job to protect all of Bodie's residents, and that includes you."

My anger overtook my warm feelings of a few minutes ago. "I thought you were different."

"I've a thought," Rags said. "Marshal, you and the judge visit the saloons starting on the south end of Main Street, and Nell and me will look for Mr. Poague starting on the north end. If'n anyone asks, Nell and me will say we're doing our rounds. It will save us all time, it will. And if'n we find Mr. Poague, we'll look for you. We won't try and arrest him ourselves."

My hackles up, I waited for Catlow to dismiss Rag's suggestion.

"That sounds okay to me," he said. "Judge?"

"That's reasonable, provided neither of you specifically asks about Poague."

"Won't say a word, Judge, not a word."

"All right then," Catlow said. "We have a plan."

Catlow flashed a broad smile my way, as if to say, "See? I'm different. I believe a young woman can be a deputy."

Of course, without his insistence, I would not be a deputy, although a second-class deputy. In fairness, I *was* still included. My attitude softened. *I will accept second-class status. For now.*

"Thank you, Marshal." I put my pistol back in my pocket. I did not return his smile.

Chapter Thirty-Three

Rags and I strode downhill past the Standard Mill on our way to the north end of town. The stamp mill hammered away as it crushed ore, its thunderous sound like a thousand blacksmiths striking their anvils. Below the mill, waste rock in the tailings pond glinted in the moonlight.

Rags pulled ahead of me a couple of paces. I had slowed. Hitching downhill put more pressure on my stump since I no longer used my crutches. "Can we go a bit slower?"

He stopped to let me catch up. "Sorry."

"Rags, do you think Marshal Catlow and the judge will tell us if they come across Poague before we do?"

"No. Neither of 'em could stand to see you hurt."

We plodded along side by side a few steps. Rags said, "Can I ask you something?"

"Sure."

"Why were you blushing when me and the judge walked into the jail?"

A cold breeze lifted the bangs from my forehead. I shivered. I didn't know what to say.

"Did that 'something' happen between you and Marshal Catlow?"

"I guess. At least, I think so."

We circled a fresh pile of horse droppings as we crossed Main Street.

I recalled the kiss I had shared with Baron Catlow. A quiver ran through me. I'd had no such thrill the one time Rags and I kissed, but he was my best friend. I liked Rags and I liked Catlow. How could I make sense of my feelings?

"I'm glad for you, Nell, most glad."

"You're not upset?"

"No."

I touched his shoulder. "Do you have a sweetheart?"

"Maybe."

We reached Smith's Dance Hall. Chandeliers inside threw trapezoids of yellow light onto the boardwalk. The piano player ended "Oh, Susanna" as we stepped through the double doors. Male customers and their dancing-girl partners, in satin dresses of green, gold and red, paused on their way from the dance floor to the bar. They stared at us. One of the dancing girls removed her customer's hand from her bottom. Mrs. Lockhart, the youngest and prettiest of the girls, stood at the bar talking to the photographer, Gideon Weed. She waved. "Hi, Miss Doherty. Hi, Mr. Wu."

The bartender, Harold Gant, gave us hard looks. "Get outta my place."

I scanned the faces in the room. No Fergus Poague on the dance floor or standing at the bar.

Three miners on our right tossed their playing cards on the table. They rose as one. The man in the middle said, "You heard Mr. Gant. You two git. We don't wants no crazy girls or any yellow bastards here."

Dust filled the creases in the miner's face, as well as his mustache. He wore his mining helmet with its metal lamp. His chest was as big around as the water barrel out front, and he was the smallest of the three men in black coats who approached us.

Maybe searching for Poague on our own wasn't such a good idea.

The three miners stood face to face with Rags and me.

"Git along now, afore I gits mad," the dusty miner said.

"We're duly appointed deputies doing our evening rounds." I hadn't seen the back room where men played billiards. I stepped to the right to get around the miners. The miner facing me moved to block me.

"Let me by."

Mr. Dusty scowled. "You hard of hearin'? I told you ta git."

Chairs scraped the floor behind us. Rags looked over his shoulder. "Our greeting party's increased by four, it has."

The man next to Mr. Dusty said, "Mebbe they don't know how to git."

Mr. Dusty crossed his arms. "Well, Charlie, we'll have'ta show 'em how it's done. Nice and proper. Gentlemen." Two of the miners behind me grabbed my upper arms and lifted me off the ground. Two others grabbed and lifted Rags.

"Put me down, dag gum it!" I twisted and turned to get free. I used my good leg to kick the man holding my left arm. If only I'd had my crutches.

"Cut that out," the man yelled when my boot connected with his thigh.

A man at the bar yelled, "Kick him good, honey."

Mrs. Lockhart shouted, "Stop it."

"Gentlemen," Rags said. "Kindly put us down. We're sworn deputies of the law, we are."

"As you wish," Mr. Dusty said. "Charlie, git the doors."

The miner next to Mr. Dusty opened the double doors. The men holding me took two steps and tossed me out the door and onto the boardwalk. I came down painfully on my wooden leg, wobbled, and fell forward. I kept myself from falling on my face by wrapping both arms around the hitching post.

Before I could right myself, the two miners holding Rags threw him head first toward the door. His head hit the jamb. His body twisted and he landed face down on the boardwalk. The bar patrons and the bartender guffawed.

"Rags," I shouted. I crawled to him. Blood oozed from under his hat.

"Damn it, boys!" Mrs. Lockhart yelled. "You had no call to be so rough." She came outside and slammed the doors.

I gently shook Rags's shoulder. "Are you okay?"

No response.

"Please, help me turn him."

Mrs. Lockhart and I rolled Rags over, and I rested his head on my lap. He was breathing, but unconscious. "Rags, wake up. Rags?" I took off his hat. His scalp had a gash in it two inches long. It bled a lot. *Could he die?* "Oh, God." My heart pounded in my chest. "Please, get me a towel or something. We need Doc Boyle. Quick."

Mrs. Lockhart went back into the saloon. She returned shortly with a towel and Gideon Weed.

Mrs. Lockhart sat beside me in her short dress. She handed me the towel, and I pressed it against Rags's head.

He groaned. One at a time, Mrs. Lockhart opened Rags's eyelids. "His pupils aren't dilated. He may not be concussed."

Gideon Weed bent over and stared into Rags's face. "He don't look so good."

I waved my hand in front of my face to lessen the smell of whiskey and tobacco on Weed's breath.

"Gideon," Mrs. Lockhart said, "Run and fetch the doctor."

"Okay, sweet Irene."

"Hurry, now."

Weed put one arm across his belly and the other behind his back and bowed low. Then he loped down Main Street.

Inside the dance hall, the piano player pounded out a waltz. The front doors opened and the bartender stuck his head outside. "Blast it, Irene, I need you to tend to customers. Get back to work."

"I'll wait for the doctor, if it's all the same to you, Mr. Gant."

"It's not the same to me."

"Then you should have kept the boys better behaved."

"We'll see about this." Gant turned and went back inside the dance hall.

Rags moaned.

I flinched. This was all my fault. He wouldn't have gotten hurt if I hadn't asked him to be a deputy.

I hoped Doc Boyle got here soon. "Thank you, Mrs. Lockhart. Thank you for coming out here to help. Will you be in trouble with your boss?"

"No. I bring in more customers than the other girls, and Gant knows it."

The towel on Rags's head slowly turned from white to red. "I'm so, so sorry."

He groaned again, but his eyes remained closed. "Wake up, Rags." He stirred. Seconds later, he blinked and tried to sit up, but I held his shoulder.

"Not too fast, deputy."

He rolled his head around and stared into my face. "Me head hurts somethin' awful."

"I'm so happy to hear you talking."

"How'd I get out here?"

"Some of the customers took offence to our presence at the dance hall."

He struggled to rise, but Mrs. Lockhart and I held him down. "Are you okay, Nell?" He looked about him. "Where's me shotgun?"

"Don't worry about that now. We'll deal with those animals later."

Rags touched the towel on his head and grimaced. "So, was Poague inside then?"

"You looking for Fergus Poague?" Mrs. Lockhart said.

I looked at Rags. He'd let the name slip. I looked at Mrs. Lockhart. "Yes."

"A bearded brute of a man that smells of horses, right?" she said. "He thinks he's a swell dancer, but I have bruises to prove otherwise. He hasn't been in this evening."

"Please don't tell anyone that we're looking for him."

Chapter Thirty-Four

After getting Rags to Doc Boyle's, I searched Main Street for Catlow and the judge. I caught up with them outside the Parole Saloon. They hadn't found Poague yet.

"They did what?" the Mashal yelled when I told him what had happened to me and Rags. "Did they hurt you?"

"No."

"Are you sure?"

"I'm fine."

Catlow marched toward Smith's Dance Hall. "Those ruffians should be horsewhipped, and I'm just the man to do it."

"There must first be a trial," the tall jurist said.

"Only if you insist."

"I do."

When we got to the dance hall, Catlow yanked both doors open and let them crash against the outside walls. Music and conversation ceased. The dancing couples froze mid-step. All eyes turned toward Catlow, the judge, and me as we entered.

The bartender, Harold Gant, shouted at the Marshal. "Have a care. You're gonna break my doors."

"Shut up," Catlow roared. He pulled his pistol from his coat pocket. He turned to me. "Which ones did it?"

Using my pistol, I pointed at Mr. Dusty who sat at a table playing faro. "He was the leader. Those four sitting over there are the ones who manhandled me and Rags."

"You vermin are under arrest for assault and battery. I sincerely hope each and every one of you decides to put up a fight." He placed the barrel of his revolver against Mr. Dusty's temple. "Especially you."

Judge Snethens waved his pistol at the other four. "I think they'll all come peaceably."

Mr. Dusty raised his hands. "We was just funnin'. Didn't mean no harm."

Catlow looked from man to man in the dance hall. "I want to make one thing absolutely clear. I will shoot the next person who so much as talks back to one of my deputies." He jerked his pistol toward the open doorway. "Get movin'," he said to Mr. Dusty.

Mr. Dusty stood.

"You, too," I said to the foursome looking down the barrel of Judge Snethens's pistol. They got up from their table and exited the dance hall. The judge and I followed them. Catlow trailed behind us with Mr. Dusty.

Soon after we left the saloon, Mr. Dusty cried out. "Aiii."

When I looked behind me, he had fallen to the ground. Catlow prodded him with his boot. "Get up, vermin."

Inside the jail, we discovered that Mr. Dusty had acquired a black eye.

The judge glared at the Marshal.

Catlow shrugged. "The man fell."

We put Mr. Dusty in the cell with Bill Hoffman. The two that picked me up went into a second cell and the other two in a third.

"Got anything to drink?" Bill asked his cell mate.

"I wish," Mr. Dusty replied.

Judge Snethens, Catlow, and I returned to the office.

"Nature's calling," the judge said. "I'll be right back."

After Judge Snethens left, Catlow took me by the hand and pulled me to him. He kissed me on the cheek and then on the mouth.

A question had been eating at me.

"Mr. Catlow—,"

"Nell, please call me Baron. My mother hoped I'd be royalty one day. I'll never be that, but you can honor her hope by calling me by the name she gave me."

"All right, Baron. I am wondering, surely you can find a woman who has ... who has both her legs."

"Oh, Nell." He sighed. "You mustn't think you're unworthy of affection. God made birds so that even those with a single leg can soar in the heavens. Why would He care less about people who lose a leg? Wouldn't He want them also to be able to soar?"

He couldn't have given a better answer. My heart swelled. I put my hands around Baron's neck and brought his face to mine. I lost myself in his soft, moist lips. Our connection, mouth to mouth, soul to soul, continued for one ecstatic minute, maybe two. Neither of us flinched when one of the prisoners called for another blanket. Our kiss ended only with the sound of the judge's boot heels on the boardwalk outside the door. We each jumped back.

The judge poked his head in the door. "Ready to go, Marshal?"

"I'm ready. Nell, you must be tired. Why don't you stay here and watch the prisoners?"

"I want to go with you."

"Three of us together may cause suspicion. Poague might hear about us visiting all the saloons and vamoose before we find him."

"It's not fair."

Baron just stared at me.

"Oh, very well. I'll be here when you bring Poague in."

"Okay." Baron winked as he went out the door.

I took a blanket off one of the bunks in an empty cell and gave it to the prisoner who'd asked for it.

"Thanks, miss. I wantcha to know, I's sorry for what we done."

"Tell it to the judge."

I sat in Papa's chair.

How long would it take for them to bring in Poague? *The sooner he's captured, the sooner I'll be able to question him about the second shooter.*

I added wood to the potbellied stove and turned down the oil lamp. I leaned back in Papa's swivel chair, rested my boots on one of the desk drawers, and closed my eyes. I fell asleep instantly.

Judge Snethens knocking on the door interrupted my new favorite thing to think about—kissing Baron.

I unbolted the office door and opened it. The judge stood there alone. They must not have found Poague. "No luck?" I asked.

"No," he said as he entered the marshal's office. "Poague seems to have vanished."

"Where's Mr. Catlow?"

"He's gone to bed. You ought to go home, too."

"Mama told me not to come home until I've quit my job as deputy. I'm not quitting, so I'm going to sit in the jail for the rest of the night."

"Nell, go home and talk to your mother."

"Talking with Mama is the last thing I'm going to do."

"Hmm. Your pertinaciousness is unbecoming, young lady."

I stared blankly at the judge. "Pert—?"

"You're stubborn. A trait, I might add, that runs in your family. I had planned to watch over the prisoners, but if you insist on staying, there's no need for me to do so."

"I'll be fine, Judge."

He gave a slight bow and left. I bolted the door behind him.

The judge would harp on my talking to Mama. Mama. She was going to have apoplexy the following day. *The Bodie Miner's* next headline would surely be: "Nell Doherty, Scandal of Bodie, Spends the Night in Jail with Six Men."

I leaned back in Papa's chair again and propped up my legs. I closed my eyes.

BILL HOFFMAN HEARD THE KNOCK ON THE DOOR before I did. "Hey! Wake up out there. Get the darned door and let me sleep!"

"Shut up," Mr. Dusty yelled.

Consciousness came to me gradually, unwillingly, accompanied by aches and pains. Papa's chair was not nearly as comfortable a place to sleep as my feather bed.

Someone knocked on the door.

"Just a minute." I got up, unbolted, and opened the door.

Mrs. Lockhart stood on the boardwalk. "I have news," she whispered.

"Come in." I closed the front door. Then I closed the door that separated the office from the cells.

Mrs. Lockhart looked puzzled. "Is it your job to guard the prisoners?"

"Not exactly. Mama's angry with me for being a deputy. We had an argument."

"She thinks a woman's rightful place is at home?"

"Something like that. Please, sit down." I took Papa's chair and Mrs. Lockhart sat across the desk from me. "What's your news?"

Mrs. Lockhart glanced at the door which led to the cells.

"Fergus Poague left town," she whispered. "He came into Smith's when I was at your Papa's funeral. I only found out a little while ago from Daisy, one of the other girls. Poague had a quick drink at the bar with Erastus Kohl."

Kohl, of course.

"Then Poague vamoosed."

"Did Daisy see which way he went?"

"He was headed north."

North. Poague was headed north. "He's going to Aurora."

Mrs. Lockhart yawned and rubbed her eyes. "Why would you say that?"

"Just a hunch. How long ago did Poague leave?"

"About twelve hours I guess."

"God, we'll never catch him."

I should find Baron and the judge. Form a posse. I should do it right now. Or in a minute, or two. I shook my head and patted my cheek to revive myself. I shouldn't have hesitated, but I was plum tuckered out.

"What time is it?" I asked.

"After two."

"Do you think Poague is sleeping now?"

"I would be."

"I'm ashamed to say it, but I'm so tired that if I chased after him now, I might fall off my horse."

"Couldn't you telegraph the marshal in Aurora first thing tomorrow?"

"Oh, I could do that."

It eased my conscience to hear that I wasn't failing in my duty to Papa if I waited until morning. Papa. Papa and Mrs. Lockhart.

"Why did you dance with my Papa?"

"Dancing with men is my job. Maybe you should be asking why he chose to dance with me."

"Why did he dance with you?"

"Miss Doherty, I've met a lot of men at dance halls between

here and Chicago. Most of my customers only want a little female attention, to spend time with a pretty lady, to be flattered. But some men are driven by lust. Their shifty eyes roam over my body. They press me too tightly against themselves. They grab me where they shouldn't. Make lewd suggestions."

"And Papa, what kind of customer was he?"

Mrs. Lockhart looked down, and then back at me. "I didn't have time, you know, to get to know your Papa, not really." She tugged on her ear. "It's hard to say what his reasons were. Some men talk freely, most men. But your Papa, well, he kept secrets. I can't say why he danced with me."

How many secrets did Papa keep? Didn't Mama make him happy?

Mrs. Lockhart shifted in her chair and changed subjects. "I'm sorry about what happened to Deputy Wu."

"Doc Boyle said he'll be okay. Thank God."

"You have strong feelings for Deputy Wu."

I stared at her. Was she one of those people who thought Chinese were vermin? "Why do you say that?"

"You treated him with great tenderness and concern. And you must be great friends, otherwise you wouldn't have chosen him to be a deputy, and he wouldn't have accepted."

"Rags and I have been best friends since I lost my leg. No one at school wanted a gimp for a friend. After I lost my leg, I was no longer *fascinating* to boys. Rags'd always been an outcast—half Irish and half Chinese. Everybody in Bodie only saw the Chinese in him, as if that was some kind of sin. We called ourselves The Lepers Club."

"So, you two are good friends, nothing more?"

Could she be interested in Rags? No. She's only just met him. "We're just friends. Why are you asking?"

Mrs. Lockhart diverted her eyes again. She took a deep breath. "I hope you won't think me forward, but I'd like to ask you something."

She better not say anything against Rags. I tensed. "Go on."

"Miss Doherty, I watched you at your father's wake. Am I wrong, or were you eying Baron Catlow?"

"I don't know what you mean."

It was my turn to look away. *Mama had caught me staring at Baron, too. Had everyone at the wake seen me watching him? Did Baron know?*

"Baron Catlow's a good-looking man, rugged, handsome." Mrs. Lockhart closed her eyes briefly and hummed a few notes from a tune I'd heard but couldn't name. "Catlow reminds me of a handsome scallywag named Harlan Wolcott of Virginia City. That dreamy gentleman near swept me off my feet."

"You loved a scallywag?"

"Not forevermore. I found out he was a swindler. After that, there could be no true love between us."

She had scruples. Maybe I'd misjudged her. She couldn't be blamed for dancing with Papa. He'd been the one to ask her to dance. And I had to talk to someone.

"How do you know if you've found true love?"

She reached across Papa's desk and took my hand in hers. "So, it's that way, is it, between you and Mr. Catlow?"

"I think so. I've never felt like this before."

"Like you're floating on air?"

"Sometimes."

"How long have you felt this?"

I blushed. "Since earlier this evening, when we kissed."

Mrs. Lockhart patted my hand and sat back in her chair. She pursed her lips. "I'd call such feelings 'attraction.' " When she saw the confusion on my face, she continued. "True love comes later, after you've had time to get to know the best, and the worst, of your beloved. If you still hunger for his touch after that, then you have true love. At least, that's the way it was with me and my husband, George."

She pressed my hand between hers once more. "I want to give

you a hard lesson. You're young and very pretty. You've no need to rush things with a man. Some men, like Harlan Wolcott, that scoundrel I mentioned a minute ago, seem charming at first, but turn out to be devils. So it's important to take your time to get to know a man. Promise me you'll take your time."

"I promise."

Chapter Thirty-Five

The sun had not yet risen the second time I awoke that morning. My aches and pains from sleeping in Papa's chair in the jail had multiplied. If only I'd slept in my own bed at home. I'd have had to listen to Mama tell me what to do though. Maybe if I can arrest Poague, she'll realize that I can do something other than be a teacher.

I added wood to the stove in the office and looked in on the prisoners. All of them save Bill Hoffman were asleep.

"Hey, Pencil-leg, can I get me a drink?"

"Is that all you ever think about?"

"No, but me thirst is topmost in me thoughts this here moment. Whaddya say, sweetheart?"

"I'm not your sweetheart and no, you can't have a drink."

A knock on the front door ended my conversation with Bill. True to his word, Rags had returned before sunup. I was pleased to see him, but Doc had told him to rest.

"Should you be out of bed?"

"I feel much better, I do, than last night. Head hardly bothers me at all. I'm ready for anything, 'cept being tossed into a post again."

"I have something to tell you," I whispered. "Fergus Poague was seen leaving Bodie yesterday on his way to Aurora."

"Blast."

"I'm hoping Aurora's marshal can arrest him. I plan to telegraph him shortly. While I'm doing that, would you fetch Baron Catlow and Judge Snethens?"

"Sure."

———————

THE SKY DIRECTLY ABOVE WAS A CLOUDLESS DARK blue. To the east, the stars faded into a pale blue sky. Like every other man, horse, or mule moving up or down Main Street, my breath created small clouds of vapor as I made my way. The lights were on at the Delmonico Restaurant. I could smell pork chops and bacon. It made me wish I'd had more than a crust of bread for breakfast.

When I got to the telegraph office, I hitched around to the back where Ezekiel Smith and his family lived. Lamplight shone behind the window curtains. I knocked on the door. Zeke's dogs —Amos, Jeremiah, and Daniel—barked and howled. A hand pulled back the window curtain, and I stared into the blackest face of any Bodie resident. Zeke's expression changed from curiosity to concern. He opened the door.

"Hush now, hush," Zeke told his dogs. "Is only Miss Nell."

Each dog had to nose or lick my hand before skittering back from the door to let me in.

"Is ev'rythin' alright, miss?"

"I'm sorry to bother you so early, Zeke. I need to send a telegram to the marshal in Aurora. It's urgent."

"Okay. Be right witcha. Lemme get my coat."

He slipped around a curtain that separated the kitchen from the bedroom of his small house at the back of the telegraph office.

"Good morning, Mary," I said to Zeke's wife. She stood at the stove, stirring porridge.

"Mornin' to you, Nell. Would you like somethin' to eat? I has coffee, too."

"Thank you. The porridge smells wonderful, but I'm in a rush." *Rats.*

Zeke reappeared from around the curtain, and we went to the front of the building and entered the telegraph office. He lit a kerosene lamp suspended from the ceiling. I wrote my message on a form Zeke handed me. I returned the paper.

"Poague, a murderer?"

"I think he shot Papa."

"I was so sorry to hear 'bout his dyin'."

Zeke rubbed his hands together, then bent over his telegraph key and waited for the clatter to stop. At a pause, he tapped out the dots and dashes of my message. "Tha's funny." He checked his batteries. They consisted of a dozen glass jars on a shelf next to his desk. Each jar held clear liquid on top and blue liquid at the bottom. "Batteries is okay, but she's not workin', Miss Nell. Line to Aurora must be down."

My stomach flipped. I had given Poague a sixteen-hour lead. *I should have gotten a hold of Baron and the judge last night and chased Poague right then.*

"I'll send George checkin' the lines, Miss Nell, soon's he can. And I'll keep tryin' to send you's message."

When I arrived back at the jail, Baron sat alone in the office. Seeing him elated me. Seeing him depressed me.

He took my hands in his. "You look sad. What's wrong?"

"I made a giant blunder." I turned away, embarrassed to face him. "I gave Poague a head start last night. He might get clean away."

Baron caressed my cheek for a second. He turned my face to his. "How'd he get away?"

I explained that Poague had been seen leaving town and that I had been too tired to pursue the murderer, figuring he could be captured by telegraphing Aurora's marshal first thing this morning. "But the telegraph between here and Aurora is down. I should have told you and the judge last night. Now it's too late. Poague is going to escape."

A frown came and went on Baron's face. He pulled me into a hug. His warmth partially melted my anger at myself. He lifted my chin and stared fervently into my eyes. I shuddered.

"Don't feel bad, Nell. You did exactly what I would have done in your place. He'll still be caught, I'm sure of it."

The front door creaked open.

Baron released me from his embrace. Rags and Judge Snethens entered the office. The judge stifled a yawn with the back of his hand. "My humble apologies. Both Somnus and Bacchus failed me last night. I barely slept a wink."

"Judge," I said, "the one to be apologizing is me. I've just been telling Mr. Catlow. Poague may escape because of my stupidity." I summarized what I'd learned about Poague and what I did, and didn't do. "The only thing now is for us to gather a posse and go after him."

The judge pushed his hat back on his head. "We have no legal authority in Nevada."

"Judge, I will chase that murderer to hell and back, badge or no."

"And go to jail along with him?"

"We can't just let him get away. We can't. We have to—"

The judge rapped his gloved hand three times on the pipe of the potbellied stove. "Hold on, now. Men—and women—of Bodie could become a legal posse if Aurora's marshal deputized our party under his authority."

The floor beneath us shook for several seconds. Was it an earthquake? I hoped it wasn't a mine. We all held our breath.

The sound of the explosion came from up the hill. Was it at

Baron's Second Chance Mine? One of the other mines? Was my brother okay?

"Oh, God," Baron said. He rushed out the door. Over his shoulder he shouted, "Miss Doherty, please stay put. Don't go chasing Poague on your own."

I held my tongue, but I was not going to wait much longer before going after Poague.

Judge Snethens tapped the stove pipe three more times. "Consider that an order, young lady. Don't budge until we have a chance to settle our plans." He followed Baron out the door.

I crossed myself and asked God to protect the miners. "Rags, please find out what's happened and come back and tell me."

"And then?"

"By then, I'll have made my plans."

Chapter Thirty-Six

I set the pot on the stove to boil water for coffee and locked up the jail. I tiptoed across the crusted ice of Virgin Alley to Main Street. At Delmonico's, I ordered oatmeal for my six prisoners. Then I visited the telegraph office.

Zeke shook his head. "I's sorry, Miss Nell. The line to Aurora's still down."

That left me no choice.

I returned to the marshal's office with a feast of hungers. A hunger to hunt down Fergus Poague, to squeeze the handcuffs around his wrists to the point they dug into his flesh, to hear him confess that he and Kohl shot Papa. I hungered to watch the color leave both their faces as I told them they would soon hang for Papa's murder. And to see their feet flail and eyes bulge as the rope tightened around their necks and they glimpsed their eternal damnation.

I hated them.

Rags stepped into the jail and dispelled my dark thoughts. "'Tis the Second Chance Mine that exploded. Sealed the entrance, it did."

"Was anyone hurt?"

"The foreman, Barnabas Rotke, is missing. It's said that the mine should have been empty. 'Twas thirty minutes before the start of the first shift when the blast went off. Mr. Catlow's organizing a rescue. Lots of questions being asked, first among them: How does an explosion happen if'n no one's supposed to be in the mine?"

"An interesting question, but I have other concerns."

Rags shook his head. "I figure you'll be wantin' to hightail it to Aurora, you will."

"With the telegraph down, I need to get the message to Aurora's marshal some other way."

"I'm thinking that's a mite convenient. What about Catlow and the judge?"

"I'll leave a note."

"Saints preserve us."

I opened the center drawer of Papa's desk and pulled out a pencil and a piece of paper. "Please go to the livery stable. Get my horse and borrow a horse and buggy."

A SHORT TIME LATER, RAGS RETURNED FROM THE stable. He gave me a boost and I mounted my pony.

Rags climbed into the buggy. He shook the buggy's reins. "Giddy up."

The sun peeked over Silver Hill and the town woke up. Smoke wafted out of the U.S. Bakery's chimney. Mr. Johnson unlocked the front door of his grocery. He waved at us. Rags and I waved back.

We continued north on Main until the last of the buildings slipped behind us. We wound through upper Bodie Creek Canyon, surrounded by low hills covered in scrub brush and patches of icy snow in the shadows. Past the toll station, the canyon narrowed and deepened. We rode past the tall rust-red fingers of rock where we found Deputy Jorgensen's body. "You're awfully quiet," I said.

Rags shrugged. "You don't want to hear what I'm thinkin'."

"The telegraph is down. We're just going to let Aurora's marshal know to look out for Poague."

"I know."

"But?"

"Poague is a big fella, like the miners who tossed us outta the dance hall."

"There's two of us."

"Poague might have friends."

For two hours, I watched the telegraph line as it drooped from pole to pole on our left. The break in the line never showed itself.

We turned east and began the climb through Esmeralda Gulch. The much-pitted road was hemmed in by scrub brush on either side.

A mile up the gulch, we reached the top of a rise. Below us lay what was left of Aurora. The town had passed its peak much earlier than Bodie. Many of Aurora's brick buildings had been taken apart and the bricks shipped to Bodie, but a few structures remained.

We passed a dozen isolated buildings on the outskirts of town. Among the broken, crumbling houses, only one showed any signs of life. Smoke rose from the chimney of a small weather-beaten cabin that sat fifty yards from the road. A barn missing part of its roof sat behind the house. A rhythmic hammering—thump, thump, thump ... thump, thump, thump—issued from the barn.

Rags and I rode past the town's graveyard, which was overgrown with scrub brush. Pine Street, Aurora's main thoroughfare, was empty. One brick building across the street from the jail was a mere façade. Only the front wall stood, rent by holes which once were its doors and windows. A sign on the front of the jail read: "City Marshal – Willard Culpepper."

We found Marshal Culpepper sitting at a desk much like Papa's, hunched over a bowl of stew. Culpepper looked me up and down, then studied Rags. "Where'dja get them badges?"

"I'm Nell Doherty, Marshal Sam Doherty's daughter. This is Wu Chao. We're from Bodie. Judge Snethens deputized us after my papa got shot."

"I was sorry to hear about yer pa." Culpepper dipped his spoon into his bowl and shoveled stew into his mouth.

"We came to deliver a message—"

"I heard Snethens was a drunk. Didn't know he'd lost his sense. Girls and yella fellas lawmen? What's the world comin' to?" Culpepper scraped the bottom of the bowl with his spoon. "Them badges is no good in my town."

"Marshal, we're here because the telegraph is down. Fergus Poague is suspected of shooting my father. He was seen riding toward Aurora yesterday. A big man with a cragged face and dark beard. If you run into him, he should be arrested and returned to Bodie."

"You got a warrant?"

"What?"

"Need a warrant." Culpepper licked the last of the stew off his spoon.

I couldn't keep the panic out of my voice. "B-but he's a murderer."

"That's as may be; still need a warrant."

Another obstacle. But Poague was not going to escape. "How do I get a warrant?"

Culpepper pulled the end off a loaf of bread. He waved the bread at me. "Some deputies you got over there in Bodie. Telegraph Snethens. Have him issue a bench warrant."

God, he wasn't listening. I counted to ten. "Marshal, the telegraph line to Bodie is down. I'll do what I can to get a warrant. In the meantime, will you look for Poague, and if you find him, will you at least hold him until we can get the warrant?"

"If I run into 'im, and that's a mighty if, I'll maybe hold him for twenty-four hours. Best have Snethens send me that warrant right away."

"Thank you, Marshal." *Thanks for nothin'.* "You should also know that Bodie's Deputy Vern Jorgensen's body was found near the junction of the Bodie Road and Esmeralda Gulch. He'd been shot in the back."

"In the back, you say? I am sorry to hear that, young lady. Looks like being law in Bodie's gotten dangerous. Makes me wonder why they let you two be deputies."

He sounded like my mother.

"One more thing: A Chinaman was found not too far from where we recovered the deputy's body. The Chinaman died from the cold."

"Marshal Culpepper," Rags said. "The Chinaman who died, he was one of four Chinese who'd disappeared from Virginia City. They all vanished at the same time a few months ago. Have you seen any new Chinese in town?"

Culpepper cocked his head. "Son, I don't have time to keep track of every yella fella comes through."

Culpepper's not going to help us. I can't believe it. We're on our own. "Since we're here, do you mind if we look around for Poague?"

Rags started. "What?"

Culpepper wiped his bowl with the hunk of bread. "I cain't stop you walkin' about, but if'n you do it wearin' them badges, I'll arrest you both."

"Understood."

Outside, Rags and I pocketed our badges. He stared at me. "What happened to 'we're just delivering a message'? I'm thinkin' you've lost your senses."

"I have to keep looking for Poague. I have to. I'll never forgive myself if he gets away."

"Ah, for the love of Mike. It's not you that's lost your senses, 'tis me." Rags rubbed his cold, red nose. "Let's start with the livery stable. If Poague's been here, he'll have left his horse with someone, he will."

I patted his shoulder. "Thank you."

Chapter Thirty Seven

We searched up and down several of Aurora's streets without luck. No one remembered seeing Poague. We had tramped down one side of Silver Street and were on our way up the other side when we stopped at Wong's Wash House. Inside the laundry, the air smelled of soap and starch. Rags and I bowed to Mr. Wong. "Nay hoh."

Mr. Wong bowed in turn and repeated our greeting. He and Rags conversed for a minute in Cantonese.

"He's not seen Poague, but he may know where the Chinese are." Rags said something in Cantonese and Wong responded.

Rags translated. "A month ago, Mr. Wong visited the grave of his brother in Aurora's cemetery, the rocky part reserved for the Chinese. Sure'n after he made an offering to the gods, he smelled fermented tofu near what he thought was an abandoned homestead. He heard faint hammering, he did, coming from the barn. Before he could get close to the barn though, a white woman flew out of the cabin yelling and screaming at Mr. Wong. She shooed him away. The woman acted so crazy, he never went back. Do you remember the barn we passed, the one missing part of its roof?"

"Yes."

"The missing Chinese may be there."

Two pieces of the puzzle fell into place. "Poague will be there, too."

"How does you figure that?"

"The gold flake. Both Poague and the dead Chinaman had gold flake. Come on, let's go arrest a murderer."

"We'll be needing help to take Poague, we will."

"There's two of us."

"The crazy woman may be Poague's friend. He might have others. We should get a posse together."

"A posse? Poague could ride off any minute." I turned to leave the laundry. "We don't have time for that."

Rags grabbed my arm. "We can ask Marshal Culpepper. That won't take but a minute."

"Okay."

Rags thanked Mr. Wong for his information and we returned to Aurora's jail.

Culpepper sat his desk. He had taken his revolver apart and was oiling it.

"Hello, Marshal," I said.

"Got your warrant?"

"No, but we think we may know where Poague is hiding. We'd like you to go with us to arrest him."

"If you don't have a warrant, I'm not interested."

I wanted to scream. "Marshal, we're talking about a murder suspect. We're pretty sure he's at a cabin just outside Aurora."

Culpepper picked up an oily rag and rubbed the revolver's cylinder. "Got proof this fella's stayin' at this cabin?"

"Mr. Wong, the launderer, told us he thinks some Chinese are staying at this place."

"And this Poague fella's fond of Chinks?"

"No. We think the dead Chinaman we told you about is one of four that disappeared from Virginia City. The dead Chinaman and Poague both had small pouches filled with flakes of gold leaf."

Culpepper's head snapped up. "Gold, you say?"

Rags stepped closer to the desk. "Might be it's the Standard Mine's stolen gold. There'd be a reward for returnin' it."

"Where's this cabin?"

MARSHAL CULPEPPER RODE IN THE BUGGY WITH RAGS and I followed on Sunrise. Smoke rose from the chimney of the weathered cabin, which sat to the left and closer to the road than the barn with the hole in its roof. We couldn't see inside the cabin because the windows were covered by dark-gray blankets. We approached the door on foot. Rags and I stood on either side of Marshal Culpepper. He knocked.

A shrill woman's voice answered, "Go away. You're trespassin'."

"Ma'am, this here's Aurora Marshal Willard Culpepper. I'd like to ask you a few questions."

The door opened six inches. Behind it, in shadow, a woman stood. "Who's that with you?"

"Two deputies from Bodie."

The woman cackled. "A Chinese and a woman deputy? How stupid do you take me for?"

"They're a bit irregular over in Bodie, that's a fact." Culpepper said. "I still have a few questions needin' answers."

"Go right ahead."

"Was hopin' I could get off my feet, ma'am. Got a touch of the gout."

The woman opened the cabin door. She stood in shadow, half hidden by the door. "Come on in."

"Thank you, ma'am."

We entered the darkened room lit only by the orange glow from the open grate of the stove. The woman pointed toward a table and chairs, the only furniture in the room. "Sit your nosey

207

selves down and I'll fetch some coffee." We sat at the table while she shut the door.

She bolted the lock and faced us with an Army Colt in her hand. "I'll have your guns. All of them, now, on the floor."

Culpepper pulled his revolver from his holster. The woman shot him before he could aim and he fell to the floor.

"How could you." I dropped to my knees next to the marshal.

Culpepper lay on his side. His mouth moved, but no sound came out. After a few seconds, the light left his eyes and he stopped breathing.

I shouted at the woman. "He didn't do anything to you and you killed him."

"You and your Chinese buddy could be next, if you ain't careful."

What have I gotten us into now?

The woman pointed her pistol at Rags. "Drop your guns, deputies from Bodie." She cackled again. "Deputies."

Rags put his shotgun and pistol on the floor. I took the revolver from my pocket and laid it at my feet.

The woman waved her Army Colt. "Kick 'em over my way."

My eyes adjusted to the faint light from the stove. As the woman bent down to pick up our pistols, I got my first clear view of her. She wore her long red hair in a thick braid that fell to her waist. Her round face was pale, except for the unusually large, permanent dark circles around her eyes. Eyes I had seen before. I had marveled at her face many times, the only woman's face among the wanted posters on the wall of the marshal's office back in Bodie. Susan Cuthbert, known as Black-Eyed Susan, was wanted in Virginia City for the murder of her husband.

"What're you starin' at, you gimpy tart?"

I looked away.

"You, yellow heathen, push the shotgun closer my way. Use your toe."

Black-Eyed Susan set the shotgun in the corner of the room

farthest from us. She undid the bolt and reopened the door. "Fergus," she yelled. "Don't you know to come runnin' when you hear shooting? Get your oafish self in here, now. And bring some rope."

Fergus? I couldn't believe it. I'd found one of Papa's killers, but only after being captured by one of his friends. Surely, if these two killed Papa and Deputy Jorgensen, they wouldn't hesitate to kill me and Rags.

I had failed. Not only wouldn't I arrest Poague, I wouldn't find out for sure who the second shooter was. My rashness was going to kill me. Worse, Rags was going to die, too.

I mouthed "I'm sorry" to him. He winked.

Was he seeing something I didn't? More likely, the hit he took on the head affected his thinking. I mouthed "What?"

Rags didn't have time to answer.

Fergus Poague stomped into the cabin with a coil of rope. "I'm busy, Suzie. Whatcha want now?"

Black-Eyed Susan pointed her pistol toward us. "Look around, you dunderhead. Use your eyes. See them, do ya?"

"Sure, I see 'em, but what're they doin' here?"

I jumped to my feet and screamed. "You murderer, you killed my papa." Hands held high, I lunged toward Poague.

The big brute didn't even flinch under my assault. He gave me a little push and I fell to the floor. I got up on my feet, planning a second attack. Rags grabbed me around the waist and pulled me back into my chair.

I wrestled out of his grasp, furious, though not with him. My anger came from knowing I'd come this close to capturing Papa's killer, but wouldn't succeed in bringing him to justice.

Poague scratched his scalp through his fur hat and squinted at me in the dimly lit cabin. "Who the heck're they?"

Black-Eyed Susan swept a strand of hair behind her ear. "The dead one on the floor's Aurora's marshal. These two say they's deputies from Bodie. I reckon they came here following you.

Now, listen close. Tie 'em up good, and I mean real good. We don't want these two gettin' away like that Chinaman. Tie 'em up and lock 'em in your bedroom."

"Why my bedroom?"

"Cuz you're a gentleman and I'm a lady."

"How long they gonna be here?"

"Not long." Black-Eyed Susan looked at me and cackled.

Poague looked at Marshal Culpepper's body. "What're we gonna tell The Boss? He don't like killin' less it's necessary."

The Boss? Who was he? Could he be the other person who shot Papa? Or was that Black-Eyed Susan?

"Never you mind about talkin' to The Boss. I'll take care of that. He'll understand this killin' was necessary."

With his pocket knife, Poague cut two lengths of rope from the coil. He tied Rag's hands behind his back. I wrinkled my nose as he tied my hands behind me. Mrs. Lockhart was right. Poague smelled like horse sweat.

"This way, you two," he said.

We shuffled ahead of him into the bedroom on the right at the back of the cabin. I held my head low. I wanted to scream, but it wouldn't have helped. Hopefully, Rags's wink meant he had a plan. I didn't have one.

Poague paused at the door. "Sit'n keep still. Suzie don't like no noise." He closed the door.

I crept up and put my ear to it.

Poague whined. "Suzie, why does I gots to cut up the leaves?"

"You'd rather hammer all day, wouldja?"

"I keeps cuttin' my fingers, them knives is so sharp."

"You let the Chinaman get away, so you have'ta take his place."

"I don't wants to be a Chinaman."

"Who would?"

"We gots another Chinaman now. He can cut up the leaves."

"No. That's your punishment for lettin' the other get away."

I looked at Rags. He stood facing me near the room's one window. His hands tied behind his back, he pointed at one of several large nails hammered into the window frame. We wouldn't be slipping out the window. I again set my ear against the door.

Black-Eyed Susan said, "Move the marshal and the deputies' horses and buggy into the barn, and then get back to work."

"Do I gots to? It's cold in the barn. And my fingers."

"After dinner, we'll have us a drink, or maybe three drinks. Maybe I'll teach you how to waltz."

"When's The Boss coming?"

"Don't you ever listen? I told you, he'll be here in three days."

"An' then I'll be rich."

Black-Eyed Susan cackled again. "Then we'll all be rich."

Chapter Thirty-Eight

I sat next to Rags on the bed in Poague's dimly lit room and lowered my chin to my chest. Rags bumped my shoulder with his and whispered, "Still want to be a Pinkerton?"

"I don't think I'm going to get the chance," I whispered back.

"I still have my pocket knife. But we need a plan. They'll have'ta to sleep, they will, probably one at a time. We should cut the ropes later, after one of them's gone to sleep. Before then, they may check on us."

"Are you sure we can't get out the window?"

"Nailed shut. We'll have to jump Poague and Suzie. One at a time."

"Well, they're planning to get drunk after dinner. Maybe that'll make it easier to overcome them. We just have to hope they don't decide to shoot us before we're ready."

"'Tis a gamble." Rags wiggled his nose. "Wouldn't ya know? I got an itch with me hands tied behind me."

TWO HOURS LATER, THE HAMMERING STOPPED IN THE barn. The sky grew dark. Half an hour after that, Black-Eyed Susan called Poague to dinner. Soon after, she said, "Time to break out the whiskey."

I sat on the bed, the room lit only by faint moonlight. Rags left his post at the door where he'd been listening and joined me on the bed. "She's tried to teach Poague to dance, but says he's got two left feet. She's going to bed, she is, despite his desire to keep waltzing."

I went to the door to listen. The other bedroom door clicked shut. Poague's boots marked out an inconsistent one-two-three waltz beat on the wooden floor. The boots stopped and Poague snapped his fingers. "Suzie ain't the only girl in this here cabin."

Uh-oh.

I hopped onto the bed. The door opened and Poague's head appeared against the orange glow of the stove. He stared at me. "We're gonna have us a party, girlie. Yessiree." Poague pulled a revolver from his belt and pointed it at Rags. "Get up now. Gonna lock you up in the barn with the other heathens."

Rags leapt at Poague. "You filth."

The big man brought his pistol down on Rags' head and Rags fell to the floor. I jumped up and raised my hand. "Stop," I yelled. I knelt beside Rags. He grimaced.

"You need to take care of your head." I looked up at Poague. "You just want to dance, isn't that right?"

Poague grinned. "Get up, heathen."

Poague's grin sent a chill up my spine. Did he plan to have his way with me? My friend Lucy said that was worse than death. *Oh, why hadn't I waited until Baron and the judge could have joined us?*

"Get up," Poague said.

Rags stood. "Nell—"

"It's all right. I'll be okay." I had gotten us into this fix. The least I could do was give Rags a chance to escape. He would be in the barn with the other Chinamen. He had his knife. Together, they could get free and then come for me, maybe. "Go on, I'll see you later."

Rags' pained look told me he knew I wasn't being honest, and also that he felt ashamed because he no longer had the strength to fight.

"This way, heathen." He pushed Rags through the door and turned to me. "Don't go no place, girlie, if you want to see your friend tomorrow, alive."

Poague shut the door. This wasn't the way it was supposed to happen. It was supposed to be two against one. Me and Rags against Poague. How could I take on the big man by myself?

Ten minutes later, he was back. "I'm gonna untie you, but if you try anything, your friend will pay fer it. You understand?"

"Yes."

Poague cut the rope binding my hands. He laid his knife along my cheek. I flinched. The flat of the blade pressed hard against my skin.

"Thought I was gonna cut ya, huh?" His fingernails lightly raked my cheek. "Not yet." He folded the knife and slipped it into his boot.

Was he so drunk he forgot I called him a murderer?

His hand slid from my neck down my back. He pinched my bottom. I jerked away from his hand into his belly. He laughed. "We're goin' to get to be real close friends."

I clamped my jaws shut to keep from calling him a pig. If I was going to catch this murderer, I had to use honey, not vinegar.

"Time to dance, girlie." He put an arm around my waist. I stiffened. Poague's odor, part horse sweat, part manure, made me gag. My eyes watered. I needed to stall. I needed time to come up with a plan.

"Mr. Poague, my name's Nell, not girlie."

"Pleasure. Now let's get down to business. You know the waltz?"

"I need to pee first."

"What? Why didn't you do that afore?"

"Did you expect me to pee on the floor? Get me a slop jar and I'll just be a minute."

Poague opened the door to Black-Eyed Susan's room. She was snoring. Poague closed her door and handed me a large porcelain jar with a lid. "Make it quick." He closed the door.

I sat on the bed and prepared myself.

Poague's patience lasted two or three minutes. He knocked. "Ain't you ready yet?"

"I need some help buttoning up my dress."

"More like unbutton." Poague stepped into the nearly pitch-black room.

I stood on the bed, against the wall next to the door. With all the strength I could muster, I swung my wooden leg like an ax onto his head. Dazed, Poague spun toward me. He shook his head. "I'm gonna strangle you." He raised his arms to protect himself. Too slow.

I hit his head again just as hard as before and he fell to the floor. I lost my balance and fell on top of him. Even unconscious, Poague gave me the creeps. I rolled off him and pushed myself against the wall.

I'd done it. I'd knocked out Poague. Was that a rustling noise in Black-Eyed Susan's room? Had she heard the noise?

I held my breath and counted to thirty. No more noises came from her room. I exhaled. When my pulse no longer pounded in my ears, I slid over to Poague and reached into his coat pocket to collect his revolver. *The Lord giveth.* I stayed on the floor and examined my wooden leg. The knee joint was broken. *The Lord taketh away.*

I hopped into the cabin's main room and grabbed the coil of rope Poague had fetched earlier. I set my stump on a chair. *Now I have five legs.* I alternated taking a step with my good leg and sliding the chair forward and shuffled back to the unconscious Poague. I took the knife from his boot and cut two pieces of rope. I tied his hands behind his back, tied his feet together, and took a deep breath.

I could hop to the barn and get Rags and the other Chinamen. But if Black-Eyed Susan woke up, she might revive and untie Poague. Then we'd be facing a gunfight. Anything could happen. Better to wake Black-Eyed Susan and march her to the barn at gunpoint.

I slid and hopped across the main room to her bedroom door. I held Poague's pistol. I listened at the door through a count of sixty Mississippis. Black-Eyed Susan snored, but the timbre had changed. I turned the knob.

In the orange light of the potbellied stove behind me, I could dimly make out Black-Eyed Susan. She lay on her back, her braid undone, her hair partially covering her face. Her mouth hung open. She blew a few strands of hair up and down. It would have been comical if I hadn't been shaking from fear.

I inched forward on my chair-leg, Poague's revolver pointed at Black-Eyed Susan. I took a deep breath and yelled, "Wake up."

Her black eyes popped open. "She-devil," she yelled. She lunged at me and grabbed onto the pistol. I twisted and fell backward onto the bedroom floor, struggling to wrench the gun free of her grasp. Black-Eyed Susan fell on me.

Our arms swung right and left, as each of us fought to gain control of the pistol.

"By God, I'm gonna kill you," Black-Eyed Susan said.

The alcohol on her breath stung my nose. Her weight on me made it difficult to breathe. I weakened.

Black-Eyed Susan cackled. She tilted her head and bit my ear.

"Dag nab it." I made the mistake of yanking my head. My flesh ripped. Rage flooded my muscles. "That's it."

My left heel found the foot of the bed. I pushed and rotated my body. Black-Eyed Susan flipped off me. Her head thumped against the wall. My ear was free.

From the other room, Poague yelled, "Hey, Suzie, I need help."

"You're not the only one needs help. Get in here."

I rolled on top of her. Both of us still held the pistol. I slammed her hands against the wall several times. She held on. I swung my arms away from the wall as if to smash her hands against the wall again, but I changed direction. I clubbed her forehead with the pistol.

She spit out, "She-devil."

Her grasp on the gun loosened, and I wrenched it away from her. I brought the pistol up over her. Before I could hit her again with the pistol, she punched me on the jaw. The gun flew under the bed. Black-Eyed Susan grabbed my throat. She cackled. "You're done for."

I grabbed her head, lifted it up, and slammed it against the floor. Again, I smacked her head against the floor. I couldn't breathe. I got woozy. I raised her head off the floor.

"I'm gonna kill you."

Using the last of my strength, I smashed her head against the floor once more.

Black-Eyed Susan went limp. She released her grip on my neck, and I collapsed on top of her. I gulped air.

My arms ached, as if I'd held a massive weight above my head, like Atlas carrying the Earth. My clothes were soaked in sweat. "Black-Eyed Susan, you're under arrest."

"The hell I am."

I picked up her head again. "You're too stubborn for your own good." I slammed it against the floor.

Her black eyes closed.

After a few seconds, I tapped her cheek. "You give up?"

Her eyes remained closed, but she mumbled, "Ne-never. You'll haveta kill me. She-Devil."

Her body went slack. She didn't respond when I poked her in

the ribs. I rolled off her and reached under the bed for the revolver. I sat against the bed. My hands shook.

The front door creaked open an inch. Light shone from outside. Without taking my eyes off Black-Eyed Susan, I yelled, "Who's there?"

"Saints preserve us. 'Tis me." Rags opened the door all the way. He held a lantern. "I've brought some new friends. I, oh, my Lord." Rags rushed into the cabin, followed by three Chinamen wearing manacles. "Are you okay? What in heaven's name happened to your ear?"

I hurt everywhere except my stump: arms, shoulders, head, and ribs. Stabbing pain emanated from my ear. Blood oozed from it down my neck. None of that mattered.

"We're alive. I've captured Poague and Black-Eyed Susan. Me, a one-legged girl." I imagined Papa beaming as I brought the prisoners into Bodie. He'd have been so proud. And now I had quite a story I could tell the Pinkertons. "Maybe now you and I'll get some respect from the townspeople. So, I'm better than okay."

Black-Eyed Susan coughed. "You won't be when I's through with you."

Chapter Thirty-Nine

We left the cabin just after sun up. Water in a tin bucket outside the cabin door had a paper-thin layer of ice on it. The sky was gray. My mood was black. I'd badgered him for two hours, but Poague denied having anything to do with Papa's murder. All Black-Eyed Susan would say is, "I'm gonna kill you."

Rags and I and the three Chinamen marched our prisoners outside toward Black-Eyed Susan's buckboard wagon. She shook her manacled hands. "What're you plannin' to do with us?"

"We're taking you to the jail in Bodie."

"Little ol' Bodie's jail?" Black-Eyed Susan cackled. "I've charmed my way out of much tougher jails than that. You're gonna be sorry you ever met us."

"You two don't worry me. Mr. Poague's going to hang for killing my Papa. With any luck he'll be joined by the other person who shot him. As for you, you'll soon be on trial for murdering your husband and Marshal Culpepper."

Two of the Chinamen helped her onto the seat of the wagon. They climbed up after her and Mr. Hong, the shorter one, took the reins.

Black-Eyed Susan scooted away from the Chinamen. "Get away from me, you yellow vermin."

Mr. Lam, who had tended to my injured ear and to Poague's head wounds, seized the chains tying Black-Eyed Susan's hands together and lifted them, shaking them in her face. He said something in Cantonese and laughed.

"Give the lady some room, will yer?" Poague said. He and the third Chinaman sat cross-legged in the buckboard's bed. Poague also wore one of the sets of iron manacles we'd removed from the Chinamen.

I stood in front of the cabin, my stump supported by the seat of the wooden chair. I didn't want to ride in the buggy Rags had borrowed from the livery stable, but I had to. Without my wooden leg I couldn't ride Sunrise. I'd fall out of the saddle. The buggy wasn't a wagon like the one Poague, Black-Eyed Susan, and the Chinamen sat in, but close enough. It had four wheels. A single horse pulled it. Same as the buckboard I rode in when I lost my leg. I felt dizzy.

"I'll drive careful," Rags said.

"You better."

He held my right arm as I hopped over to the buggy on my left foot. I took a deep breath and let it go. "I guess it's now or never."

Rags held me tight around the waist. I grabbed the seat back.

"When I say three."

"Okay."

I put my foot on the step. "One, two, three." I pulled and Rags shoved. I flopped onto my stomach on the seat and sat up. My bonnet slid to the side of my head and I straightened it.

Rags scurried around to the other side of the buggy and climbed in. Mr. Hong flicked the reins and the wagon made for the road. Rags and I followed behind in the buggy, leading Sunrise and Poague's large chestnut-colored Morgan. At our feet were two flour sacks full of gold flake, the butt end of a gold ingot with the letters "dard Mine" stamped on it, and my broken leg.

"How's your ear?" Rags asked.

"It stings. Maybe that's the herb Mr. Lam put on it before wrapping my head in a bandage. How's your head?"

"Poague hit the other side of me head. Sort of balanced out the pain. 'Tis tolerable. About going to Bodie, we're in Nevada. We should be takin' the prisoners to Aurora's jail, shouldn't we?"

"I want you to be seen by a doctor as soon as possible. Not only is there no doctor in Aurora, but they've lost their marshal, too."

"Oh, right."

Not long after we left the cabin, a half-dozen men on horseback appeared, galloping toward us from the direction of the Bodie Road.

Rags picked up his shotgun and cocked the hammers. "Think Suzie and Poague have friends?"

"I hope not." I pulled my revolver from my pocket and leaned forward, trying to make out who the horsemen were.

One of them removed his Stetson and began waving at us. Baron Catlow. Judge Snethens rode beside him.

"They're friends," I said. I pocketed my pistol.

Baron and Judge Snethens were followed by my brother, Patrick, the photographer Gideon Weed, and two others. The horsemen flowed around the buckboard and took up positions on either side of the buggy. Black-Eyed Susan growled at them like a cougar.

Baron rode up next to me. "We were worried. I, uh, we, feared the worst."

Judge Snethens fixed a stern gaze upon me. "You've been reckless, again."

"I may have been reckless, Judge, but Rags and I captured two murder suspects, including Poague, freed three Chinamen held against their will, and found some of the Standard Mine's missing gold."

"Impressive, I grant you," the judge said. "But your achievements appears to have come at a cost. What happened to your head?"

"Black-Eyed Susan bit my ear, but I'll be all right."

"Anyone else injured?"

"Black-Eyed Susan killed Aurora's Marshal Culpepper."

"Willard's dead?" the judge said.

"Yes. I'm sorry. Rags and Poague and Black-Eyed Susan were all hit on the head. They seem okay this morning, though." I hoped Rags was okay.

"*Audaces fortuna iuvat.*" The judge frowned. "Fortune favors the bold, but you were very lucky. Very lucky indeed. When we get back to town, we need to confabulate."

That didn't sound good.

"Marshal," I said, "what happened at the mine? Was anyone hurt in the explosion?"

"Sadly, we lost Barnabas Rotke, my foreman. He was a good man. We don't yet know what caused the explosion—Barnabas didn't normally handle dynamite. I'll continue to investigate what happened while we clear debris and re-timber the mine entrance.

"Judge, we should send someone to Aurora to let them know about Culpepper."

"An excellent idea," Judge Snethens said. "Charlie, will you and Silas please ride into Aurora and let them know about their marshal being killed. Nell, do you know where his body is?"

"In the barn."

Charlie said, "We'll see to it, your honor." He and Silas rode off.

Patrick nosed his horse up next to the buggy, edging out the judge's horse. "Is you all right, sis?"

"Pretty much. Thanks."

"Did I hear right? You captured two murderers?"

"Yes, with help from Rags."

"That's something. Papa would be proud."

I teared up at the mention of Papa. "Thanks, Patrick."

"Mama's really upset, though, what with you not coming home last night. Scared her somethin' awful. She'll be fixed to give you hell."

"Thanks for the warning." *Lordy, I'm in trouble with everybody.*

Gideon Weed rode up next to Baron. "Miss Doherty, I would very much like to take a photograph of you and Mr. Wu and your prisoners. Maybe get a photograph including all of Bodie's officers of the law. What do ya say, Miss Doherty? Marshal?"

Baron stared at me, smiling too broadly not to be noticed. I smiled back, not caring who saw. I caught Patrick looking at Baron and then at me. He was sure to say something to Mama. And Mama would be scandalized.

"Did you hear my question?" Weed asked Baron.

Baron answered while keeping his gaze upon me. "Um, uh, sure, Mr. Weed, was it? You can take our picture."

Black-Eyed Susan threw back her head. She cackled and cackled for some time as the buckboard rattled its way along Esmeralda Gulch.

Chapter Forty

I stood on the boardwalk in front of the jail and leaned against Baron. He held his arm around my shoulder. My wooden leg was unusable and I didn't have my crutches, so standing still on one leg would have been difficult without someone's support. His nearness warmed my insides.

Judge Snethens stood to the right of Baron, and Rags took up the rightmost position of our foursome. All of us faced the street where Gideon Weed crouched under his tripod camera's black cloth, which rippled in the cold breeze. He waved his hand sideways. "Judge, Mr. Wu, move in a little closer to the marshal. That's good. Miss Doherty, turn your head a bit more to hide the bandage. Good. Good." Weed slid a glass negative into the camera, removed its dark cover, and removed the lens cap. "Hold still."

I grinned in triumph. Almost singlehandedly I had captured Fergus Poague and Black-Eyed Susan. I imagined Papa standing in a cloudy heaven, smiling down on me. Everyone on Earth would have to see me differently, too. I'd proved I could be a deputy. The newspaper editor, Mr. Reeves, and even Mama would have to admit I was capable. She'd have to lessen her opposition to my being a deputy, a little. What gladdened my heart most was knowing that if I could do a deputy's job, I could make it as a Pinkerton detective.

Weed re-capped the camera's lens. "That's it. Thank you kindly. I'll have prints to show you tomorrow." He'd already taken a picture of me and Rags with our prisoners, but only after Baron yelled at Poague and Black-Eyed Susan to keep still and stop complaining about standing in the cold.

As Weed folded up his camera, I took Baron's arm and hopped alongside him on my one leg into the office. The judge and Rags followed. Baron helped me lower myself into Papa's swivel chair. The judge took the chair opposite me. He scowled. "Did we, or did we not, tell you to stay put and not take action on your own?"

Why's he so angry? "Poague had left Bodie and the telegraph was down."

The judge took a deep breath. "You didn't answer my question."

"You, um . . ." I bit my lower lip. "You told me not to budge."

Tapping his finger on the desk for emphasis, he said, "You disobeyed a *direct order*. You put yourself and Mr. Wu in grave danger. How can I trust that you won't do the same again?"

"We captured two murderers and nobody got seriously hurt. Well, except for Marshal Culpepper."

Judge Snethens shook his head. "Marshal Culpepper was a good man. If he'd been backed up by a posse, he might still be alive."

"Are you blaming me for his death?"

"No. He shouldn't have drawn on someone pointing a gun at him. I'm just reminding you that rashness can have dire consequences. You and Rags were lucky. You may not be so lucky next time, and I'll not have your life on my conscience. Nell, I commend your determination. You've done a superlative job as a deputy, but you've stirred up a hornet's nest of protest. I could lose my judgeship over it."

"Everybody loves you."

"Public opinion can be fickle." The judge pulled a folded *Bodie Miner* from his coat pocket and smoothed the newspaper out on the desk. On the front page, next to a story about the mine explosion, sat an editorial entitled "Contravening Nature."

> *The hiring of women as peace officers offends our notions of what is good and proper. We demand that Miss Nell Doherty be removed from the office of deputy marshal. The reasons are obvious.*
>
> *First, women lack the strength to force compliance with the law. This is particularly the case with Miss Doherty who has a wooden leg. Her deficits in the physical realm were made plain the other day when several ruffians threw Miss Doherty out of Smith's Dance Hall.*
>
> *Second, it is not in the nature of the fairer sex to be capable of facing the horrors perpetrated by criminals, nor are women fit to mete out the violence that is part and parcel of a peace officer's life. What parent would want their daughter to be sullied by the corrupting influences of the criminal element?*
>
> *Just as the Almighty intends that husbands rule over their wives (Ephesians 5:22, "Wives, submit to your own husbands ...") only men should be enforcing the rules over our citizenry.*
>
> *We can only hope that Judge Snethens will come to his senses and take Miss Doherty's badge from her. If he does not do so soon, then come this November, voters may decide the old reprobate is unfit for the job.*

I looked up from the paper. "Judge, as you just said, I've done a good job as a deputy. This poppycock is just the opinion of one narrowminded man."

"It's an opinion shared by most of the town, including your

mother. For your protection, and for my own, I must ask you for your badge."

"But—"

"I'll suffer no disputation on this matter."

"This isn't right," Rags said. "Not a bit."

Baron had supported me before. I turned to face him.

He averted his gaze. "I'm afraid I agree with the judge. Nell, I couldn't bear to have your death on my conscience."

I pounded my fist on the desk. "Have you forgotten? There's still Kohl."

Judge Snethens released an exasperated sigh. "We don't have any evidence proving that Kohl is guilty."

"One of Papa's killers is still out there, loose. Who's going to catch him?"

I glowered at Baron.

"Nell, you know I'll do everything I can."

"You'll be busy repairing your mine."

"We got some good news," Baron said. "The county sheriff is sending one of his deputies to take over as marshal."

"Then let me keep my badge until he gets here."

"No," the judge said. "These aren't common criminals we're dealing with, but hard-hearted killers."

"This isn't fair."

"No, it's not. Some days, the whole world is unfair." The judge pulled his flask from his coat and took a swig. "Now, please hand me your badge."

Rags removed his badge from his coat and placed it and the shotgun on the desk.

"Ah, Mr. Wu, you may keep your badge, if you like."

"What!" My anger burst like a firecracker. I lunged forward in my chair. "You're letting Rags keep his badge just because he's a man?"

"There's more to it than that. I trust he won't run off on his own and get himself in a bad scrape. We could use his help guarding the prisoners."

I was struck speechless by anger. My jaws clamped tight enough to split a fireplace poker.

"Your honor," Rags said, "if Nell has to give up her badge, after all she's done, I've no stomach to keep mine."

"I understand and appreciate your loyalty, Mr. Wu."

My hands shook as I unclasped and pulled the badge from my coat. I threw it on the desk. It bounced and landed on the floor.

Baron offered me his arm. "May I escort you home?"

"No, thanks." *Traitor.* "Rags, would you do me the kindness of fetching my crutches?"

Chapter Forty-One

Judge Snethens got up from his chair. "Nell, I'm sorry. Perhaps, one day, society will accept women as deputy marshals."

"How can people accept women as deputies if they never see them acting as deputies? I guess that will never happen because there aren't any men brave enough to deputize women."

"I risked my life countless times in the war. I've no doubt of my bravery." The judge crossed his arms. "I understand your anger, Nell, but I'm not changing my mind."

The judge left the jail.

"I'll get your crutches," Rags said. "And while I'm about it, I'll drop off your wooden leg with Doc Boyle so he can repair it. See you shortly."

Baron sat on my side of the desk and took my hand in his. *This must be one of those 'bad times' Mrs. Lockhart talked about that would test my love for Baron.* "I'm really, really angry with you." I didn't remove my hand from his.

His eyes bore into mine. "I know."

"Why didn't you support me?"

"Because of how I feel about you."

How he feels about me? Does Baron mean he loves me?

I looked away.

If Baron loves me, why doesn't he insist I stay on as a deputy? He knows how important it is to me to find both men who shot Papa.

His thumb stroked the back of my hand. I closed my eyes to try to concentrate. His hand was warm. His touch was lulling me to sleep. It had been such a long day and a half. Such a struggle capturing Black-Eyed Susan and Poague.

I opened my eyes.

There was one more task to perform before Baron and I would have time to just sit and hold hands. "Baron, who's going to chase Papa's other killer?"

"I told you, I'll do what I can." His thumb caressed my hand, his touch light. "Did the prisoners say anything about the man they called The Boss?"

"Could be Erastus Kohl."

"Do you have any real evidence against Kohl?"

"No." There was no point continuing to argue that Kohl was involved. Like the judge, Baron wanted more evidence. *And now, I can't search for it. Worse, no one might look for it.*

Baron released my hand and pulled his watch from his vest pocket. He leaned toward me and whispered, "I have to appoint a new mine foreman, but I promise to come back in an hour and interrogate the prisoners. I expect I'll get something out of 'em." He took my hand again. Soft as a feather, his thumb floated across my skin. "If I lean on 'em, hard, will that make you feel better?"

"No. Not yet. Maybe. I don't know."

I wanted to be there, to question them, to trick them into revealing The Boss's name. But I was no longer a deputy. It wasn't fair.

Baron leaned closer and kissed me on the lips. My anger fought against my desire. The anger won out and I turned my head. Baron's kind eyes gazed at me. A wisp of a smile, thin as a new moon, graced his face. *Why does his gaze make me limp?*

"Do you love me?" I asked.

"Yes, I love you."

Wooden leg and all, he loved me. I couldn't believe it—not the words. But I believed the soft glow of his face and the intensity of his stare.

Black-Eyed Susan cackled from her cell. She yelled, "Sounds like you're pitchin' woo, marshal. You do all your courtin' in the jail?"

Baron stood and stomped to the door that led to the cells. "Black-Eyed Suzie, if you don't shut up, I swear I'll gag you."

She cackled again. "Ha. I'm already gagging."

Baron slammed the door between the office and the cells. He took a deep breath. "I'm sorry." He took another deep breath. "I'll discover who the other gunman is. I promise he will get what's coming to him." He left for his appointment at the mine.

FIFTEEN MINUTES LATER, RAGS ARRIVED WITH MY crutches. We left the marshal's office. I swung on my crutches and Rags strolled beside me down Virgin Alley toward Yong Liao's Mercantile. The afternoon sun hid behind a thick layer of pale gray clouds. On the way, we passed the young prostitute Huang Min emptying her slop jar into a small pool of muck between her crib and the brothel next door. Rags waved to her and she bowed her head slightly.

"What is it you want to talk to Yong Liao about?" Rags asked.

"The paper with Chinese writing on it that Papa signed. I found it in my pocket when I pulled out my gloves."

"If you're tired, I could give it to Yong Liao, I could, and let you know later what the paper says."

"His store's on the way home. It shouldn't take long."

An excited Bobby Wu, Rags's youngest brother, met us half way down Virgin Alley. He carried a wicker basket full of laundry.

"Oh, hello, Nell. Hello, oldest brother." Bobby's eyes sparkled. "I've a terrific idea. I've decided to become a detective. I could work for Pinkerton, too. Oh, wouldn't that be grand?"

Rags shook his head. "Given up your dream of becoming a pirate captain, then?"

"That's old news. Detectives lead exciting lives without breaking the law. Oh, Nell, don't you think it'd be wondrous to be detectives?"

"If that's what you want." I repeated the warning Papa had given me. "You know, detectives' lives aren't always exciting."

Bobby shifted the weight of the wicker basket onto his hip. "Oh, I knew you'd understand, Nell. You're the best. See ya."

Bobby went north up Virgin Alley.

Rags watched his brother go. "Bobby has a head only for adventure. The idea of carrying a gun attracts him. He's no notion of what it means to use one."

"He's only fourteen."

"He's the very definition, he is, of one of those ten-dollar words you taught me—impetuous."

If anyone was the definition of impetuous, it was me. *Rats. Why couldn't I be the definition of some other word, like bold. A bold person would have done what I did and still have her badge.*

YONG LIAO STOOD BEHIND THE GLASS COUNTER INSIDE his store. He held an abacus. Alternately, he read a document lying on the counter and flipped the beads of the abacus up and down.

"Nay hoh, Uncle," Rags and I said together.

"Good day. Please, sit." We took our places on the black-lacquer drum stools near the potbellied stove. I lay my crutches on the floor. Yong Liao pushed the beads back and forth a bit longer, wrote something on the document with a pencil, and then sat in his rocking chair.

"Congratulations, Miss Doherty and Wu Chao. You catch murderers. Very remarkable."

"That may be so, but the judge took our badges," I said. "Well, actually he took mine and Wu Chao resigned in sympathy."

"Editor Reeves' doing, in part. In part, your doing. Too much brave become reckless."

"I know, Uncle. I am sorry if I have disgraced Wu Chao."

"No dishonor in taking friend's side."

I reached into my pocket and pulled out the document with its rows of Chinese characters interrupted twice by a note in English from Papa and his signature. I handed it to Yong Liao. His left eyebrow rose. He glanced at the document a moment. He looked at Rags, then at me.

"Where find?"

"In Papa's coat. What does it say? Is it related to Papa's death?"

"Wu Chao not explain?"

"He wasn't able to read it all."

Yong Liao glanced at Rags, then back to me. He set the paper on a round table between us. "Is business contract. Private business."

He doesn't want to tell me. Why? "Private business? Of Papa's?"

"In part."

"Uncle, why are you not telling me everything?"

"Cost of knowledge may be high."

"I want to know."

Yong Liao reached into his pocket and pulled out his long-stemmed pipe and a box of matches. He lit his pipe and puffed on it as he rocked in his chair for a minute or two. He gave no indication he would stop.

"Uncle?" I said.

"You very young."

"I'm too young to understand?"

"That is question."

What could it be that I'm too young to understand?

Yong Liao spoke to Rags in Cantonese, and Rags answered in kind. Yong Liao grunted then spoke one word. He kept rocking and smoking his pipe.

"What?" I asked Rags.

"You were born in the year of the ox—you're stubborn."

Yong Liao stopped rocking. "You cook?"

"Yes, Uncle."

Yong Liao set his pipe on the round table between us. From the shelves behind the counter, he retrieved two small jars and returned to his rocking chair. "This," he raised the jar in his left hand, "sugar. This," he said, raising the jar in his right hand, "salt. In kitchen, different jar for sugar, different jar for salt, don't mix, yes?"

"Yes." *Salt and sugar?*

Yong Liao put the jars on the round table. "You make *new* jar —here." He pointed at his heart. "Don't mix."

"Oh-kay." I didn't understand. I hoped his meaning would become clear as he went along.

"Play poker one night. Liao, Papa Marshal, others. Mr. Deng from Virginia City lose many dollars. Not able call. You understand 'call'?"

Papa once explained poker to Patrick and I had listened. "I know a little bit about the game." I had no idea where his story was going.

"Deng ask, okay to bet contract? Better than cash, he say."

"He called the bet using the contract."

"Yes. Only Liao, Marshal, and Deng still in game. Marshal and Liao accept contract as cash. Deng lose hand. Marshal and Liao have same cards, so split pot two way. Each get half contract."

"So, what's the contract for?"

"Now, please, take lid off new jar here." Yong Liao pointed again at his heart. "New jar for contract only."

"Okay. I'm ready." *I guess.*

"Hmm. I hope true." Yong Liao rocked forward and stopped. He held my eyes in his gaze. "Contract is for Huang Min."

"What? Oh, no. Nooo." *He couldn't mean that.*

"Before he call, Deng own Huang Min. After he call, Marshal and Yong Liao own Huang Min."

Papa owned a sixteen-year-old soiled dove? I squeezed my eyes shut. How could Papa do such a thing? My heart thundered. I couldn't accept that Papa owned this girl. I held the sides of my head. My mind was going to explode. "You knew what the contract was. You and Papa saw it was owning another person. How could you accept it? How could you?"

"Deng say he pay cash in one week, take contract back. We say, okay. Two night later Deng go to opium den. Fall in snow on way home, die of cold."

"I can't believe this. You and Papa kept this girl, you kept her as your, uh, prostitute slave."

Papa would never do such a thing. He wouldn't.

Yong Liao picked up the contract from the little round table. "Look here." He pointed to Papa's second signature under his handwritten sentence: *The terms of the contract have been fulfilled.*

"Your Papa decide to free Huang Min."

Of course. Papa wouldn't keep a prostitute. My heartrate slowed.

"Night your father shot, he was to bring contract for Liao to sign."

That was the night Mama and Papa argued. The night I listened to them through the wall. I'd assumed they had fought over Irene Lockhart. I'd been wrong. That's why Mama hadn't gotten angry when Mrs. Lockhart showed up at Papa's funeral. Mama and Papa hadn't argued over Mrs. Lockhart, they'd argued over Huang Min. *Oh, Mama.* "How long ago did you and Papa, uh, win Huang Min?"

"Two month ago."

"Two months? Two months? And all this time she continued to see customers?"

"Yes."

"That's horrible. You and Papa should have freed her immediately."

Yong Liao tipped his head from side to side. "Where she go then? How she live? Family in China, they sell her, no want back. She keep money she earn now."

I wanted to object again. To yell and say what he and Papa had done was both illegal and sinful. But I remembered my own situation. As Mama reminded me too often, without a husband, my options were few. If Pinkerton wouldn't have me, and if I couldn't become a teacher, I might starve. Huang Min could at least survive as a prostitute, but that should have been her decision.

"You say Huang Min can keep the money she earns, but you kept her a slave. If you'd freed her, she might have chosen to do something else."

"You want Huang Min make choice for self."

"Well, of course."

Yong Liao removed a fountain pen from his jacket pocket, laid the contract on the little round table, and signed his name under Papa's signature. He handed the paper to Rags. "Perhaps you wish tell Huang Min?"

Rags blushed. "Thank you, Uncle."

Why was Rags blushing? Was it because he'd seen her without clothes? My thoughts were interrupted by Yong Liao.

He tapped his heart with his finger. "Miss Doherty, remember little jar? Put Huang Min, contract, all this talk, into jar. Put top on jar, not open again."

236

Chapter Forty-Two

"Thank you for your honesty," I said to Yong Liao. I picked up my crutches. Rags and I bowed and we left the mercantile. Outside, the wind had picked up strength. The air had chilled further. I stopped my three-legged walk and faced Rags.

"What?" he asked.

"I'm so mad at Papa. I can't believe he owned a slave."

"I'd like to give you ancient Oriental advice, I would."

"If you must."

Rags scowled at me. "Master Confucius said, 'We learn three ways: by reflection, which is noblest; by imitation, which is easiest, and by experience, which is bitterest.' "

"That's a big help."

"Yong Liao'd say, 'Having had a bitter experience, 'tis time for reflection.' "

"You want me to be noble?"

"Let this new information simmer."

"I don't know if I *can* keep it stuffed in its own little jar."

"'Tis why I'm repeating Yong's suggestion. Don't go spoiling your good feelin's for your Papa with this new knowledge. Keep the sugar and the salt separate."

"And just *accept* the fact that Papa owned a slave who was a fancy lady?"

"Aye. Everyone's got good and bad in them. We have to take the bad of those we love to get the good."

I studied my friend. A touch of sadness had deepened his voice. He'd spoken as if he'd experienced having to accept the bad with the good. I had a hunch. "Why did you blush when Yong Liao asked if you'd like to tell Huang Min she's free?"

Rags blushed again. He stared at the ground. He was acting so silly. He must like the girl. That's what his brother Bobby couldn't tell me. He couldn't tell me Rags was in love with Huang Min, a soiled dove.

I laid my hand on his shoulder. "Huang Min's your sweetheart, isn't she?"

"Yes." He didn't look up.

"Huang Min being what you call a hundred men's wife, that must be hard on you. Do you have a little jar for all those things she does? Are you able to keep the lid on it?"

"'Tis hard that, but it isn't only that. She won't say how she feels about me, teases me awful. Says if I'm wantin' to be hers, I need money. Six-hundred dollars. She won't tell me what it's for, though she's desperate to get it."

"Well, maybe she'll appreciate you when you tell her you freed her."

"But I didn't."

"Who's going to say different?"

Rags tired eyes met mine. "Nell, you're an angel, you are." He hugged me. "I'll see you tomorrow. Keep that jar closed."

He ran north, toward Min's crib. I hitched south across the frozen ground toward home, expecting a frosty reception from Mama.

JUST BEFORE THREE IN THE AFTERNOON, I OPENED OUR front door and entered the house. Mama stood at the kitchen counter at the back of the big room, chopping carrots. She looked over her shoulder.

"About time you came home." She wiped her hands on her apron and threw her arms open wide. "Come here, darlin'."

I crossed the room and she enveloped me in an embrace. I was home.

"Where's your wooden leg?"

"It broke." I wasn't going to tell her how. "Rags took it to Doc Boyle to fix."

Mama lifted my bonnet from my head. Her eyes went wide when she saw my bandaged ear. "You've been hurt."

"It's not hurting much now and the bleeding's stopped. It's only my feelings that really got hurt."

"Your feelings?" She pulled back and held me at arm's length.

"The judge took my badge from me."

"One of my prayers answered." She looked toward the ceiling. "There's another matter I've prayed over. Patrick saw you and the new marshal making eyes at each other in front of God, the judge, and them murderers, too. So, I'm wonderin', what's this Mr. Catlow to you, then?"

"I'm trying to sort that out."

"I see. Has he touched you?"

"Mama."

She pulled me closer. "Has he touched you?"

"We held hands. We kissed."

"Jesus, Mary, and Joseph." She crossed herself. "Have you no shame?"

She's acting like Baron's the devil. "He's been a perfect gentleman."

"Perfect gentleman, my eye. What's he doin' sniffin' around a young girl like you? He must be twice your age."

"He's only thirty."

"Don't be quibbling with me, young lady."

"Papa's nine years older than you." I almost said 'was' older.

She wagged a finger in my face. "Don't be sassin' me neither. Your seeing him is unseemly and nothing good will come of it."

"Just because Papa did bad things, doesn't mean Baron will, too."

Mama grabbed my face and squeezed. "Don't you *ever* say anything against your Papa."

"How can you say that when Papa and Yong Liao owned Huang Min and kept her as a prostitute? It's wicked."

Mama held her hand to her bosom. "What? What did you say? He owned that yellow girl? He not only had congress with her, but he owned her?"

Congress between Papa and Huang Min? Papa wouldn't do that. No, no, he wouldn't. No. Although, that could explain why Papa held onto the contract for two months. But, no, he wouldn't do that to Mama. Of course, I'd never thought he would own a slave.

Mama's face paled. "Tell me, did he truly own the girl?"

"I thought you knew. I thought that's what you and Papa argued about the night he was shot."

"I'd only heard a rumor that he'd visited her crib." Mama sniffed several times. She turned away from me. "I have to sit. Come join me on the couch."

Mama wiped her eyes with her handkerchief. "How do you know this?"

I told her about discovering the contract in Papa's pocket and having Yong Liao translate it. "I'm so sorry. I should have kept my mouth shut." *Should have kept the jar closed.*

"It's part of my penance, it is. I always knew your Papa was a bit of a rogue. I accepted it because of all the sweetness in him. Swept me off my feet, he did, despite my being engaged to Seamus O'Connor. Your grandma never forgave me for that."

"You broke an engagement?" I couldn't believe it. Mama

never did anything the least bit improper. Had I not known either of my parents?

"Your father in his uniform was a sight to behold. Everyone said so. Just a minute." Mama went into her bedroom and returned carrying her favorite picture of Papa, a hand-tinted photograph of him in his Union blues. He held a rifle alongside him. The tip of the bayonet stood taller than he did. His dark-blue sleeve had three golden V-shaped stripes. The brim of his hat was turned up on the left side.

"So handsome. Don't you think?"

"Very handsome. Why didn't you tell me you'd been engaged before?"

Mama's finger circled Papa's face on the picture. "My, he could dance. And his smile, how it dizzied me."

It touched me deeply how much Mama still loved Papa, even after he'd angered and disappointed her. She accepted Papa with all his faults. Like Yong Liao, she kept her salt and sugar in separate jars. This must be what Mrs. Lockhart had meant by true love. Maybe someday I could forgive Papa, but I couldn't imagine it. I hoped Baron would never hurt me like Papa had hurt Mama.

Mama took the photograph back to her room and returned to the couch. "Now you're over this nonsense about being a deputy, you should write to Aunt Agnes and tell her you'll be attending the state Normal School after all."

"We agreed I could work for Pinkerton for a year."

"Your father agreed, not me."

"And, there's Baron. He says he loves me."

Mama rolled her eyes. "Oh, darlin', all men say that. Not one in ten of them knows what love is."

"Baron may be the one."

"He's too old for you. I don't want you seeing him again, do you hear? I forbid it."

"I won't throw away my feelings for Baron just because you say to, no more than I'll forget being a Pinkerton."

241

Mama leveled her eyes at me like two cannons. "Listen here—"

"I didn't sleep last night. Can we call a truce for now?"

I kissed her on the cheek, hoisted myself onto my crutches, and swung off to bed. I changed into my nightgown and pulled the stocking off my stump. I rubbed extra liniment into the puckered, red flesh and pulled the covers over me.

What was I to think of Papa? Owning Huang Min was bad, but having relations with her, too? It was a grievous sin, yet Mama forgave him. Her acceptance confused me. On the one hand, letting Papa do as he pleased showed weakness. But at the same time, her acceptance showed strength. Through her forgiveness she endured, and she kept her love alive. Love seemed so complicated.

Lord, what a day. I learned things about Papa I didn't want to know. Caught Poague and Black-Eyed Susan. That pleased me no end. But losing my badge was so unfair. I pounded my fists against the feather mattress. Hadn't I shown that I could be as good a deputy as anyone else? How will I catch your other murderer, Papa?

I stared at my dresser top, at Pinkerton's *Thirty Years a Detective* and the stack of magazine clippings of Conan Doyle's Sherlock Holmes stories. *A lot of good you did me today, Mr. Pinkerton, Mr. Holmes.*

Misters.

Not marshals, not deputies. Misters.

I didn't need a badge. I pulled the blankets up to my chin and closed my eyes. *Tomorrow, I will be a detective.*

Chapter Forty-Three

I snuck out of the house before sunrise. I did not want another argument with Mama over my future. Two inches of new powdery snow covered the ground and more drifted down from the still-dark sky. In my right coat pocket, I carried the pistol Yong Liao had given me. My left pocket held a candle, matches, a small notebook, and a pencil—my detective gear. I only lacked my own "Dr. Watson," and I found him sweeping the floor of Yong Liao's Mercantile. I rapped on the door. Rags unlocked it and let me in.

He leaned on his broom and looked at me askance. "What mischief are you about?"

"How's Huang Min?"

"Never you mind changing the subject, Nell Doherty. I know that crazed look, I do. Spit it out."

"Remember the night we got thrown out of Smith's Dance Hall?"

"Of course. Me—my—stitches remind me every time I move my head."

"Remember what I wanted to do, before we decided to search the saloons for Poague?"

"Must have been knocked out of me."

"I wanted to search Poague's house for clues. He's behind bars now, so it will be safe."

"Sure'n I'm the biggest fool ever. My mind brings up arguments against your plans, when I know perfectly well my thoughts are of no use." Rags set the broom against the glass counter. "I'll ask Bobby to finish sweeping and let Yong Liao know. Back in a minute."

Bobby arrived before Rags.

"Mornin', Nell," Bobby said, as he entered the store. "Missed you. Oh, I hope we can soon resume me lessons." He picked up the broom and began sweeping. He looked toward the door and turned back to me. In a whisper, he added, "Thanks again for not tellin' Rags what I told you about Huang Min bein' a hundred men's wife. Mr. Hundred-and-First wouldn't appreciate it."

"You call Rags Mr. Hundred-and-First? Shame on you."

Bobby grinned. "Oh, not to his face, I don't."

"You shouldn't make fun of your brother. None of us can control who we fall in love with." I wouldn't have thought I'd fall in love with a man twelve years older than I.

"No, I reckon not." Bobby gazed at me, expectantly, as if I had uttered a Confucian pearl of wisdom, and would soon reveal another.

"When you're grown up, you'll have a sweetheart, too. You won't want others making fun of you then."

Bobby straightened his back. "I'm grown up. Ma says I'm very old for fourteen."

The door opened and Rags entered the shop. "I'm ready."

"Bring your pistol," I said.

"Planning to shoot up Poague's empty house, are you?"

Bobby waved his hand excitedly. "Oh, can I go, too? Please?"

"No," Rags said.

Bobby pouted.

"We're only going to look inside his cabin," I said.

SUNLIGHT BEGAN TO LIGHTEN THE CLOUD-COVERED SKY as we made our way to Poague's shack. Feather-light snow continued to fall, melting on my eyelashes. We passed Dean Howell driving his wagon packed with milk cans.

Rags and I plodded up the hill past the Standard Mill and its tailings mounds. We turned on to Wood Street.

"What do you hope to learn?"

"Proof of who is the second gunman that shot Papa."

"Still certain Kohl did it, aren't you?"

"Yes."

I stopped twenty feet in front of Poague's cabin. Snow had collected along the horizontal edges of the flattened tin cans that covered the walls.

"Having second thoughts, are you?"

"No. I'm trying to think what Sherlock Holmes would do. I guess we can go straight in. It's too late to study footprints outside the shack."

Poague's one-room home had a table, two mismatched wooden chairs, and a neatly made bed. The table held an oil lamp, a mostly empty pint bottle of whiskey, and the issue of *The Bodie Miner* with the article on my becoming a deputy marshal. I took the matches from my pocket and lit the oil lamp.

The room held no dishes or cookware, no food. Three shirts and two pair of denim pants hung on nails. Affixed to the wall above the bed, two postcards of actresses in full-body tights provided the only decoration.

"Doesn't look like there's much here," Rags said.

"Check under the bed."

I went through Poague's pockets and found a used handkerchief and a gold Knights of Pythias pin identical to the one I found next to where Papa had been shot. This must be the replacement he bought that tipped Judge Snethens off that Poague might have been in Virgin Alley the night Papa was shot.

Rags lifted the edge of the blanket and pulled a wooden crate out from under the bed. "Found something. Well, maybe."

I looked around the nearly barren cabin for other places Poague might have left a clue to the other gunman. Only the stove remained. I opened the ash door at the bottom. Almost empty. Poague must have cleaned it out recently. I took the newspaper off the table, unfolded it, and began scooping out the contents of the stove onto the paper.

Rags sat on the bed, pulled objects from the crate, and set them on the blanket. A tin wash basin, a bunch of rags, a razor, soap, four shotgun shells, a small leather pouch, and a bottle. "What the devil? I gave her this me-self." He held the bottle up. Oriental Toilet Water.

Rags lowered the bottle and dropped his head on his chest. "It's the only one this size has left the store. I gave it to Huang Min as a gift."

"You can't be thinking Min liked Poague. He's ugly. He smells like a hard-ridden horse that's rolled in its own droppings. Poague probably stole the bottle from her." I left unsaid that Poague might have been one of her 'first hundred husbands' and that she might have given him the perfume to mask the man's horsey odor. "The bottle's also a clue. Pettibone couldn't remember anything that happened the night Papa was shot, but he remembered smelling Oriental Toilet Water. Poague having this bottle is more evidence that he shot Papa."

Rags still stared at the floor. "Blast."

"We know Min may have seen Papa get shot. Maybe she saw Poague and was too afraid of him to say anything. But he's in jail, now. Maybe now she'll tell us what she saw, including the identity of the second shooter."

"That would be somethin', it would. Okay, when we're done here, we'll have a talk with her."

I scooped another handful of soot out of the stove. "What's in the pouch?"

Rags opened it. "Well, I'll be. More gold leaf cut up fine. What's with this gold leaf, do you figure?"

"Beats me." I sifted through the ash with my gloved fingers and found several burnt fragments of paper. One was the bottom corner of a letter, which bore the signature, partially burned, of Gideon Weed, Esq.

I held up the charred paper for Rags to see. "Why do you suppose Poague would burn a letter from Gideon Weed? Do you think Weed could be The Boss that Poague and Black-Eyed Susan mentioned?"

"Sounds farfetched."

"I'd agree, except he's such a busybody, always lurking around. At Papa's wake, he was eavesdropping on me and Judge Snethens while we were talking about Poague."

"Really?"

"He also arrived in Bodie about the same time as the first gold robbery."

Rags closed his eyes. "Gideon Weed a killer? I dunno. When I look at him with that beard of his, I see Honest Abe, not a killer. Whoever this Boss is, he must be somebody like Yong Liao or Judge Snethens, someone who's really smart. Do ya think Weed is that smart?"

"I don't know. Let's see if he was in Virgin Alley when Papa was shot."

"How d'ya intend to do that?"

"Ask him."

Rags removed his hat and gently fingered the stitches on his scalp. "Nell, have I told you how much I've always admired your subtle way of confronting people?"

"I'm sorry." I went back to searching the ash. I found two more scraps. One of them held part of a drawing, the top half of a cylinder with a curlicue tail. The second fragment held hand-written directions.

the alarm
Wind the cloc
3. Attach battery wi
bomb in

Bomb?

"Rags, look at these." I handed him the two burnt pieces of paper.

He looked at them and whistled. "Looks like one o' them Fenian time bombs, it does. Do ya think it coulda been what exploded in the Second Chance Mine? T'would make Barnabas Rotke's death a murder."

"Poague expected to get rich. How would he get rich by blowing up the mine?"

"Maybe the Standard Mine wanted no competition."

"I don't believe that. I wonder. The papers with Weed's signature and the one with the bomb instructions were burned at the same time. Maybe they're connected."

"Meanin'?"

"Well, photographers use flash powder. Maybe Weed would know about other kinds of explosives, too. Maybe he wrote the instructions."

"Let me see the paper with his signature."

Rags compared that to the note about the bomb. "Blast. Can't tell if they were written by the same person. His signature's script writin'. The instructions're printed."

"Do you still think Weed is as honest as Old Abe?"

"'Tis something to think about."

"We'll let Baron and the judge know right after we talk to Huang Min."

I stirred the ashes some more and flipped over a few more quarter-sized scraps of singed paper. Nothing.

Rags looked under the bed again. "Hmm."

"What?"

"A lot of feathers." He pulled the blankets off the bed and poked the mattress. "Found something else." He flipped the mattress over and revealed a fist-sized hole. He put his hand inside and pulled. Out came a puff of feathers, and a shotgun.

Chapter Forty-Four

Rags blew feathers off the shotgun he'd found hidden in Poague's mattress. "Odd, this is. Never heard of anyone hiding anythin' but valuables in a mattress." He examined the gun, turning it over in his hands. "Got some initials on it: H.W. You know anybody has initials H.W.?"

H. W.? H. W.? "I can't think of anyone with a last name beginning with W, except you and your family."

"You don't suspect us, do you?"

"Of course not, silly. Help me think."

"There aren't many in Bodie with first names beginning H. I can only think of Doc Boyle, his first name is Hiram. But I don't think this shotgun is his."

"I don't either."

We were quiet for a moment.

"There's Harold Gant," I said, "the owner of Smith's Dance Hall." I remembered something Mrs. Lockhart said. "She told me about a scoundrel named Harlan Woolcott. She said he was a swindler in Virginia City. Maybe this HW stands for Harlan Woolcott, and he's using an alias in Bodie."

"Could Poague be this Woolcott fella?"

"No. Mrs. Lockhart knew Poague. She'd have told me if they were the same man. Anyway, she said Woolcott was handsome."

"Would ya call Gideon Weed handsome? His last name starts with W."

I pictured Mr. Weed in my mind. "He's a bit gaunt, but I suppose you could say he's handsome."

"So, Weed and this Harlan Woolcott, they could be one and the same."

"After we talk to Huang Min, we'll ask Mrs. Lockhart about Mr. Weed."

I put the Knights of Pythias pin in my coat pocket.

Rags pocketed the bottle of Oriental Toilet Water, the gold pouch, and the extra shotgun shells. "I'm going to keep the shotgun. Just in case."

I blew out the oil lamp, and we left Poague's shack. Outside the sun had climbed above Silver Hill. A blanket of new snow covered my world: the streets, the houses, the Standard Mill, and the mountains. Deceptively pure, like life. Our footsteps broke through the gloss as we trudged along Wood Street.

"Oh, deputies," a woman trilled at our backs after we had turned onto Main Street. "Deputies."

I stopped on the boardwalk and hopped around on my crutches to greet Widow Grimsby, who carried her little schnauzer under her arm. She and her dog wore identical coats and bonnets of bright red, yellow, and green plaid. Supposedly, the bright colors made it easier for her husband's ghost to locate her when they communed each full moon.

"I was on my way to see you. I've had my fill of his assaults, and I want the man arrested—this instant. He's vile. He frightened King Charles half to death. So much so, the poor A-N-I-M-A-L—he thinks he's human, you know—the poor thing soiled his night shirt."

I'm trying to catch a murderer and she wants to tell me about

251

her dog soiling his night shirt. I counted to ten while she droned on.

"Look at how droopy King Charles's beard has become, ruined his whole outlook for the day, maybe the week, though he might perk up if he saw that blackguard in jail."

Rags touched the brim of his hat. "Mornin' Mrs. Grimsby. Uh, which blackguard might you be talking of?"

"That good for nothing Kohl, of course. As if you couldn't guess. He's been pestering King Charles for over a week now."

She had my full attention. "You mean Erastus Kohl?" I said. "What's he done?"

"Well, first the beast yelled at King Charles. Then he chucked tin cans at him." Mrs. Grimsby lifted her dog's chin and spoke in cooing tones as if to a baby. "Didn't he dearest little one?"

King Charles woofed in agreement.

"On the New Year—yours, dear," the widow said to Rags, "not ours—the devil tossed firecrackers at King Charles, and last night, the final straw, Mr. Kohl took arms against him. Shot at King Charles twice, twice I tell you."

Kohl had lied again. He did have a gun. I fought to keep my fists from clenching. Why would he lie about that unless he'd shot Papa? "Are you certain Kohl shot at King Charles?"

"Absolutely. I couldn't believe it either. Can you imagine my horror at the thought of King Charles being fired upon, possibly wounded, or even killed?" Widow Grimsby looked expectantly at me and then at Rags. "Well, dears, what are you standing there for? Go arrest the man."

"Sorry to say," Rags said, "we're no longer deputies."

"Oh, I know you two were unpopular choices, but you needn't be coy with me. It's all over town that you've been appointed deputies by the honorable Judge Snethens. And, just between you and me, the ladies of Bodie's Freethinkers Society think you're setting a fine example, showing dunderheaded men that women can do anything we set our minds to."

I wish Mama felt that way. "That means a lot to me, Mrs. Grimsby. Thank you. But Wu Chao is telling the truth. We really can't arrest anyone now because—"

She waved away any possible objection to her demand. "Yes, yes, I understand. You may, of course, have other duties to attend to, duties you think important no doubt, but really, King Charles and I deserve protection as much as anyone. This is a matter of life and death. What could possibly be more important? Isn't that right, King Charles?"

The dog woofed his assent. From beneath his bushy eyebrows, he shot a pleading glance my way.

"Mrs. Grimsby," I said, "we will go straight to the jail and discuss this with Marshal Catlow. He wouldn't want Wu Chao and me to try to arrest a man as dangerous as Erastus Kohl by ourselves."

"Very well, dears, if you think that best. But please do be quick about it. If King Charles catches another whiff of that man's scent, he may shiver himself to death."

We took our leave of the widow and continued along the boardwalk.

Rags glanced at me sideways.

"What?"

"You're thinking that Kohl lying about having a gun means he shot your Papa."

"Which is perfectly logical. He did it, Rags. He's Papa's second killer."

"His lie's suspicious, it is, but not enough proof for the judge."

"I know. I know. That's why we're going to talk to Huang Min before we see Baron. All we need to hang Kohl is for Min to admit she saw him shoot Papa."

Rags hunched his shoulders. "Min's Chinese. She might not be allowed to testify in court, not against a white man."

A chill swept through my body. Surely Judge Snethens would

allow Min to testify, although, he allowed Huang Min to be enslaved because it was *customary*. It was also customary that Chinese couldn't testify in court. But not this time.

"If Min saw Kohl shoot Papa, I'll make the judge put her on the stand." I swung down the lane on my crutches, frightened and angered by the prospect that Papa's killer might get away. "I'll make the judge do it, if it's the last thing I do."

"Dare I mention Mr. Weed? Are ya still interested in him?"

"One thing at a time."

We made our way to Main Street and turned north. We passed a pair of miners on the boardwalk. They stared at me and Rags walking together. I glowered back. They were smart enough not to open their mouths. Maybe our reputation had improved.

It was early in the morning; not many people were out and about. Rags and I made the first boot prints in the snow that lay between a pair of buildings that fronted Main Street and backed up to Virgin Alley. Outside Min's door, I rested on my crutches. Rags knocked and said something in Cantonese.

"Rags," I whispered, "do me a favor and don't mention the bottle of toilet water. I want to focus on who shot Papa."

"I'll ask her about that later, then."

After a minute Rags knocked on the door louder.

From inside the crib came, "Go 'way."

Rags shouted in Cantonese.

"Go way, Irish boy. Come later."

I touched Rags's shoulder. "Let me try. Min, it's me, Nell Doherty. We need to talk to you."

"Talk before. Go 'way."

"Rags, tell her I'm not going away. Remember, I'm crazy. I'm coming in whether you want me to or not, even if I have to kick the door in again."

Rags repeated what I'd said in Cantonese. Min uttered a string of what I assumed were Chinese curses. After a bit of rustling around inside, the crib door opened. "Come, Crazy Lady. Irish Boy, make tea."

Min sat on her bed, a blanket wrapped loosely around the pink silk robe she wore. Lao Fu, her tiny calico cat, lay on the bed pillow, eyeing me and Rags warily. I sat in one of the two chairs on opposite sides of Min's small table. Rags poured water from a stone jar into a brass teapot and put the latter on Min's potbellied stove.

Min pulled the blanket more closely around her. "What want?"

Just a miracle. I wanted Min not to be afraid. I wanted her to name the second son of Belial that killed Papa. "Rags, tell her I want to know who the second gunman was."

Min responded in a few Cantonese syllables.

"She says she didn't see anyone."

"Tell her I don't believe her. We know she looked out her window. No, wait. Tell her instead that I greatly appreciate the advice she gave me. Tell her I need her to do what she told me to do. I need her to 'be strong.' "

Rags translated my words. Min shouted in Cantonese. She jabbed her finger repeatedly at Rags.

She couldn't mean Rags shot Papa. Bill Hoffman said that, but he was Bodie's biggest liar.

After a solid minute of shouting, Min stopped. She covered her face with her hands.

Rags said, "She's afraid."

"Was that all? She sure took a long time to say that."

"She was mostly telling me how angry she is with me for waking her up."

"Tell her we'll protect her. Rags, tell her you'll go to the jail right now and ask Marshal Catlow to join us."

Rags translated.

Min screamed, "No tell anyone." Tears formed in her eyes.

"You can trust us. You'll be okay. Rags, go get the marshal."

Min lunged and grabbed the shotgun Rags had set against the end of the bed. She pointed the gun at my face. "No get anyone."

The prospect of imminent death focused my attention on the barrels of the shotgun. A yellowish speck on the left barrel caught the light. I started a prayer, then remembered something Rags had told me. "Tell her she doesn't know how to use a shotgun. She doesn't know about cocking the hammers."

Rags translated what I'd said and it had the desired effect. Min took her eyes off me to check the weapon. As she did that, I grabbed the shotgun by its barrels and yanked it away from her.

She put her hands together as if in prayer and cried. Her body shook. "Please, no tell anyone."

"Tell her we'll protect her."

I looked at the end of the gun barrel and the shiny object that might have been the last thing I would see. A tiny bit of what looked like gold had melded itself to the end of the barrel. I opened the shotgun and extracted one of the shells. The paper at the end of the cartridge looked like it had been opened and refolded. Jamming the point of my pencil into the shell, I loosened the wadding at the top. Instead of lead shot, the shell contained flakes of gold leaf. That meant ...

The ground fell away beneath me. I had stepped off a cliff and plummeted toward oblivion. I rocked forward and back in the chair, unleashing a guttural moan.

Rags rushed toward me. "Nell. Nell, what's wrong?"

I kept rocking. "No. It can't be. It can't be. Oh, God." Tears flowed down my cheeks. An intense pain exploded in my stomach. I couldn't breathe. I wrapped my arms across my cramping belly. "No, it can't be. It can't be."

Huang Min knelt next to me. She laid a hand on my arm. "Okay, you learn *show* soft. Now, try *be* strong. Yes?"

"I don't think I can." I rocked back and forth.

Rags said, "Nell, stop crying. Tell me what's wrong."

I handed the shotgun shell to Rags. I continued rocking.

Rags looked inside the shell. "Gold leaf?"

"Remember Old Nate Briscomb, the prospector who used to give us cigarettes? He said something once. 'Never trust a mine owner who'd lost his gold watch and chain. Means he used the gold from the watch to salt his mine.'"

"Salt his mine?"

I wiped the tears from my cheeks. "Add gold to the mine's ore to make the mine look more valuable than it was. The owner could then sell the mine for an inflated price. That's what this shotgun was used for, to salt the Second Chance Mine. Poague was night watchman. He loaded the shells with gold flake and went into the mine at night when no one else was there. He fired the shotgun here and there scattering gold flakes amongst the ore."

Min said something in Cantonese and Rags answered in kind. "She wants to know what's going on."

I sniffed, then took Min's hands in mine. "I think I know who the second man is who shot Papa. I just need her to confirm it. Tell her if she'll be brave, I will protect her with my life."

I watched Min's eyes as Rags translated. She sobbed for several seconds, then got control of herself. "Be brave, yes, I be brave." She squeezed my hand and told her story.

"The man took her younger sister," Rags translated. "He keeps Min's sister in Virginia City, a hundred men's wife, same as Min. The man told Min if she doesn't do what she's told, her sister would be hurt."

"That bastard."

"Who is it?" Rags asked.

"I need to hear it from Min."

Rags said something in Cantonese and Min continued.

"The man told Min to tell Poague he must shoot the marshal. If Poague didn't shoot the marshal, Min would tell the marshal that Poague killed a man in San Francisco."

Min sounded hysterical. Rags pulled her into an embrace. He stroked her head. Between sniffles she whispered to Rags.

"Min says she's sorry. She had no choice. She's very afraid of this man. He waited outside her crib with a rifle. At the same time that Poague shot the marshal, this man also shot the marshal. She saw it from her window."

"Tell me his name." Hot tears streamed down my face. "Min, what's his name?"

"Cotloo."

Chapter Forty-Five

I didn't know I could suffer so many different torments at once. I'd been wrong about everything—about Kohl, about Baron. How could I have been so stupid to think he loved me? That I had loved him hurt even more. Like frostbite, the part of my heart that had been dormant before Baron burned with a frozen anguish. My body shook as if I had a fever. Sharp pains stabbed the top of my head. *Baron, Baron, how could you have done all these horrible, evil deeds? Bastard. Murderer.* I hoped his hangman failed to break his neck and left him dancing in the air, gagging on the noose for eternity.

Rags hugged Huang Min and spoke to her softly in her native tongue. He looked at me over Min's shoulder. "Now what do we do?"

"We arrest him."

He snapped his fingers. "Just like that, though we've no badges, or nothin'."

"He won't be expecting it. We'll just walk up to him, all smiles, pull out our pistols and threaten to shoot him if he so much as blinks."

"You could do that? Shoot Baron?"

My anger and hatred spoke. "He's not Baron to me anymore. He's Papa's murderer."

He had been my love. Could I really shoot him?

Rags's pinched expression suggested that he, too, doubted my resolve. "We have to at least get the judge."

"Agreed."

"I'll take Huang Min to Yong Liao's so she'll be safe. Then get the judge."

Thank God Rags could be logical. "I'll wait for you here."

"You promise?"

"I promise."

Huang Min changed clothes while Rags and I faced the door. Min put her cat in its wooden box cat bed. I flinched when I saw the cat's nest contained two mismatched socks, brothers of the ones Papa had worn the night he was shot. Oh, Papa, how could you have visited Min? I needed to keep the lid on that jar. I had a murderer to arrest.

Rags and Min left for Yong Liao's Mercantile at the south end of the street.

Gideon Weed had set up his tripod camera in front of The Mother Lode bordello, next to Huang Min's crib. Weed waved to me. "I'm doing a study of Bodie's architecture."

What kind of person would be out taking photographs with three inches of snow on the ground? I waved and closed the crib door.

I had so many questions. Baron shot Papa, but why? Had Papa suspected him of being involved in the bullion thefts? Did Papa know about him salting his mine? I hit my knuckles against my forehead. Oh, why hadn't I seen that Baron was a foul criminal like Mrs. Lockhart's Harlan Woolcott?

Could it be? Baron was in Bodie. He was a good-looking man, if an evil one. Mrs. Lockhart had described Harlan Woolcott as a good-looking scoundrel. Woolcott's shotgun was used to salt Baron's mine. Were Baron and Harlan the same man? But if that was true, why hadn't Mrs. Lockhart told me? Did she still love him? Could she have been jealous of me and Baron? Was that why she had me promise to go slow with Baron? Was she involved in his crimes?

Gideon Weed's voice grabbed my attention. I swung toward the window on my crutches and peeked out.

Baron sat on his pinto talking to Weed.

I wanted to scream "Murderer," but that would warn the bastard that I was on to him.

Baron held the leads of Poague's tall chestnut-colored Morgan and a dark-brown mustang with white-stockinged legs. Baron could ride up to the jail. He could free Poague and Black-Eyed Susan.

Hurry, Rags. Hurry.

Baron continued to talk with Weed.

Weed's signature had been on one of the notes Poague burned. Could Weed be the leader of this outlaw gang? Did Baron work for Gideon Weed? I had to know what they were saying.

I swung to the crib door. I cracked it open.

"The prisoners'll be safer in Bridgeport," Baron said. He clicked his tongue. He and the three horses moved toward the jail.

Bridgeport. The county jail was there. But Baron wouldn't be taking Poague and Black-Eyed Susan to the county jail. Was Baron lying to Mr. Weed, or to me? If Weed was 'The Boss,' he might have told Baron I was in the crib.

Mr. Weed waved at Baron's back. He turned a bit and waved a second time at the backs of buildings that faced Main Street. Odd. He and Baron were the only people in Virgin Alley.

Baron was nearly at the jail. *God, what am I going to do? Could I shoot him? Might he love me?* I had no daisy to pluck petals from.

He loves me.

He loves me not.

Can I shoot him?

Can I not?

261

I'd promised Rags I'd wait for him. I couldn't. Baron would escape, along with Poague and Black-Eyed Susan. I had to act, for Papa's sake. I'd promised him first. Baron didn't know that I knew he was a murderer. I could surprise him.

I poked my head out the crib door. Mr. Weed was strolling in the direction of the jail with his tripod camera slung over his shoulder. The three horses were tied up outside the jail.

I looked in the opposite direction, along the row of two-storied bawdy houses and small, boxy cribs, toward King Street and Chinatown. No Rags. No judge.

Poague and Black-Eyed Susan stepped onto the boardwalk in front of the jail. Black-Eyed Susan looked stranger than usual—she wore men's pants. Both she and Poague were manacled.

I couldn't let Papa's killers escape.

I hitched past Mr. Weed, who had set up his camera in front of Madame Soto's Parlor several doors up the street from Huang Min's crib. Weed whispered, "Miss Doherty, you should go back to the shack."

Weed didn't look like a villain. He looked concerned. If he was The Boss, he was a clever actor. I waved as I passed him. "Just want to say goodbye before Baron leaves."

I trudged toward the jail on the snow-covered lane. I wished Doc had fixed my wooden leg. If I leaned on the right crutch, held my revolver in my left hand, and aimed, I wouldn't be able to hold onto my left crutch.

Baron stood seventy-five yards away. With my crutch, I waved at the black-hearted devil. Could he sense the menace in my smile? He waved back. Was I too late to surprise them? I picked up my pace.

Weed yelled, "Miss Doherty, can you help me—please?"

What could he want now? Is he trying to distract me?

"Miss Doherty."

I didn't turn around. I just needed a minute to get close enough to Baron and the others to get the drop on them. Weed would be too far away to do anything, even if he was The Boss. Rags and the judge would be there soon, too.

Baron helped Black-Eyed Susan mount the white-stockinged mustang.

I was fifty yards away from the jail.

Baron helped Poague onto the saddle of the tall Morgan.

"Wait." I yelled.

Baron looked at me. "Sorry, Nell. No time." He handed Poague and Black-Eyed Susan the reins to their horses. Poague said something and Baron shook his head adamantly. I hitched toward him, twenty-five yards away.

"We have to go," Baron said, "before a mob tries to hang the prisoners."

He's lying. Everything's been a lie. His love, too, nothing but a lie.

My arms pumped. The crutches dug into the new snow. My good leg swung. Almost there. "Baron, wait, just a minute."

"See you when I get back." He mounted his pinto.

Across the lane from the jail, Mrs. Lockhart stepped out the back door of Smith's Dance Hall. She had a dark-blue shawl tightly wrapped around her. Did she plan to tell Baron goodbye?

Poague turned the chestnut Morgan my way. He yelled, "You hurt me bad. Gonna hurt you back."

Baron shouted at him, "We have to ride before a necktie party forms. Ride."

Baron's protecting me.

Black-Eyed Susan cackled. She pulled a pistol from under her coat. "Go on, stupid, shoot her."

Poague pulled a pistol from under his jacket.

Fifteen yards from him, I froze. They're all armed. Three against one. Or was it four to one? I looked behind me. Gideon Weed stared my way, but he held his camera not a pistol.

Baron yelled at Poague and Black-Eyed Susan. "What are you

doing? We need to ride." He looked my way. He saw I knew the truth. "Aw, damn it."

Poague aimed his pistol at me.

I reached for my revolver. The hammer caught in my coat pocket. I yanked on it. "Come on. Come on."

Poague fired. The bullet whizzed past my head.

I wobbled and nearly fell over.

I yanked on the pistol, not caring if I tore the fabric. No luck.

Mrs. Lockhart screamed, "Gideon!"

"Coming," Weed yelled.

I glanced behind me, tugging and cursing my pistol.

Weed tossed his camera to the ground. He pulled a pistol from his pocket and ran toward the jail. He shot at the fugitives as he rushed forward. So, he wasn't part of their gang. But why was he shooting at them?

A bullet struck the ground next to my foot. Smoke surrounded Poague.

I needed cover. Could I get behind the outhouse? Not as fast as someone on a horse.

Mrs. Lockhart drew a short-barreled revolver from beneath her shawl. She stood thirty feet from the murderers. She shouted, "Harlan Wolcott, tell your friends to throw down their guns."

She knew Baron was Harlan Woolcott. *What's going on?*

"Time to ride," Baron yelled. His pinto hopped and spun around.

Poague and Black-Eyed Susan turned toward Mrs. Lockhart. They each fired a shot at her. She fired back.

Weed passed by me, running toward the outlaws outside the jail. He fired another round. The fur hat leapt from Poague's head.

Poague turned toward the photographer. "Hell-fired devil. You're a goner now." He shot at Weed. The bullet went wild, shattering a window of one of the bordellos.

Black-Eyed Susan took another shot at Mrs. Lockhart. Her

brown mustang snorted. It danced right and left, stirring up the new snow.

Rags, where are you?

I yanked again. My pistol came free.

Mrs. Lockhart, Weed, Poague, and Black-Eyed Susan shot at each other. Clouds of smoke enveloped them.

Baron shouted, "Let's go."

I let my left crutch fall to the ground, took aim at Poague and pulled the trigger. Smoke billowed around me. I had missed.

Black-Eyed Susan cackled again, then sprouted a blood-red eye in the middle of her forehead. Her mustang reared. She pitched backward onto the snow-covered ground.

"Suzie!" Baron spun his horse around. He pulled his revolver from his holster and shot Mrs. Lockhart. She fell against the rough exterior of the dance hall and slid to the ground.

"No." Not Mrs. Lockhart. Weed stood between me and Baron. I hopped sideways on my one leg, steadying myself with the remaining crutch.

Poague fired again at Weed. The photographer stumbled forward two steps. He fell to his knees and collapsed face first onto the snow.

Poague turned to me. Uh-oh.

"Come on, Poague," Baron yelled.

"Gotta git one more."

Poague fired twice. The second bullet nicked my left arm. It burned something fierce. I gritted my teeth and cocked my pistol.

Poague screamed, "Damnation." He tossed his pistol to the ground. Out of bullets. He roared and spurred his giant horse toward me. I took aim.

Something exploded to my right.

Poague's neck blew apart. Mrs. Lockhart, gun hand stretched in front of her, fell sideways onto the snow.

Poague leaned forward in the saddle. Blood gushed from a hole above his collar.

The Morgan galloped straight at me. Ten feet away. I was done for. I closed my eyes.

The tall Morgan's hooves shook the ground in front of me. He passed by. He hadn't run me down, but the toe of Poague's boot caught my crutch and wrenched it away. I spun and fell.

Only Baron remained upright.

I pushed myself up and wobbled on my one leg. I wiped snow off my pistol. I pointed it at Baron. "Stay where you are, or I swear, I'll shoot you. You're under arrest."

He laughed and holstered his revolver. "So long, Nell." His smug grin angered me.

"Don't do it. I will shoot you if you try to leave."

"No." He winked. "You love me."

Did I? Could I love Papa's murderer?

Baron turned his horse and trotted away. Balancing on my good leg, I took aim. I fired.

Baron raised and lowered the Stetson from his head. He continued on.

I could barely see through my tears.

I shouted at Baron, "I loved you. I loved you, so much." I wiped the tears from my cheeks. "But I loved Papa more."

Held up by one leg, I swayed. My hand shook as if with palsy. I pulled the trigger a second time. Baron whipped his pinto.

I gripped the pistol with both hands. Aimed. Fired a third time.

Baron jerked backwards. The pinto slowed to a stop. Baron pitched sideways and slid off his horse.

My body convulsed. Hot tears stung my face. I threw my pistol at the ground.

Behind me, Rags shouted, "Nell! Are you all right?"

"I'm not going to die," I yelled over my shoulder. Not physically.

I hopped up and down, rotating a little with each effort. Rags and Judge Snethens ran toward me, shotgun and pistol at the ready. When the judge realized the shooting was over, he stopped running, leaned forward, and grabbed his knees. Soiled doves and madams poked their heads out doors and windows. Several Chinese appeared at the far end of the street, including Yong Liao. Rags' brother Bobby had opened the window to the family's apartment. He waved vigorously at me.

I shouted to Rags. "Mrs. Lockhart and Mr. Weed have been shot. Fetch Doc Boyle."

I hopped on my good leg across the snow to my nearest crutch, picked it up, and hobbled to Baron. I knelt beside him. He coughed. Foamy blood stained his teeth and oozed over his lips.

He grabbed my coat and pulled my face to his. "I would never have hurt you."

Fresh tears stained my cheeks. "You couldn't have hurt me more."

Baron coughed again. His blood splattered my face. "You ... you shot me in the back."

"Same as you shot Papa, you filthy bastard. I warned you."

He half gurgled, half coughed. "I'm cold."

"Hell will warm you up."

Baron's body fell limp and he released his grip on my coat. He stopped breathing.

I tore Papa's badge off Baron's coat. "Murderer," I screamed. I beat his chest with my fists. "Bastard." I pounded on his chest twice more. "You kissed me. You kissed me and each kiss was a lie. How will I ever be able to trust a kiss again?" My tears puddled on his coat.

Sweat trickled down my spine. I was dizzy and threw up. I needed to get away, to put distance between me and Baron. Trying to stand, I slipped on the snow and fell. I got to my knee for a second attempt.

Judge Snethens extended his hand. He helped me up. "You all right?"

"Yes. Baron—"

"Wu Chao explained it all to me." He put his arm around my shoulder. I winced.

"What's wrong?"

"A bullet grazed my arm."

The judge shook his head. "You are one tough little lady."

I handed him Papa's badge.

"Nell, if it was in my power, I would bring your Papa back to life, but I can't. I do have the power to do one thing though. Can you stand on your own a second?"

"I think so."

The judge waited for me to get my balance. Then he leaned down and pinned Papa's badge to my coat. "You've earned this, Marshal."

Chapter Forty-Six

Three days later, Mama and I sat on the couch in our parlor. My canvas suitcase and Gladstone bag sat on the floor of my bedroom, packed.

"Handing over the marshal's job was the right thing to do," Mama said. "As Mr. Reeves pointed out in his editorial, women aren't meant to do such work."

I huffed. "Mama, Mr. Reeves is an idiot. I didn't quit the marshal's job because of him. I quit so I could go to Chicago and become a Pinkerton detective." *If they'll have me.*

"Nell, running off to Chicago on the small chance you'll get hired by the Pinkerton Company doesn't make any sense. Even if you were a man, they'd still want someone with two good legs."

I pressed my palms against my forehead. "Mama, I may be a cripple in some people's eyes, but I'm strong. I captured a gang of murderers. I stood toe-to-toe with them in a gun battle. I did that, Mama. Me, Nell, a girl with one leg."

"Detective work is dangerous."

"I'll be careful. Have faith in me. Papa did."

Mama sighed. "Being a detective is still unladylike."

I counted to ten. I was not going to argue that issue again.

Mama couldn't accept the fact that I wanted to be a detective any more than I could accept being a teacher.

I handed her an envelope. "This is for you."

She pulled out the greenbacks and counted them. "Four-hundred and fifty dollars? Where on earth did you get so much money?"

"From the superintendent of the Standard Mine. It's a reward for returning the gold bullion stolen by Baron Catlow and his gang. I gave Rags half and kept fifty dollars for myself. The rest is yours."

"Lordy." Mama began crying. "You really mean to leave, don't you?"

I teared up. "I'm going to Chicago, but not forever. I have to give it a try, Mama. Being a detective is what I was meant to be."

Mama hugged me and squeezed hard. "I'll miss you somethin' fierce."

"I'll miss you, too."

Mama handed me a hundred dollars from the envelope. "Take it. You may need it. We still have Patrick's wages." She wiped the tears from her eyes. "I'll worry so. Who'll protect you?"

"Oh, Mama, I'll protect me."

AT NOON, THE PEOPLE I WOULD MISS THE MOST gathered around the stagecoach in front of the Wells Fargo office to see me off. The sky was a bright blue. An inch of new powdery snow covered the ground. The driver loaded my bags into the rear boot and climbed into his seat. My chest tightened with the weight of leaving my family and friends.

Doc Boyle doffed his hat. "Good luck, Nell."

"Thanks again for repairing my wooden leg. How is Mr. Weed doing?"

"Still delirious, but I believe he'll pull through."

"Mrs. Lockhart?"

"Haven't seen her since I patched up her shoulder."

I had looked for Mrs. Lockhart the last couple of days without success. I still didn't know why she and Mr. Weed took part in the gunfight.

Rags and Huang Min approached. "I'll miss you," Rags said. He wrapped his arms around me. Tears sprouted in my eyes. I blinked them away. I'd promised myself I wouldn't cry. Rags hugged me quite a while, until Huang Min grabbed his arm.

"Enough, Irish boy." She pulled him away and kept her arm wrapped around his.

"You make a lovely couple," I said.

Rags and Min gazed at each other. "We can't thank you enough," Rags said, "for sharing the reward. We'll have us enough to free Min's sister. Yong Liao said he'll contact a friend in Virginia City and arrange it."

Rags and Min stepped back to let Yong Liao speak to me. I bowed. He bowed deeply to me. I'd never seen him offer such respect to another. Maybe that was an omen. Maybe the Pinkertons would see what Yong Liao saw and hire me.

"Miss Doherty, Yong Liao will miss you."

"I will miss you, too, Uncle."

Yong Liao took my hands in his. "The Master said: 'Some plants spring up but not flower; others flower, but not bear fruit.' My heart say: You will bear much fruit. Best wishes for good life."

"Thank you, Uncle."

He bowed and stepped aside.

Judge Snethens bent down and kissed me on the cheek. "I would grace you with felicitous words of advice or other hortations, but my head is scramblebrained, not by strong drink as you might expect, but by the sorrowful events of the last week. Here's a little something to remember me by." The judge handed me a Colt revolver, engraved silver with pearl grips. "For the next time you get in a tight scrape."

The revolver, with its magnificent scrollwork on the barrel and cylinder, was both a work of art and a weapon, a necessary tool for a Pinkerton.

I hugged him. "Thank you. Thank you for the vote of confidence."

"If you need a letter of reference, I would be most gratified to take up pen and compose a testimonial for you, Marshal."

I smiled and slipped the pistol into my coat pocket. I turned to enter the stagecoach.

Rags's youngest brother, Bobby, stood before me. "Oh, I so wish you weren't leaving. Or that I was going with you. Sure'n it's more than I can stand. Oh, if only ..." He grabbed me in a bear hug, kissed my cheek, and released me. He stammered, "G-good-bye, Nell," and ran off. Scents of oranges and sandalwood joss sticks lingered in the air.

Mama looked shocked. Judge Snethens hid a laugh behind a gloved hand. Rags chuckled. "Guess you've another reason to come back to Bodie, you do."

The stage driver yelled down from his seat. "Time to git, miss."

I hugged Patrick and Mama. "I'll write you every week." With help from Patrick, I climbed into the coach. The driver yelled, "Giddup," and we were off. I stuck my head out the window and waved to Mama until the stage reached the bend in Main Street, and she left my sight.

Suddenly, the driver shouted "Whoa," and brought the team to a halt.

I wasn't the only one leaving Bodie.

In the snow-covered road, two battered suitcases beside her, stood Mrs. Lockhart, her left arm supported by a sling. The stage stopped and the driver jumped to the ground to load Mrs. Lockhart's bags in the boot. He helped Mrs. Lockhart into the coach. Another cry of, "Giddup," and we were off again.

Mrs. Lockhart had taken the bench opposite me. "Surprise."

"I've been looking for you."

"I know. I had some things that needed tending to."

"I'm grateful to you for saving my life."

She tilted her head to the side. "How are you?"

"I'm excited to be leaving. Sad to be leaving Mama and Patrick and Bodie. Nervous about what lies ahead."

Mrs. Lockhart stared at me intensely. "You shot and killed the man you loved. That must have pained you grievously."

Once again, the crushing anger, despair, and sense of loss bore down on me. "The worst of the hurt came before I shot Baron. The worst was when I figured out who he was, and that he'd shot Papa." I swallowed hard. "Were Baron Catlow and Harlan Woolcott one and the same?"

"That's right."

I slapped my hand on the seat. "Why didn't you tell me?"

"Nell, you were in love with him. If I'd told you, you might have told him. As it was, I risked giving myself away by telling you he was a swindler."

"Risked giving yourself away?"

Mrs. Lockhart pulled a piece of paper from her sling and held it out to me. "Read this."

I batted the paper away, and it dropped to the floor. "I don't care about some silly old paper. I want to know what you were doing in Bodie. How did you know about Baron, Harlan, whoever he was? Why did you and Mr. Weed join the gunfight?"

"Will you try not to be angry with me, Nell? I couldn't tell you earlier."

"Tell me what?"

"I'm a Pinkerton detective."

My mouth fell open.

"Gideon Weed is, too. The Standard Mine hired us to discover who had stolen their gold shipments. Your father and Deputy Jorgensen knew who we were, but no one else. The night you saw your father and me dancing, we were discussing the case, nothing more. We both suspected Baron Catlow, but we didn't have any evidence—not until you found Poague, Black-Eyed Susan, and the gold."

Did you hear that Papa? They couldn't have done it without me.

Mrs. Lockhart pointed at the paper on the floor of the coach. "You really should read that."

It was a telegram addressed to her. "I concur. Stop. Hire Miss Doherty. Stop." The telegram was signed William Pinkerton. *Hire me. William Pinkerton.* My breath caught in my throat. "Does this mean—"

"Nell, if you want it, you have a job with Pinkerton's National Detective Agency."

"Really?"

Mrs. Lockhart beamed. "Yes, really."

My dream had come true!

But at a terrible cost. I wouldn't have gotten this offer if Papa hadn't been killed. It wasn't fair that my joy was accompanied by sadness, my jar of sugar paired with one of salt. I remembered Yong Liao's words: *Put top on jar, not open again.* I put the lid on the jar holding Papa's death. I would occasionally want to peek inside it, but not that day. I opened a new jar, which held my future.

"Mrs. Lockhart, I accept."

Nell: Pinkerton Detective

Book Two of the Nell Doherty series

In her second adventure, Nell battles counterfeiters, murderers, and Chicago politicians. If she's successful, she'll become a permanent operative of Pinkerton's National Detective Agency. If unsuccessful, she'll likely die.

Turn the page for an excerpt...

CHAPTER ONE

Chicago, March 1892

I gave Mrs. Thorp a head start, then slipped out the front door of the mansion. In the semi-dark of the gas-lit street, she wouldn't realize that I followed her if I stayed far enough behind. I could do that, though as a new operative, I wasn't supposed to. If Mrs. Thorp saw me, little Davey Markus might die.

Smoke thickened in the air as we proceeded from the large homes in the Markus's neighborhood toward downtown. Chicagoans were equal in one respect. Some days, piles of foul-smelling garbage lined the streets of both the rich and poor districts alike. I covered my mouth as I passed the carcass of a horse rotting in the roadway. Gaps in its hide exposed some of its ribs. A rat poked its head out. I thought of my pony back home and nearly retched.

I stopped now and then to keep my distance because Mrs. Thorp walked so slowly. She reached Eighteenth Street and halted. She looked in her hand bag as she glanced behind her. I was partially hidden by a couple walking arm in arm between me and Mrs. Thorp. Still, I hid my face by re-tying the ribbon of my bonnet to secure it against the chill wind coming off nearby Lake Michigan. Had she recognized me? She continued to walk as before, the same slow pace. No more furtive glances in my direction.

Mrs. Thorp waited for a one-horse carriage to pass. She lifted her hem, crossed the street and stood at a cable car stop amid a cluster of men and women in winter coats on their way home after work. Lucky them. I worked for a company with the motto 'We Never Sleep.'

I felt bad that I suspected Mrs. Thorp. She had treated me kindly since I assumed the position as tutor for the Markus's daughter two days ago. My initial fear that she knew I was a Pinkerton agent receded after realizing that what disconcerted me about her gaze was the uneven set of her eyes, the left a half-inch lower than the right. I hoped my suspicions about her were wrong. It didn't seem possible that a gray-haired woman of fifty could be a criminal. But Mrs. Thorp had eaten supper with the rest of the household staff and said she lived alone. Why else would the housekeeper sneak food from the kitchen than to feed the Markus's missing son?

I crossed the street slowly to hide my swinging gait as best I could and joined the queue as the cable car came to a stop. Several men stood between me and Mrs. Thorp. I hunkered down a little to lessen the chance she would see me. As she boarded the front of the car, I thanked my lucky stars, walked toward the rear and took a seat at the back. Everything was working out just fine. I suppressed a hurrah. I, one-legged Nell Doherty, had followed Mrs. Thorp without being seen. I was a detective.

The conductor rang the horse-drawn trolley's bell and we lurched forward. At Halsted Street, we switched to a cable car. Mrs. Thorp disembarked at De Koven Street. I got off at Taylor and hitched back down Halsted to catch Mrs. Thorp. Her slow pace turned out to be a good thing. As I turned the corner, she climbed the steps which led to a three-story tenement halfway down the block. Mrs. Thorp disappeared into the building and I hastened after her. Three young girls, six to ten years old, played jump rope out front in the semi-dark. They stared at me. I smiled at them and climbed the steps. A hand-written list of tenants had been tacked to the wall of the first-floor landing. No Thorp was listed.

I went outside and addressed the oldest of the girls playing jump rope. "I'm sorry to interrupt. I've come to visit Mrs. Thorp, but her name's not on the list. Can you tell me which apartment she lives in?"

"I don't know you," the girl said.

"Mrs. Thorp's in 2-B," a young redhead said. "Lives with Mr. Mattison."

"Sally, we's not supposed to tell strangers. In case they's one of the baduns."

I leaned down and brought my face even with the little redhead. "Sally, thank you." I stood up. "I'm not a bad person." Mrs. Thorp might be.

Sally pursed her lips. "How come you walk funny?"

"I have a wooden leg."

"Oh."

I reentered the tenement and climbed to the second floor, good leg followed by wooden leg. The hall smelled of onions and boiled beef. A novice musician in apartment 2-A practiced scales on the violin. In 2-B, a man and a woman shouted at each other. And a child cried. He sounded about four-years-old. Davey Markus? I put my ear to the door.

The man said, "...have to move him tonight. Too many's heard the little brat squawking. Shut your mouth you little--"

"Hush, Davey, dear," Mrs. Thorp said. "He means you no harm."

I found him. I found him.

Davey's sobbing continued. Poor thing. To be four-years-old and to have been kidnapped, he must be scared out of his wits.

"There, there, Davey. It won't be long 'til you see your parents. We wouldn't be in this fix, Bart, if you hadn't asked for more money. Mrs. Markus said they've hired Pinkertons."

I smiled.

"We've been through this before," Bart said. "We need money to overthrow the capitalists. What better place to get it than from the damned capitalists themselves."

"Mind your language, Bart."

"Mind your place, Dolores. Get the boy to eat. Sean and Fred'll be here in fifteen minutes to take the little snot."

Uh oh.

"But who'll look after him?"

"Never you mind that."

There's no way to contact the office. If I left to summon a police-man, these radicals might spirit the boy away before I could return with help. I wasn't supposed to take action on my own. Mr. Pinkerton had told me just to keep my ears and eyes open at the Markus's house. But this might be the only chance of saving the boy. In fifteen minutes, I'd face four opponents instead of two. Could I force my way into the apartment and subdue Bart and Mrs. Thorp quickly enough? Mrs. Thorp seemed concerned about Davey. Maybe she'd help me.

I drew my pearl-handled Colt from my coat pocket, held it behind me and knocked on the door. "Mrs. Thorp, it's Nell Doherty. Mr. Markus has sent me to fetch you back to the house. Mrs. Markus collapsed."

Davey's whining stopped. Only indistinct whispers could be heard through the door.

"I'm sorry to hear that, Nell," Mrs. Thorp said. "But I'm not feeling well myself."

"Mr. Markus is greatly distraught given all that's happened. He's just below in his carriage. Could you at least come down and talk to him?"

More whispering. If only they'd open the door.

"Please, Mrs. Thorp. You're really needed back at the house."

The door opened just wide enough for Mrs. Thorp to slip through it. "I'll come down to talk to Mr. Markus, but only for a minute."

I let her walk ahead of me so there was less chance she'd see my pistol. She shuffled along even slower than before and braced herself with a hand against the wall of the dimly-lit hallway. "It's my stomach. I get cramping sometimes. It's worse than usual."

"I'm sorry to hear that."

We descended the stairs to the lobby.

Mrs. Thorp looked out the glass door. No carriage outside. No Mr. Markus. Her eyes went wide. Her face paled. "You. You're, you're one of 'em." She turned toward the staircase.

I grabbed her arm and pushed the barrel of my revolver against her ribs. "Mrs. Thorp, I know you and Bart have Davey upstairs. I've come to take him home."

"Bart will kill Davey before he turns him over to the likes of you."

"I know you care about Davey. You can save his life. If you help me, I'll testify for you in court."

Mrs. Thorp pressed her palms against her forehead. She shook her head. "Bart'll kill him. I know he will. Davey's family are nothing but blood-sucking capitalists to him."

"I only need you to open the door. I'll take care of the rest. Or you can go to prison for the rest of your life."

I held my breath as Mrs. Thorp chewed her lip for ten or fifteen seconds. Finally, she said, "All right. I'll help you."

We climbed the stairs to the second floor, Mrs. Thorp in the lead. She knocked on the door. "It's all right, Bart. I'm alone." She winked at me.

I had an ally. Maybe. In either case, I was going to get Davey back to his family safe and sound. I only needed to get inside the apartment.

A key turned in the lock and Mrs. Thorp opened the door. I shoved her to the side and entered the apartment.

Bart stood in the middle of a small room lit by a kerosene lamp on a dining table. He took one look at me and grabbed Davey's arms.

Davey looked up at me. His hair was matted. Food stains dotted the boy's shirt.

I pointed my Colt at Bart. "Let go of the boy."

"Not a chance," Bart said.

I cocked my revolver. "Release him. Now."

He grinned, but not at me, at something behind me. I side-stepped to my right and turned.

Mrs. Thorp smashed my shoulder with a rolling pin. My shoulder screamed in response. Thank God I had moved.

Mrs. Thorp raised the rolling pin to strike me again.

I pointed my Colt toward her. I pulled the trigger. In the small room, the gun's blast sounded like an explosion of dynamite. Smoke enveloped me. Davey screamed.

A hole in the wall showed that I'd missed my attacker. Unwounded, but frightened, Mrs. Thorp stumbled backwards, fell against the wall and slid to the floor.

"Stay put," I yelled.

I turned and faced Bart. He grabbed the sides of Davey's head.

"Let go of the boy, or I'll shoot."

"You can't shoot worth a darn. You don't frighten me. Drop yer gun, Missy, or I'll break his neck."

"Two months ago, I faced down a whole outlaw gang. Back away from the boy, now."

Bart leaned away from Davey. He waved his left hand at me. "Don't shoot."

I relaxed my finger's pull on the trigger.

Bart's right hand slipped into his pocket. With a flick of his wrist he produced a straight razor. The blade gleamed in the lamplight.

I raised my pistol and took aim at Bart's head. His grinning face, half hidden in shadow, took on the appearance of the last man I'd shot. Not again. No, not again. I shook my head to clear it, to chase away the ghostly image, to see only Bart standing there threatening Davey. I took a deep breath.

Bart placed the blade against Davey's neck. "Drop it."

I fired my pistol.

Author's Notes

Peace officers in Bodie held different titles. Some were constables, some deputy sheriffs. I chose to give Nell the title of marshal to distinguish Bodie's chief police officer from the county sheriff.

In some cases, I have changed the locations and/or names of buildings in Bodie. Currently, the jail is located at the intersection of King Street and Virgin Alley (Bonanza Street). In my novel, the jail sits at the northern end of Virgin Alley. I based this location on a detailed map of the town from 1880. It was common in Bodie, especially after a fire, for buildings to be relocated.

Acknowledgments

Creating *Nell: Marshal of Bodie* was not a solitary effort. Many friends and family members assisted me. Apologies to anyone I failed to mention below.

First of all, thank you to Mark Clements, Paula Bonilla, Nancy Horgan, Ken Kaplan, Jennifer Karp, Laura Kelly, Deborah Larkin and Michelle Traher Neff of Mark's Wednesday Night Read and Critique Group some of whom sat through multiple drafts of the novel.

Thank you, also, to David Putnam and Mary Putnam for hosting the De Luz Writers meetings in their home. I benefitted from their advice and the advice of the other De Luz Writers including Mary Ames, Judy Bernstein, Roberta Davidson, Claudia Ermey, Richard Goldsmith, R. Daniel Houston, Linda Moore, Jeff Nichols, Janet Rendall, Gerry Tarantino, Lona Tomlinson, and Susan Walsh.

I gratefully acknowledge the editorial help I received from Larry Edwards, Jennifer Silva Redmond, and Laura Taylor. Thank you for being a part of my team.

Joan Neumann, David Redfearn and Sharlene Liu were kind enough to read early copies of my novel. Thank you all for your suggestions.

Thank you to Hannah Linder for your wonderful cover design, and to Catherine Posey for the internal formatting of the book.

Finally, thank you Susan for giving me the space I need to write and for lending me a hand.

About Bodie

Bodie is a real and magical place. Dozens of buildings from the 19th and 20th centuries remain standing (or leaning) in this ghost town that is now a California State Historic Park. The town is located north and east of Mono Lake in the eastern Sierra Nevada mountains. Note that the last three miles of the main road into the park are not paved. There are restrooms, but no other services. Bring food and water.

Bodie has been called the last of the old-time mining camps. At its peak around 1880, the town boasted a population of 8,000 people—miners who blasted and dug the ore out of shafts hundreds of feet below the surface and stamp mill operators who crushed the ore to a fine powder and processed it with mercury or cyanide. These workers were attended by shopkeepers, gamblers, speculators, barkeeps, and ladies of the evening.

For more information on Bodie, visit the California Department of Parks and Recreation at https://www.parks.ca.gov/?page_id=26330 or the Bodie Foundation at https://www.bodiefoundation.org/

The foundation raises money to keep the town's buildings

from deteriorating further. The foundation offers tours of the town including the Standard Mill which processed millions of dollars of gold and silver over its roughly 50-year lifetime. If you can, I recommend that you visit during the annual Friends of Bodie Day celebration held annually in August.

Made in the USA
Las Vegas, NV
06 September 2023

77136152R00173